DOUBLE CROSS

Tania Park

ISBN: 978-0-6485565-2-7 (Paperback)
ISBN: 978-0-6485565-3-4 (Ebook)

Printed & Channel Distribution: Lightning Source | Ingram (USA/UK/EUROPE/AUS)
Cover Designed—Laila Savolainen, Pickawoowoo Publishing Group
Publishing Consultants/Interior Design—Pickawoowoo Publishing Group

Publisher
Tania Park Publishing
For enquiries, write to: rights and permissions via publisher.

Also by Tania Park

Mistaken

'He never got around to telling me why he wanted me dead.'

When Bella's new boss whacked her across the head and dropped her over a cliff, her life changed in an instant. She became a naïve pawn caught in a very dangerous game.

Retribution

Living with a new identity in a different state on the other side of the country, Amy Masters is stunned and terrified when her ex-husband turns up at her place of work. After almost killing her, he is supposed to be still in jail.

Blind justice

'Panic turned to terror at the sudden onrush of two sets of feet. A rough hand clamped over her mouth to silence her.'

Piano bar pianist, Christine Mears, becomes involved in a murder investigation when she meets Detective Ben Somers. She unwittingly becomes the main target of an unscrupulous gang of drug dealers. To them she is worth two million dollars and the gang goes to extreme lengths to snatch Christine to use as ransom.

Road Trip

'Something inside her broke apart, leaving an intense sensation of emptiness. It was like he'd taken a huge chunk of her heart with him and he was only her brother.'

Madison Brown, 20 and Gemma Tomas, 17, are complete opposites in almost every way but have a unique bond tying them together. When Gemma lands a job in Brisbane, she sweet-talks Maddie into driving with her across Australia. To save money, they camp along the way. Gemma's impulsive behaviour leads them into some awkward predicaments as they drive through the outback from Perth. Their friendship becomes fractured as Maddie tries to extricate them from difficult and life-threatening situations.

Stalked

'A triumphant sneer shot from the corners of his mouth as he thought of one way he could leave his mark to let her know she belonged to him.'

The only man to ask the insecure university student, Emma Nicholls, out, is a possessive bully. After Emma finds the courage to break the relationship, Greg Saunders doesn't take it kindly and begins stalking her to get revenge. Despite moving to a new house several times to hide from him, he keeps finding her, even when she returns to the remote family farm for the Christmas break.

The Swan

'I was seven years old. Do you honestly think I would tell the truth so that I could get beaten again the minute the police left?'

Just as an elegant swan emerges from the gaucheness of a young cygnet, Melanie Jones struggles to escape the darkness of a terrible abusive life. Deep shame and fear are constant companions.

Her music is the one haven where she is able to find temporary reprieve from the awfulness of her life. Her mother's tragic murder is the turning point in Melanie's life.

Dedication

I was fortunate enough to be accepted into a three-day residential workshop at the Katherine
Susannah Pritchard writing centre in November 2017, when only three chapters of this book were at first draft stage.

The facilitator, Laurie Steed, author of, You Belong Here, gave me so much encouragement about my writing style and where the book was heading, I knuckled down to get it finished.

A huge thank you, Laurie, for your structural analysis and suggestions. Despite re-writing large chunks, getting rid of superfluous characters and changing direction in several areas, I actually enjoyed the re-writing process and learnt a lot.

My heartfelt thanks also go to Kaye Hawley, a member of my writer's group who has a very handy red pen. She delights in finding the teeniest error in punctuation and grammar before handing back a manuscript, you thought was pretty well perfect, covered in red marks.

Hyphens, Tania, you must get the hyphens right!

To my fellow writers at St Stephen's Writing Group in Forrestfield, Western Australia, thank you for you continual support and encouragement.

Chapter One

His head shot up. Ears alert, he waited, unsure what the unusual noise was.

There… again… a definite footstep on the veranda.

Unnerved, he clicked *save*, shut down the programme, slid the thumb-drive out and slipped it into the side of his shoe. By wriggling his foot, the rectangle of metal and plastic worked its way under his instep. Although his heart was winning a world drumming competition, he took the time to gather together the five sheets of paper he'd been working from, folded them in half and shoved them under his jumper, tucking the ends into the waistband of his jeans. Wondering how many weird things could happen in one day he huffed out his held breath while shuffling the manuscript to give it an untidy appearance as though it was what he'd been working on. Satisfied there were no traces of his research to be seen, he stood.

Now he could investigate.

At another scrape, Shane Douglas reached over and flicked the light switch, leaving the house in darkness except for the dull glow from the oven and microwave electronics in the kitchen, which never went out unless there was a power outage. It took a couple of seconds for his eyes to adjust, during which, he'd snuck the two metres to the side of the window nearest the front door, twitched back the edge of the closed venetian blind and spied the huddled form crouched in the corner behind the only pot-plant he owned. It only remained on the edge of the veranda because it had survived three years of neglect with only sporadic watering. Despite its neglect, the shrub had flourished as though it knew, one day it would make a decent hiding spot.

Her long hair hanging in a ponytail was about all he could make out in the shadows. Although some men grew their hair and tied it back, he'd never seen a man with hair so long.

'Who are you and what are you doing here?'

There was a muffled squeal as the woman jack-knifed around, emitting a curse at the same time she slumped in a heap. Her shock mystified him for it was obvious someone was home with the light being doused or maybe she thought he was retiring to bed and didn't know she was there. So, her fear of out there was greater than what was inside the home. Interesting. So, what was out there? He crossed the carpet and unlocked the two deadlocks of the front door. Although everything of importance was now out of sight, he wasn't about to unlock the security screen door, at least not until he was certain it was safe.

'You want to tell me what's going on?'

'Shh, I'm hiding.' She hadn't moved but there was a definite tremor to the hushed voice coming from the darkness.

'From what?' he whispered.

'Two guys.'

'What about them?' He peered around searching for signs of anyone else being out and about but spied nothing moving or out of place. Everything looked normal. The row of still unemptied garbage bins could be hiding someone, as could the odd variety of front fences in various states of repair and disrepair. It was an ordinary, but attractive, outer-suburban Perth street, housing middle-income families. Some were poorer than others, some more house and garden proud. He was on the higher end of the income but lower in the pride stakes. Streetlights lit up the road and pathways but apart from a squashed Chocmilk carton and an empty cigarette box, the length of street as far as he could see, was empty.

'They were following and threatening me. I was terrified so I ran.' The shape moved to a sitting position with Lycra clad legs stretched out in front. Her back was against the far wall but from the street she would still be unseen. And it was a woman: he'd pity any guy who had such a sweet melodic voice.

'How do you know they haven't followed and know where you are?'

'I made sure I wasn't seen.'

A sliver of doubt crept in before it turned to a shiver of unease which quivered across his shoulders as edges of hidden pages prickled tender skin, reminding him to be cautious. Now he wished he'd taken the time to hide the work. This intrusion, on top of the weird behaviour of his peers at work earlier, was enough to send his anxiety level off the chart.

'So why here? Why, out of all these houses, did you pick this place to hide?'

'Well, I was hardly going to lead them back to my place.'

'And where would your place be?'

There was a hitch in her breath. 'Why do you want to know?' she stuttered after a lengthy pause, which turned the shiver of unease into a piercing stab.

'Well if I was going to see you home safe I'd need to know where I was going. If it's far away I'll need the car. Close by and I can walk.' To let her know he meant no harm, he turned the key of the flyscreen lock and stepped onto the veranda. The moist night air kissed his skin, a brief but welcome change of atmosphere from the stuffiness of his study but it did nothing to ease his tension.

'Oh, umm, there's no need. I'll be fine. I'll wait here for a few minutes.'

The answer didn't sound quite right. If she feared a couple of louts, surely she'd welcome a man ensuring she got home safe and sound. Or maybe she didn't trust him either. The thought hurt for he considered himself trustworthy.

'Hey, you up there.'

Startled by the shout, Shane glanced up. Two men stood at the gate, which was forever open, mainly because the hinges needed replacing and required a monumental shove to either open or close it. Less than a metre high it wasn't a deterrent for visitors, welcome or not, so it was a darn sight easier leaving it jammed open. It, along with a myriad other maintenance jobs, was on his *to do* list but at the moment he was time poor.

'That's them,' the woman whispered.

'Yes? You talking to me?' Shane called as he took another step towards the edge, keeping an eye to his side for any sudden movements.

'Yeah. You seen a woman?'

'I've seen thousands.'

'No need to be a smart-arse. In the past couple of minutes. Did you see a woman run past here?' The taller of the two men began walking up the path. Hands were fisted in the pocket of a dark bomber-jacket which looked to be leather. Shane wondered if the fists were hiding a weapon, but the pockets didn't seem to be large enough for a handgun, knife or bludgeon. Dark pants and shoes matched the man's hair. The face was shadowed, completing a formidable image. Shane understood why the woman would be scared.

To head him off, Shane moved to the edge of the veranda. 'No,' he said when it became necessary to say something. In a sense it was the truth. The woman he'd seen was huddled less than three metres from him. He sure hadn't seen her running.

'Then who were you talking to?'

Damn, how long had they been standing there and where did they come from? 'I was talking to myself, trying to figure out the best way to write my next paragraph. Seeing which way sounded better.' As an excuse it was lame but as a writer of sorts it was second nature. 'What's this woman done?' It was impossible to make out features with the man's face shadowed. The other man was half turned away as though he was still searching the street, or maybe it was a deliberate ploy to not be seen. His wariness shot up another notch and he took a step back. Worry began to niggle and prod. What if this was a deliberate ambush?

'She broke into my house.'

Well this information changed things somewhat. 'Have you rung the police?' Shane called at the same time he heard a whispered obscenity from the female housebreaker.

'No, not yet.'

'Maybe you should. After all it's their job to track down burglars and they can collect fingerprints and DNA. Now if you'll excuse me, I've got some work to finish.' As he turned to go back inside, he peeked over his shoulder to make sure the two men were leaving and not rushing forwards. Once he was behind the relocked screen door, he paused and watched the two make their way down the street. It seemed strange they weren't searching down driveways and front yards as they went. They looked as though they were simply on an evening stroll chatting quietly to each other. The anomaly worried him. Satisfied they couldn't hear he turned to the woman. 'You've got ten minutes to leave, before I call the police.'

'Aren't you going to invite me in?'

The question threw him. Two minutes ago she refused his offer to see her home and now she wanted to get inside. Why? 'Not likely. I don't know you and from what those two said, I certainly can't trust you.'

'They were lying, I didn't break into any house.' She shuffled forwards on her backside, reminding him of a caterpillar humping along the ground. Now she was less than a metre from him, he could make out some features in the dull rays of the streetlight. About thirty, he guessed, and unremarkable in looks. She appeared to be tall and lean but fit, if he took into consideration the muscular shape of bare arms. She certainly wasn't some prissy dolly type.

'Says you. They said different. I trust you about as much as I trust those two.' He indicated with his hand in the direction the two had gone. 'You didn't want to tell me where you lived, didn't want me to see you home. Said you were fine. And now you want inside my home? I don't think so. One of your minutes is up. Nine to go before I call the police. Goodnight.' He shut and relocked the heavy front door, laughing aloud at the less than favourable mutterings from his unwelcome guest.

Normally he'd be a little more understanding and a heap more welcoming but with vitally important papers stuffed down his pants and an uncomfortable jut of a more important thumb-drive telling him to be wary, he wasn't taking any chances. More than one person would love to get their hands on the statistics from the research he was analysing, although only three other people knew he had them. So far, none of those three had ever done or said anything to indicate they couldn't be trusted – until today. The over-eager looks on their faces when he'd told each about the meeting he'd called to announce the results of his research, had been the first nerve-twitching indication. Pointed questions, when each had made individual visits to his lab, had created full-alert status to those tightened nerves. He'd been so concerned he brought all his research materials home for the first time. Now, he was more than thankful the files and thumb-drives were locked in his home safe. Results had been leaked before with devastating consequences. The perpetrator of those leaks hadn't been discovered. When he really thought about it, the only person he could rely on in the trust department was himself.

Without turning on any lights, he made his way to the guest bedroom, eased the papers from his abdomen and straightened them. He opened the wardrobe door and dropped to the floor on his knees. Two heavy boxes of books hid the safe which was concreted into the end wall. He was the only person who knew the combination. His fellow workmate, Steve Richards, thought he knew it, but Shane had deliberately given him a false combination. Steve had four digits whereas the old but solid safe needed six. And the four Steve had were way off the real ones, well, as way off as you can get with only ten digits to work from. Minimal noise was made as he unlocked the safe, slid the papers inside the top file, removed the thumb-drive from his shoe and put it alongside everything else in the safe before relocking it.

To give the impression he was a normal everyday guy doing normal everyday things, he went to the bathroom, flushed the toilet and turned on a few taps while carrying out ablutions before retiring to bed. As he re-hung the towel, a thought inched its way to the forefront of his mind. He said he was going to finish some work so maybe he should make out he was doing so. The woman still had two minutes if she was still there.

When he crept back to the front room on the balls of bare feet, it stunned him to see a beam of light flickering through the edges of the blind. Up and down it went, honing onto each of the three pictures on the wall, to the chair in the corner where it paused on the mess of papers on the seat. He scoffed to himself. She could read all she wanted of the minutes from the most boring meeting he'd ever attended. The local cricket club had nothing to hide and a measly amount of money to pilfer. As a favour to Justin, his workout buddy, Shane had been the required non-member needed to preside over the Annual General Meeting. Before Saturday, when he was meeting up with Justin at the gym, he had to verify the minutes as correct and sign off.

The light flickered across the wall, catching only the far edge of the desk. The nerve of the woman. What was she hoping to achieve? One hand brushed through his hair and down his face as he thought. His initial gut reaction had been correct. He grinned. Time to find out exactly what she was up to.

The moment he switched on the light the flashlight flicked off. For a second the intense silence was unnerving. It was broken by a whisper of a footstep. He waited for the creak of the central few boards which needed re-nailing. It was another job on his ever-growing *to do* list but time to do these menial tasks was almost non-existent until his research was finalised.

The expected *squawk* came, followed by another few seconds of silence. A *thud* indicated the woman had jumped the half metre from the veranda. With the light on, peeking through the edge of the blind would be a dead giveaway, so he shot across the passage into the rarely used sitting room. When his nose tweaked at the mustiness, he figured the room needed airing over the weekend. To prevent any light filtering from the other room, he shouldered the door shut and peeked through the edge of the blind in time to catch sight of her rear end disappearing around the corner of the house, heading for the backyard.

The sneaky little witch!

It took less than ten seconds to race down the passage to the laundry. Here the windows were not covered but he didn't much care since it faced into the backyard. Nobody should be out there but anyone peering in would see the obligatory sink, taps, washer, drier and a bench so tiny it was almost useless. Skinny overhead cupboards and an equally thin broom cupboard weren't anywhere near large enough to hold the essentials, but he managed by having the contents packed in rigid places. The room was too pokey to hold anything else but there were plans to make it larger when he began the next round of renovations – when he had the time.

In the dark it would be difficult for anyone to make him out unless they were standing slap bang against the windowpane but the running figure heading for the back fence was easily discernable. She moved with fluid grace and now she was unfolded, he could see she was taller than he had at first thought. It was impressive the way she vaulted the six feet of corrugated iron fence with ease, confirming her fitness level. Now he understood how she had arrived without being seen, giving some veracity to her story.

It was more than possible he saw evil intent in any unusual behaviour because of the information he had in his possession. Even after she had disappeared, he considered going after her to see where she lived but decided not to. No harm was done. Yes, two guys were looking for her, which also confirmed her story. The bit about her breaking into a house? Could be true but could also have been an excuse on the men's behalf. The only suspicious behaviour was the flashlight. He visualised himself in the same position. Would he be curious enough to sneak a peek?

Hell, yes.

Chapter Two

He was going to be late. A two-car bingle had blocked both lanes of Guildford Road, causing a massive snarl. After being at a standstill for almost ten minutes he'd managed to wangle his way into a side street to weave a way through back roads before re-entering the main road. Having slept in hadn't been a brilliant start to the day. That damn woman had been the cause of him sleeping through the alarm. Too edgy to relax, he'd lain awake into the early hours waiting for the sound of her return. Or maybe it was the two guys his overactive mind had been expecting, which was ridiculous because he'd turned on the security system. Anyone breaking in would have set it off with a wailing siren loud enough to waken the entire neighbourhood, resulting in the security firm ringing his mobile number as well as the police.

Deep down he knew he'd been over-cautious, but the knowledge hadn't eased his nervous tension one iota. Maybe he should do the analysis at work and not bring any home. But it was equally hard keeping things under wraps at the office. Being the head honcho of research meant fellow workers were free to seek him out for advice at any time. If he sequestered himself in some deep dark corner or locked the office door for any length of time, everyone would know he was working on something vital.

The sight of his favourite café was a relief. He glanced at his watch. Thirty minutes late. The meeting would have begun. Too bad and another five minutes wasn't going to make an ounce of difference. Since breakfast had been nothing more than a thought as he'd rushed through a brief shower and dressing, he indicated, glanced into the rear-vision mirrors and seeing it was safe, slowed and pulled into a parking bay to one side of the cafe.

The aroma of fresh pastries, brewed coffee beans and sizzling bacon set digestive juices flowing in both his mouth and stomach, which rumbled in anticipation. Being so late with the office crowd already fed and watered and now at work, what was normally a long queue, was now thankfully short. After placing his order he stood back to wait, frowning at the trill of his phone. Gut instinct told him who it would be but still he slid it from his pocket and pressed the green arrow.

'Where are you? Have you forgotten the meeting?' Steve sounded anxious.

'Sorry, got caught up in a traffic jam. Give me ten. I'm not far away.'

'You could have rung.'

'I could have, but like now it wastes time and I don't use my phone when I'm driving.' His name was called so he hung up, grabbed his large long-black coffee plus egg and bacon roll.

The rest of the journey was short and without hold-ups except someone had parked in his designated spot. Just dandy, he thought as he coasted a circuit of the jam-packed parking lot to find not a single vacant bay. Frustrated, he bumped over the kerb and parked in the only place possible, a strip of weeds between carpark and the pathway running along the edge of the road.

Instead of heading for his office on the second floor, which contained the medical research labs and executive offices, he turned right and strode down the passage to Conference Room Three. It was smaller than the other two, making it suitable for more private meetings. Conference room was a misnomer since it only had seating for ten around a circular table. A conference to him was a crowded auditorium with discussion papers read by experts in their field. Not a tête-à-tête among four. With breakfast in one hand and computer bag in the other, he shouldered his way through the door and came to a grinding halt.

A stranger stood next to the other three executives around the credenza. What the hell was going on? This was supposed to be a private discussion, so why was there another person? He sighed and slid his eyes shut. Yesterday and last night's events were more than enough to send his nerves twanging. Adding another stranger into the mix was beyond co-incidental and he didn't do co-incidence to this extent.

'About time,' growled Steve as he took a step forward. He looked as he always did; kind of scruffy. His greying hair was too long and seemed to have been finger-combed, highlighting the ruddy complexion and slightly sagging features. He wore a navy suit; coat unbuttoned revealing a striped shirt and red power tie sporting an obvious grease spot at the base. Steve never looked like the chief accountant of a research and analysis company. Shane could never figure out why. Despite being well renumerated for his position, Steve spent little on his appearance. Either that or he was a complete slob. It didn't take much effort or money to have the tie dry-cleaned or buy another. Shane visualised Steve's wife. Apart from the wedding, he'd only met Grace a few times at office functions. She was a pretty little woman. Not beautiful but sweet in both looks and nature. But in recent times her eyes always looked haunted. They held a deep sadness which didn't disappear when she smiled.

The C.E.O, Bill Hazelby, on the other hand, could model for the front cover of a men's fashion magazine. Tall and well built, he was always impeccably presented in the latest up-market business attire and never had a hair out of place on his perfectly groomed head. His wife matched him. Lisa was what Shane classed as high maintenance, always dressed in the latest fashion and wearing an outrageous amount of jewellery. Shane guessed it was of the fake variety for Bill would never be able to afford so many items of the real stuff. For some reason, Shane had never taken to the woman; she always gave the impression she was above everyone else and reminded him of a strutting peacock, showing off to gain attention.

Like Shane, the General Manager, Chris Evans, was somewhere in between: clean, neat and tidy, without being over the top. Of late, there was something about Chris which didn't gel. He'd been less sociable than normal, but his annual leave was coming up so maybe he was plain tuckered out after a year of ups and downs. The lowest of lows was when the results of important research had been stolen and sold to an opposition company, losing them a large sum of money. Now he thought about it, Chris seemed to sink into the background around that time so maybe Chris took the theft personally since he was the general manager.

Shane could relate to needing a break for he was getting to the stage of being exhausted. Because of the critical stage of his research, he'd deferred his own annual leave and was now regretting it.

He nodded to Bill as he set down his laptop and dropped the food next to it. The coffee was number one priority. He thumbed off the lid, inhaled a long whiff of the aroma and sighed as he sipped. He wasn't a coffee tragic like most of his workmates who depended on cup after cup of caffeine to keep them going. But one strong early morning brew was his weakness. It seemed to kick-start his motor. He guessed he appreciated it so much because he wasn't a coffee souse. One a day, but the single cup was rich, strong and aromatic. For the rest of the day he stuck to water while at work. It kept him hydrated and didn't interfere with thought processes while overseeing rigidly controlled chemical tests.

Chairs were pulled out and bodies folded into each. Wondering what the heck was going on, Shane took his sweet time. He settled in a seat apart from the others, placed the computer bag by his feet and tore the grease-streaked paper bag apart. Since no-one said a word, he lifted the roll, studied it, licked away a dribble of oozing barbecue sauce and sunk his teeth in. An appreciative rumble from his stomach was loud enough to cause a couple of snickers from his colleagues. Apart from a shrug of his shoulders he ignored them but as he chewed, he eyed each man. The expectant silence was unnerving so to break the ennui he swallowed and indicated the stranger.

'What's going on?'

'Ah, this is Will…' said Chris, in a tone giving the impression Chris was as unhappy about the man's presence as was Shane.

'Tyson,' the stranger interrupted with a grin.

Shane turned to Chris. 'And?' A gut feeling of dread threatened to send the mush of bacon, egg and bun right back up.

'Will is our security expert.' Wow, Chris was peeved.

Shane glanced at the new man as things began tumbling into place. 'Who owns a dark blue Range Rover and can't read,' he said and grinned at the audible gasp. He was pleased the owner of the car residing in his parking space had the good grace to look embarrassed. Ignoring splutters from his three peers, he took another bite and chewed but breakfast wasn't as palatable as he'd hoped.

'I think I may have parked in his spot. Sorry, I didn't know.' Will Tyson sounded genuine.

Shane swallowed before raising one eyebrow at Tyson. 'It's a big sign saying it's reserved for my number plate.' He knew he was being rude but damn it all, he hadn't been a party to a monumental decision. He had the same number of shares in this company as the other three and the same amount to lose if the opposition got hold of the details of this new product. If the efficacy of this new cancer drug was as good as tests indicated, and he was now certain it was, he was on to something big, which would be worth millions.

'Have you got a report?' asked Steve.

Shane stared at him. Steve wanted to discuss results without divulging the reason behind the presence of Mr Security? Not going to happen.

'No.' He took another bite.

'Why not?' came from Bill in a tone which indicated displeasure. Well, he wasn't the only one feeling pissed.

Taking his time to chew and swallow, Shane placed the remains of the roll on the bag, lifted his head and eyeballed each man. Since they were playing games, so would he. 'There's a requirement of natural bodily functions. It's called sleep. Without enough, the brain doesn't compute so well. Analysing pages and pages of innumerable test results, accurately,' he emphasised the word, 'requires a clear functioning brain. When figures start blurring together and make no sense it means the brain is begging for respite. I went to bed. Hence the reason I was running late this morning. My body refused to rouse at my alarm because it hadn't had enough sleep.'

Sitting back, he popped the last piece of breakfast into his mouth, relishing the stunned looks on all present, although Tyson looked more amused than stunned. 'I have some results,' he added after an uncomfortable silence.

'Are they as good as we hoped?' asked Bill.

'No,' he lied.

'No?' Steve thumped a fist on the table.

The coffee wavered so Shane swept one hand around it to prevent spillage. 'There's an anomaly but I'm not going to discuss it.'

'Why not?' asked Bill.

Not liking the look on Bill's face, Shane pointed to Tyson. 'There's the reason. You guys want to tell why he's here?'

'Bill suggested it,' said Chris.

'Why?' Shane questioned Bill over the rim of the cup.

'We can't afford a leak. Like last time.'

Shane didn't buy it. 'If we'd stuck to our agreement there wouldn't have been a leak.'

'There was last time,' said Steve, sounding a lot more vehement than the others.

'And we still don't know who,' butted in Bill.

'But last time a whole heap more people knew,' said Shane. 'This time we agreed to keep it to us four only.' He sighed. 'And already we have five.'

'You guys want me to leave?' Will stood.

Shane indicated the chair. 'Sit. I'm not discussing results in any case.'

'But that's what this meeting is for.' Bill sounded way too put out for Shane's liking. Already twitching nerves tightened even more.

'It was… until you brought in a new man without bothering to discuss it with me.' He crushed the paper bag and shoved it into his pocket. Disgruntled with the outcome of the so-called private meeting, he hefted his computer bag from the floor, grabbed the remains of his coffee and stood. 'Now if you'll excuse me, I've got work to do.' As he rolled back his chair his mobile phone rang. The coffee went back on the table before he slid the phone from his shirt pocket. The number was unfamiliar, so he took the call.

Adrenalin spurted and his breakfast threatened to surge back up his throat at the message.

'I've got to go,' he said as he grabbed the coffee. 'My house has been broken into.'

Chapter Three

Despite being desperate to get home, Shane took the time to remove the council-issued parking ticket from under the windscreen wiper and transferred it to the recalcitrant blue Range Rover. It was nothing more than a childish message since his number plate was scrawled on the ticket, but he wasn't in the mood to deal with it right now. In the end the company would pay the fine.

There was a tight swelling in his throat by the time he turned the last corner. What had taken him over an hour to drive earlier was halved without the bottleneck of rush hour traffic being brought to a standstill by an accident. Fast as he was, the police had been quicker. Blue and red strobe lights flashed from the top of a marked police car. There was no need for sirens for they would have been drowned out by the strident eardrum shattering wail coming from his house. One officer stood on the front veranda with a finger stuck in each ear. Shane was almost at the veranda before he remembered what was sitting in full view on the front seat of his unlocked car. After rapidly retracing his steps, he shoved the computer bag under the passenger seat and ensured the car was locked by tugging on the door handle.

On his return trip up the brick-paved pathway, he was met by the officer who had removed fingers from ears and dropped them to either side of his hips. One hand rested on a holster and the other on a still-furled metal baton. It was difficult to see if the item in the holster, was a gun or taser and he didn't relish the idea of finding out.

'This is a crime scene; you can't come in.' The huge officer stood firm, feet shoulder width apart and chest puffed out.

'This is my house. If you want the alarm turned off you're going to have to let me pass.' Shane didn't wait for the man to give him the okay but stepped around him and jogged the last few metres. He didn't stop at the open front door but strode down the passage and into the kitchen where he shouldered his way past another officer who was studying the control panel for the security system. Shane punched in the code he changed every few days.

The sudden silence was intense but didn't stop his ear drums and the tiny bones behind from tingling in echoing quivers.

'Mr Douglas?' the officer asked.

'Yes.'

'Thank, God. I've never heard such a loud alarm. The code the security firm gave didn't work.'

'I changed it this morning but haven't had a chance to let them know.' It was only then Shane noticed the mess. He ran a hand through his hair as his brain absorbed the emptiness of hanging out drawers, the contents of which were strewn over the floor. Open cupboard doors indicated they had been searched and what had been the contents of his fridge looked like a giant mushy fruit and vegetable salad, swimming in a juice and milk dressing. He glanced at the officer. 'How long did it take for you guys to get here?'

'Five minutes after we received the call. Security company said it was a priority. We were in the vicinity.'

Shane spun on his heel to inspect the rest of the house. Five minutes was not long. Add a few minutes for phone calls to be made. Ten minutes at the most. Maybe. Hopefully it wasn't long enough to make a thorough search.

It was impossible to believe he hadn't noticed the mess when he'd stalked through but at the time, he was hell bent on killing the alarm. He stood in the doorway of his bedroom and swore. The bed he hadn't had time to straighten earlier was stripped with the mattress now leaning on one end, against the side of the bed. Sheets and doona were unceremonious heaps scattered over the floor with the four pillows filling up any other spaces. How stupid did they think he was? The only thing anyone would find under his bed was six months – maybe more, of dust bunnies. Side tables were empty, ditto the wardrobe shelves and drawers. Hangers had been swept up and down with those shirts, jackets and trousers still actually on the hangers, all askew. Half of his clothes were gaining a new set of creases on the floor, wasting his dry-cleaning bill for the month.

The bathroom had an overpowering aroma of aftershave from a bottle which was now no more than glass shards drowning in the contents. Shane grinned. He'd never liked the brand but had never had the heart to tell his mother. A conscience meant he only ever splashed on his father's old favourite when he drove the 200 kilometres to visit the amazing woman who had single-handedly raised him and his two older sisters after his father had died way too young from pancreatic cancer. His heart hitched at the thought of the woman he loved and admired above all others.

As he headed towards the third bedroom he'd set up as a study when he'd first bought the house, but was now rarely used since creating the den, a single thought centred in his mind. If whoever was responsible for this invasion of his privacy had wasted time searching various rooms, they didn't know about the safe. Which eliminated Steve as the leak, which felt good. He related to and liked Steve the most.

The study was untouched, probably because the door had been shut giving the impression of an unused room. Maybe they hadn't thought to peek in as they passed, or maybe time had run out. He stood in the doorway and cast his eyes around. The room looked as he'd left it. Next stop, the guest bedroom and the safe. He turned and pulled up short. 'What are you doing here?'

Will Tyson shrugged his shoulders as a cynical smile crept from the corners of his mouth. 'I'm employed as the security expert and it appears you're in need of my expertise.'

'Go to hell!' Shane stalked down the passage and turned into the front room he'd been working in the previous night, cursing under his breath when he saw things askew.

The room wasn't tipped over but the intruders had been here. He took care studying the contents, visualising how he'd left things before he'd crawled into bed not long after midnight. This room he loved and used the most. Tucked in one corner was a large desk and office chair where he now did most of his work. Family photos were scattered around the room and his favourite art pieces hung on three of the walls. A couple of small side tables sat within easy reach of each seat. This was his den, the place he could kick back and relax. A sense of revulsion settled around his shoulders. How dare they invade this sanctum?

His eye caught a single sheet of paper which had slipped down the side of the desk. Shane crossed the room and bent to retrieve it. A quick glance and he burst out in laughter. 'Well, hell,' he muttered when he gained control over his mirth.

'What's so funny?'

Shane spun around to see Tyson leaning against the door jamb. 'Why are you still here?'

'Where's the safe?'

'Excuse me?'

'Richards said you had a safe and I needed to check it.'

Which put Steve right back on top of the suspicion list. A hard ball of regret jammed into his throat. But no way was Shane going to divulge anything about the safe. He needed time to think things through - to play what-ifs and maybes. But he didn't have time. What he did know for sure was he needed to get rid of Mr Smarmy Expert.

'It's in my office.'

The man straightened. 'Right, which room is your office?'

'One floor directly above where we met.'

'Pardon?'

'There's a safe in my office at work. Feel free to go check it out. Here, I'll give you the combination.' As he stepped over to the desk, he could feel his body quiver in anger. Control of a shaking hand while he scrawled random numbers between lefts and rights, was non-existent. It didn't require his three university degrees to figure out something was badly amiss. He snorted. *Amiss* was a poor word choice with its meaning of things being not quite right. Last night's little adventure suited the meaning. Now, *disastrous* or *catastrophic* were more apt. A few more came to mind, none of them pleasant. It had taken less than twelve hours for his world to be tipped upside down. This time yesterday he was brimming with joy, for test results indicated he'd found *the* formula to kill a very nasty strain of cancer cells. It had become a top-secret project after initial research tests had looked promising. Only four people knew about it. Now it was more than obvious someone he thought he could trust with his life, had blabbed. But who? And why? Well, the why was obvious – money and lots of it.

Turning back to the man he suspected was lead accomplice, he stuffed the scrap of paper into Tyson's hand. 'Now go. I don't have any work material here at home,' he lied.

'That's not what I was told.'

Shane baulked at the belligerent tone and stared at the man. 'Nobody, and I mean nobody but me, knows what I do after hours. I spent eighteen hours in the lab yesterday. Why would I bring more work home when exhaustion had set in?' An idea hit. 'Whoever broke in here got what they wanted. I was editing a manuscript. It's gone. It's the only thing missing.'

'A manuscript? About what?'

'What business is it of yours? I didn't write the damn book. I was doing someone a favour by offering editing suggestions. Now get out. I've got enough to deal with without you butting into my private life.'

When the man looked as though he wasn't going to budge, Shane grabbed his elbow and despite the size of the man, dragged him back to the kitchen which was now a hive of activity with forensic officers splashing grey dust over every freakin' surface. His newly renovated ultra-modern kitchen which seemed to be vast, now emanated a claustrophobic sensation. Crammed with six large male bodies stepping over and around piles of kitchenalia and spilt food, its proportions suddenly seemed inadequate.

'Officer, could I suggest you question this idiot about the break-in? He's dropped a few clangers indicating he was a party to this.' Shane shoved Tyson into the arms of the stunned looking officer who'd tried to disarm the alarm, spun away and retreated to his den, slamming the door behind him, which set up a wave of rattles as pictures on walls and small items on furniture responded. A grin spread across his face faster than water going over Niagara Falls as he listened to the scuffle and protestations. The prat should now be tied up for a few hours.

Adrenalin flooded through his veins, causing him to pace while trying to get an over-active and confused brain to calm, clear and make some logical sense. After the nth crossing of the carpet, he yanked the seat from under the desk, spun it around and plonked into it. It felt as though every single cell in his body was vibrating with tension. 'Come on, man,' he muttered to himself. 'Relax. Think. Figure out what the hell's going on and what to do about it.' He was a research scientist, used to analysing and reaching logical conclusions. He should be able to nut this out. One hand grubbed through his hair while the other drummed on the desktop. 'Think, man.' Determined to get his body to relax, he sank back into the seat, spread his legs out and apart while huffing out a long breath. He sucked in another lungful of oxygen as he inhaled. In, two, three, four, five. Out, two, three, four, five. Eyes shut, he continued controlled breathing until he felt the tension ease and the mush of garbled brain cells began to sort themselves out. Clarity arrived. Somehow, he had to stop this madness. The best way was to ensure thumb-drives and paperwork were well hidden.

Thumb-drives. Hell. He shot from the seat and raced through the house, down the path and yanked on the door handle of his car. Still locked. Relief surged.

'Douglas, help me here.'

Shane glanced up and grinned. Those cuffs looked good wrapped around Tyson's wrists.

'Tell them it wasn't me.'

It felt darn good to see the man looking panicked. Shane took his time ambling towards the three men. The two original officers had Tyson jammed against the side of the squad car. The giant officer, a sergeant by the stripes on his sleeve, was studying the piece of paper on which Shane had scrawled a make-believe safe combination. A laugh escaped. It looked so convincing as evidence. He wondered if he could bring himself to admit the truth.

'Tell them you gave me those numbers.'

Poor man was actually begging. 'Why?'

'Because it's the truth would be a good reason.'

And Shane was an honest man. He'd been brought up to be honest, amongst other things. His mother had instilled many good values into her children. Sound morals, strong independence, respect for others and a good dose of honesty and integrity. He nodded to the sergeant. 'I gave it to him. It means nothing.'

Tyson slumped on a long breath which whistled through his teeth. 'Thank you. Now you can get these cuffs off me.'

The sergeant shot Shane a questioning quirk of one eyebrow. Shane thought. Doubts stabbed but so did his conscience.

'Look, Douglas, I was at the meeting the whole time you were. I was *on time*, waiting half an hour for you to turn up. No way could I have been the one who broke into your house. Why would I? I've been employed to avoid this happening.'

Shane straightened. 'True, you weren't the one who broke in but…' he sucked in a long breath. 'I know nothing about you. Don't know why you were even at the meeting. For all I know this whole shemozzle could have been planned – by you.' He stabbed a finger in the man's chest and enjoyed the resultant wince. 'You *say* you are a security expert. I've seen nothing to prove your claim. Don't know your credentials. Hell, I hadn't even met you before this morning. Put yourself in my shoes. What conclusion would you come to if you were blindsided by the presence of a stranger at a top-secret meeting? Followed by a break-in at your house at the same time. Rather a convenient coincidence, don't you think?'

'Yeah, when you put it like that, I can see your point. To be honest I was surprised you didn't know about me being there this morning. Someone screwed up in the communication department.'

'Someone more than screwed up.' Shane turned to the sergeant and sighed. 'Can you check his credentials? He wasn't the one who broke in. But I still don't trust him… or anyone else right now. Ah, hell, let him go but I want him checked out.' He turned away. 'I need to get my car off the street,' he added as he flicked the remote to unlock the car. It wasn't the car he was concerned about but more what it contained and the sooner he got everything locked in the garage the better he would feel.

Chapter Four

Shane shouldered the door shut behind the last police officer. It was ridiculous how he had been made to feel like the criminal while being questioned at length. It had been difficult giving in-depth answers without lengthy explanations about things he couldn't reveal. They were real interested in the happenings of last night but the descriptions he could give were generalised. If he'd known at the time he would need to describe all three late night visitors in detail, he would have taken a darn sight more notice. Yeah, he knew the adage about hindsight but right now it fitted the bill most aptly. Who knew a simple break-in could cause so much activity? All the little cases of powder, brushes, cameras and the myriad of bits and bobs needed for finding evidence had been packed up. Most of it had been useless. Whoever had broken in had been wearing gloves. There were a few smears and smudges, dirt from ripple soled shoes: picked up from his own back yard, a few footprints which had been photographed and cast but little else of value. Unless one didn't consider the gaping hole in his laundry window which he'd covered with boards until he could get the glass replaced, and an unholy mess in three rooms.

Where to start? A drink. He needed a drink. A shower and the shave he'd foregone this morning, would go down well plus a good ten hours of sleep. Drink first. In the kitchen he stepped over scattered cutlery, the remains of his fresh food supply, various food packages and cans and opened the refrigerator door. Not being a big consumer of alcohol, he scanned the almost empty shelves and spied the remains of a bottle of Sauvignon Blanc he'd opened over the weekend. Assuming it was still okay he unscrewed the lid, sniffed – smelt okay, so he sipped and it tasted fine. The first glass he could find was the small tumbler he'd used before rushing off to work. After rinsing it he shook out the water, filled it to the brim and sipped, savouring the sweet but dry coolness as it slid over his tongue.

Scanning the room, he figured it was going to take what was left of the day to put things away and clean up the mess. But first things first. Now he was alone, he could investigate the one place he hadn't dared look while anyone was around.

An edginess which had simmered all day, rose to a boil as he entered the guest bedroom. It looked the same as he'd left it. After shutting the door behind him, he checked the blinds on the side window were drawn so prying eyes couldn't see in. Nerves prickled as he neared the closet. It was stupid to be so uptight but his breath stuttered and held the moment he gripped the wardrobe door handle and swung it open. Held breath whooshed out at the untouched sight. He knelt. Holding another breath, his fingers grasped the edges of the boxes and tugged.

The safe door was locked. Since he was the only person who knew the combination his tension should have eased but his innards tied themselves into tight knots as he worked the dial backwards and forwards. Slowly he edged the door open and the breath huffed out. It was all there. There sat the results of his success. The formula worked. After months and months of tweaking, calculating, testing and waiting – it had worked.

Huffing out a long breath of relief, Shane sank back on his heels. He should be overjoyed but serious unease shimmied through his innards. Someone else knew or thought they knew. And they wanted it. He wasn't sure what to do about it and for a man who was always self-assured, his indecision rankled. At the moment, it was safe. But for how long? What lengths would his unknown adversary go to get their hands on *his* formula? As though the enemy was looking over his shoulder, he glanced around, shut the safe door, reset the lock and slid the boxes back.

While sipping the wine, he downloaded all the important files from his laptop onto a series of thumb-drives. Everything was backed up three times before erasing every file relating to work. If anyone managed to steal the laptop they'd find nothing of importance. They were welcome to read his emails and he didn't do the social media thing. Couldn't see any sense in jabbering about his private life – not that he had time in any case. And who would be interested in what he ate for breakfast, or his opinion on some inane sensationalist piece about some actor's misadventures or indiscreet misdemeanours? Who cared? For the time being he added the thumb-drives to the safe. He'd have to find a new hiding place quick smart.

Next job was cleaning up the mess. He wasn't sure where to start. Another tour of the house and his inner voice said, 'Do the easy bits first.' The den. Of the rooms which had been done over, it was the easiest. Not much had been touched but it still stabbed to know some unknown had invaded his privacy. It was ridiculous to feel it, but the room felt dirty. He wanted to scrub the place to rid it of the filth of violation but instead settled for putting things in their correct places, lingering on the single page of manuscript. Sometime soon he would have to ring his mum and let her know someone was so enamoured with the book, they stole it. The darn thing was probably now residing in a garbage can. Once the perpetrator realised how innocuous his mother's family story was, they would have screwed it up in frustration or torn it to shreds. Deep down, Shane knew the intruders had taken the manuscript, believing it to be a copy of his notes, at the very last second before hurtling out the front door. He was certain they escaped via the door for the police said it was open when they arrived. It was karma they grabbed something so unimportant to anyone except a few members of a family. Karma was something he believed in. Everyone got their just deserts in the end. He grinned. In this instance they received it sooner than expected.

Next, he tackled the bedroom. Bed first. It beckoned, especially after so little sleep last night. Once the bed was made the room didn't look half so bad. Strewn bedding took up a lot of space and looked untidy. It still felt kind of spooky knowing some lowlife had been through his things, but it didn't feel as bad in here as it did in the den. Which really didn't make sense for this is where he put his head on the pillow each night and slid into unconsciousness, supposedly safe in his own home. It was also the place he shared with his latest female conquest for more interesting activities. But any lady friend was rarely invited into his den, a place where his mother and sisters were welcome. Mystified, he perched on the side of the bed. Why was there no issue with his family invading his den, but he baulked about inviting the women he dated into the same domain? He scoffed as he shrugged his shoulders. What the hell did it matter?

What had started out as nothing more than a broken bottle of aftershave had morphed into a choking abyss of stench. The moment he stepped into his en-suite, tears swept across his eyes and his throat gagged and closed. No wonder he hated the stuff. Shane turned back into the bedroom, sucked in a lung full of clean air and held it in while he eyed the shattered bottle and wondered how he could get rid of it. The glass was the problem. A bucket of water tossed over the liquid would dilute it and wash it down the drain but glass in the sewerage system was probably not a good idea. He bet a year's pay the smell would linger. But it was possible the stuff would kill any microscopic nasties residing in his drains. Maybe he could try the formula in his next round of tests to kill off cancer cells.

His stomach threatened to eject the wine he'd enjoyed as he dropped long lengths of paper towels over the puddle. While osmosis occurred, absorbing the moisture, he fetched a dustpan, brush and plastic garbage bin. Back in the bathroom he scooped up the sodden paper towel with the pan and tipped it into the bin.

It felt like forever before he'd rid the tiles of glass shards and splinters and wrapped the towels in sheet after sheet of newspaper. The lot went into the now empty garbage bin he retrieved from the front verge. The stench lingered. It seemed to have infused itself into his clothes and skin. Two buckets of water thrown over the bathroom floor washed the remaining liquid down the drain. He left the rest of his strewn belongings where they were, tore off his clothes and stood under the stinging hot shower. He wasn't sure whether to wash the clothes or bin them. He eyed the trousers; his favourite pair so he hooked them with one wet foot and dragged them into the shower stall followed by his shirt and underwear. They could soak a while for they were worth preserving if the smell could be washed away.

As he stepped from the shower, he heard the phone ringing. Snagging a towel, he draped it around his waist and raced to the bedside table. When the phone slipped from wet hands, he scrambled to catch it with wet fingers. Finally succeeding, he jabbed it against his ear.

'Shane, where are you?'

'Carol, dinner, damn.'

'You forgot.'

'Sorry, yes.' A long sigh escaped. 'It's been a hell of a day. What time is it?' His eyes went to the digital bedside clock. It wasn't blinking. He scoffed. He'd put it back but forgotten about the basics: switching on the power.

'Seven thirty. You aren't coming, are you?'

Shane grimaced. Carol sounded miffed and he couldn't blame her. She had taken the time to cook a meal after a day at work. 'If I leave now, I can be there in twenty.' And it was the last thing he felt like doing.

'Don't bother,' she growled. 'It's obvious I'm not important to you.'

Damn it. 'Carol no, please let me explain. My house was broken into and has been left in a mess. The police took ages to investigate before leaving and I've only just had the chance to shower and shave.' He scrubbed a hand through still dripping hair.

'Oh, okay. What if I bring dinner to you? It's only a casserole and salad.'

'You will? I can still come over if you want.'

'No, I'll come to you.'

'Thank you and, Carol…'

'Yes?'

'You are important to me. You know that.'

As he hung up, he mused over his relationship with Carol Maguire. He'd even considered marriage until he'd brought the subject up and been met with a stone wall of horror. After being introduced at a work function by Chris, they'd begun their relationship as social friends enjoying outings together, which over the months turned into friends with benefits. At the time neither was seeking a commitment of forever after. Carol was a career girl only halfway up the ladder to where she wanted to be in a job she loved but somewhere along the line Shane's feelings had grown more intense. He enjoyed her company and the sex was great. She made him laugh with her witty repartee. They enjoyed the same things and listening to the same type of music but when he'd suggested they would make a great husband and wife team the hackles went up. The look of horror on Carol's face was something he'd never forget so he'd backed off, assuring Carol he was joking. Since then he hadn't had time to think about what it meant, but they still dated on a regular basis, at least twice a week, usually on Tuesday and Friday, with Carol insisting she kept the weekends free to spend with her widowed mother.

While waiting, he cleared a path to the kitchen table, dumping cutlery into a sink of soapy hot water. While they soaked, he scooped up the mushy food with a large ladle and shovelled it into a couple of plastic bags. He didn't really want to put it in his own bin since it had only been emptied. It would be an entire week before the next collection; a week for the revolting mess to ripen with a stench he didn't relish. Instead he dropped the securely tied bags outside the garage door. Tomorrow morning he would dump them in a city bin near work which was collected daily.

Although he kept the kitchen clean and tidy, everything would have to be washed thoroughly. He worked with microscopic organisms and knew exactly how quick they attached themselves to anything and reproduced to massive numbers in a very short space of time. A certain amount was beneficial in building and maintaining the body's immunity but floors, no matter how clean, harboured an amazing array of germs. Especially after the number of feet which had traipsed over his floor in the past few hours. His floor would be microbe heaven and the little critters would be having a full-on orgy.

By the time he heard Carol knocking on the front door, the table was cleared and graced with enough sparkling clean cutlery and china for two people to enjoy a meal.

'Coming,' Shane called as he strode down the passage while wiping damp hands on an even damper tea-towel. He swung the door open and smiled. 'Hi.'

'Hello, what happened?'

Shane unlocked the screen door, instantly reaching out to rescue a large plastic bowl teetering on top of a foam food box. 'Someone broke in this morning. Made a bit of a mess.'

'Why?' As Carol stepped inside Shane brushed his mouth against her cheek, frowning when she stiffened before rushing past.

'Only the perpetrator knows.' Perplexed, he watched Carol rush down the passage. *What the hell is wrong with her? Ah, she's miffed because he hadn't turned up as planned.*

'Phew, what's the smell?' Carol asked as they neared his bedroom.

Shane laughed. 'Broken bottle of after-shave.'

'Not your usual brand.'

He felt chuffed she would recognise the difference. 'Thank goodness. They did me a service by getting rid of it, but it could take a while for the smell to dissipate.'

When she reached the kitchen, Carol paused at the entrance. 'Wow, I see what you mean.'

Shane was forced to stop at her rigid back. 'Sorry, I haven't had time to get it all tidied up,' he said over her shoulder, 'but we have clean cutlery and plates. It's as far as I've got.'

'I can help but let's eat first. The casserole should still be hot enough.' Carol busied herself emptying the food box. The moment the lid came off an aroma of spices filled the room.

'Something smells really good,' Shane said as he peeked into the salad bowl before setting it on the table. A colourful array of chopped salad vegetables was coated in a creamy dressing. Carol lifted out a china dish tied in a tea-towel, unknotted it and lifted the lid.

'I'll get the wine,' said Shane as he wheeled away and retrieved the remainder of the wine and poured a glass for Carol. The last thing he needed was more alcohol. What he'd consumed so far had taken the edge of his tension but after the happenings of the past twenty-four hours he couldn't afford to lose the ability to focus and think straight.

Dinner was a delicious but quiet affair. Shane couldn't figure out why the silence. Yes, he was dog tired and socialising of any kind was way down on his priority list, but the usually effusive Carol was equally as quiet, which concerned him. Maybe she was mad at him.

'I'm really sorry for forgetting about dinner tonight.'

She jolted, losing the forkful of food she was about to put in her mouth. 'That's all right. Truly, I understand.' She refilled her fork and delicately slipped it into her mouth. When her eyes skittered away, he wondered why she couldn't hold eye contact.

'Then what's wrong?'

'What do you mean?' A tell-tale blush stole up her neck as her eyes jerked back to him.

'You seem distracted.'

A frown crept between her eyes. 'Distracted? I don't know what you mean.'

'You've hardly said a word. I figured you were mad at me for forgetting.'

'Oh, no, I'm not mad.' Her laugh sounded forced, leaving him wondering if he was in some crazy time warp and this whole day was only some weird dream. Everything about the past twenty-two hours had been surreal.

'I'm feeling a bit tired and was really wondering about this?' A hand swept around, indicating the mess.

'Yeah, same here. I can't figure out why anyone would want to ransack my house. Especially since nothing of value was taken.'

'Nothing?'

'No, all my electronics are still here. My good watch, gold chain and loose coins were overlooked even though they were in full view.'

'So, nothing was taken.'

'Nothing important.'

'But something is missing? What?'

The bad side of his conscience yelled at him to not disclose anything, which was ridiculous. If there was anyone he could trust, it would be Carol and she didn't know about his research results. Speech defied him. To cover the silence, he settled his knife and fork across the plate and shoved it to one side while his mind see-sawed. Tell her all or tell her nothing. Since he'd made a pact with his workmates to not talk about the research results until an announcement was made, he would abide by the promise, so nothing won. 'A pile of scrap paper.' Well, it was a half-truth. It was in a pile and after his mother had typed in any corrections he suggested it would have been scrapped. Now he was glad he hadn't had time to edit more than three chapters for he'd have to do it again.

'Why would they take scrap paper?'

'Beats me. I think it was grabbed at the last minute so whoever took it didn't have time to scan the pages before running. Do you want coffee?'

'Umm, no. I need to make tracks.' Carol stood and began gathering plates and cutlery. Without looking at him she piled them on the side of the sink as though he wasn't in the room.

This sudden haste to leave was disconcerting. 'You're not staying the night?' And what happened to the offer to help clean up?

Her back stiffened before she turned slowly. 'No, I'm pretty tired and have an early meeting.'

In a sense he was glad. It would be a struggle to give a session under the sheets the attention Carol deserved. He scoffed to himself. Said a lot about their relationship when he was thankful Carol wasn't staying. To assuage his guilt, he took her in his arms, hauled her close and kissed her until she pulled away, gasping for air. It took a moment for him to come to his senses, enough time for Carol to pile her dishes in the food box and head for the passage. Still dazed, Shane followed and held the door open for her. His sanity returned in an instant when Carol walked straight past him, across the veranda, down the steps to her car and opened the door without looking back or saying a word. She simply drove off leaving him both stunned and mystified. What the hell just happened?

Chapter Five

'I'm sorry, my little friend. I hate doing this to you after all we've been through but right now, I can't see any other way.' Shane inserted the fine needle into the top of the tiny jar, tipped it upside down and held it up to the light. He slowly dragged the plunger out, keeping his eye on the markings until he had enough Ketamine to do the job. After withdrawing the needle, he pushed the plunger a tiny way to rid the fine steel tube of air bubbles. Sadness settled into the pit of his gut as he studied the white lab rat. *Fighter*, he'd called it. His eyes tracked across to the other cage where *Winner* worked his whiskered jaws on a tasty pellet.

As he wrestled one hand through the flap of Fighter's cage, his pulse raced and thrummed through his ears. One finger stroked the silky white hairs on Fighter's head. The rat gave him a look which said he knew what was about to happen, causing Shane's heart to twist and tighten.

'I'm sorry,' he muttered as he gently lifted the animal and settled him between his forearm and chest. He tugged on the scruff and took utmost care inserting the needle before injecting Fighter with enough of the drug to end the poor animal's life. Deed done, he dropped the syringe onto the bench and stroked the white fur until Fighter's eyes slid shut and breathing ceased. Moisture swept across Shane's eyes, making it difficult to see as he placed the animal back in his cage and covered him with a thin layer of straw, making it look as though Fighter had nestled there to sleep.

It was no easier euthanising Winner. Overwhelmed, Shane plopped his backside onto the lab stool and dropped his head into his hands. No way should he be affected by the loss of a couple of lab rats. He'd become inured to the necessary task but these two had become special. By testing the new drug, these two little guys had fought off and overcome cancer. The tumours had shrunk and all but disappeared within weeks. They had been his success story and this was some sick reward he was giving them.

'I'm so sorry, guys,' he mumbled as he rose and raced to the bathroom where he bent over the basin, fighting down serious nausea. It was a good ten minutes before he felt he could continue the early morning tasks. To rid himself of the gut-wrenching sick feeling, he dunked his entire head under the running cold tap and patted the moisture away with paper-towels. As a final gesture he finger-combed his hair. When he straightened he caught sight of his image in the mirror. The reflection sickened him, so he spun away and returned to his private laboratory.

The rows of Petrie dishes and phials were clinical in neatness, each wearing a detailed label. Having spent the past twelve months concentrating on this one project, Shane knew exactly what each contained and could reach by instinct for a particular test. The dishes he wanted were to the far right in the top row. From the far end he removed four and placed them in order on the sterilised stainless-steel workbench. Two minutes was all it took to inspect each. The surfaces looked as though they were riddled with black poppy seeds, but each dot was a cluster of dead cancer cells. Next, he went to the cryogenic unit, unscrewed the lid with heavily gloved hands and searched for the correct phial amongst the misty condensation. It didn't really matter what he used to set things up but in case Steve, Bill or Chris asked another chemist to do a test, Shane wanted things to look authentic. He'd thought long and hard about this, adding as many what-ifs he could think of. Tense nerves felt as though they wanted to ping apart while waiting for the live cancer cells to thaw.

His being here at five in the morning wasn't so unusual. Sometimes he did all-nighters when experiments had to be watched, studied and recorded at regular intervals. Fellow scientists often did the same but right now there was nothing they were working on requiring such a level of intense scrutiny.

Utmost care and fierce concentration were needed to withdraw enough fresh cells and drop a few to hug some of the dead cell clusters. 'Not too many,' Shane muttered under his breath, or it would look contrived but at the same time he needed enough to make his claims appear legitimate. A deep sigh shuddered out when he'd finished. He leant back and studied each dish. Happy with the way they looked, he replaced the live cell phial in the freezer and slipped three dishes into their climate-controlled slots. The used instruments went into a sharp's repository bin in one of the other labs. The final dish he placed next to the microscope. Using a specimen from the dish, he readied a slide, set it in place under the clips and put his eye to the lens to examine the cells. Perfect. He peeled off the latex gloves and dropped them into the bin labelled *Contaminated Refuse*. Looking into the mirror was not an option as he sterilised his hands in the remote chance live cancer cells had transferred to his skin.

There was one more task to do. He glanced at the large round clock on the wall behind him and realised he had to hurry. Shane pulled off the protective lab garments before scooting back to his office where he pressed the button on his computer. While waiting for it to boot up, he slid the fingers of one hand into his pants pocket and eased out three new thumb-drives. It was a good job he was meticulous in maintaining files under correct headings, he thought as he downloaded only the information relating to *Prancer*, the codename he used for the cure for pancreatic cancer. When the last file was downloaded, he deleted the relevant files from the database and set about renaming a few irrelevant and not so important files bearing the same name. If anyone wanted Prancer information they would only download those with that name without opening each to check what was in the files. They would be time-short especially since his computer was password protected. Snoopers would need to waste time getting past his password, which wasn't an impossible task, especially with the level of I.Q. inhabiting this complex. Almost every employee was above average in the computer savvy department. Given adequate time many could retrieve deleted files, but he had no intention of giving anyone the required amount of time needed. Happy everything was done Shane went in search of breakfast.

Worried thoughts tumbled through his brain as he slid along the back-wall bench of a cubicle in the eatery three buildings down from the laboratories. It wasn't his favourite dining establishment but would do since it was the closest. Scanning the menu was a useless exercise because he knew what he would order but reading ingredients eased his mind while waiting for the server. As he slotted the menu into its holder the sound of a loud scrape had him glancing up.

Shane scowled. 'I'm beginning to get a complex. Why are you following me?'

Will Tyson wedged his powerfully built body between the wooden arms of a chair which looked way too small for the task. Tyson wasn't fat but Shane bet there were well-toned muscles under the navy suit. He was a large man with giant sized shoulders.

'I'm not following you. Like yesterday, I'm here for breakfast. It's the closest café to your building and I need to eat. More to the point, what are you doing here? You're supposed to breakfast at home, bring a packed lunch and either eat at home in the night or dine out with your lady friend.'

Shane stood to leave but a large hand gripped his wrist.

'Wait, let me explain. I've done background checks on everyone.'

'Everyone?' Disbelief kept Shane's feet super-glued to the floor.

'Everyone including the cleaners. Here.' Tyson pulled folded papers from an inside pocket. 'My credentials.'

Shane was in two minds about staying but he grabbed the papers and regained his seat while opening them out. He scanned each of the sheets with care, to ensure he missed nothing important. Will Tyson was head of his own private security firm and had clearance from not only the state and federal police but also the American C.I.A.

'C.I.A?' Shane asked as he re-folded the pages.

'Yes, and if I tell you why I'll have to…'

'Kill me, such a well-worn cliché but I get the picture.' A server arrived. Shane turned the sheets over. He might not like or trust the man but he wasn't stupid. Some things needed to remain private and he wasn't about to be responsible for allowing roving eyes to glance at Tyson's papers. When Tyson added his order, Shane became resigned to the fact they would be up close and cosy for at least the next half hour. The moment the server left Shane took his time to read every darn word of Tyson's credentials. He was indeed an expert in his field. Shane handed them back. 'I still don't trust you.'

Tyson's frown turned into a smile. 'I can't blame you. Not the way things panned out. Is there anyone in the firm you don't trust?'

The answer didn't require thinking about. 'You would be better off asking me who I do trust. The list would be a darn sight shorter.'

Tyson tried to sit back but it was more than obvious he was in a lot of discomfort stuffed into the too small chair. He stood, glared at the chair then eyed Shane and his long bench. 'Shove over.' Without waiting he sidled around the table, perched on the bench, deliberately thumping hip to hip. Shane laughed at the man's audacity as he slid along the vinyl seat. Giving in, he moved the cutlery, paper serviette, side plate and filled water glass in front of Tyson.

'So, who do you trust?' wavered in his left ear as he moved his own place setting to his end of the table.

'At the moment there's only one person, me.'

'Not the other execs?'

'No, not if they can get you here without discussing it with me first.'

'You're a part owner.'

'Four equal parts.'

'Which is why you're a tad put out.'

'Tad is not the word I would use. I'll be asking questions the minute each man walks in the door this morning. Who contacted you?'

'Richards.'

'Steve? That surprises me.'

There was silence while coffee was served. It smelt so darn good. Eager for the caffeine hit, Shane wrapped his hands around the mug, sniffed and sipped, recoiling at the sharp sting of still boiling water. The coffee wasn't as good as the one from his favourite café but wasn't undrinkable. He transferred a splash of cold water from glass to mug to take the edge off the heat. The next sip was more cautious followed by a large gulp. He'd been looking forward to this and it didn't disappoint.

'Why surprised?'

Shane was getting a bit tired of these probing questions. 'Because Steve's the one I like and trust the most.'

'I'm not sure it was his idea.'

'Then whose?'

'Not sure.'

Thank goodness breakfast arrived. The scent of fried bacon hit before Shane saw what was on the plate. As it lowered, his mouth salivated. Two fried eggs were hugged by a nest of crispy bacon strips, the way he liked them. Four triangles of buttered granary toast were piled on one side and two halves of grilled tomato teetered on the other. Tyson's plate looked the same except his eggs were a fluffy yellow pile of scramble. Not bothered with the niceties of etiquette, Shane hoed in.

The silence at their table was accompanied by metal cutlery chinking against china, a rumble of voices from other diners chatting quietly to each other, hisses of steam from the coffee machine and occasional grumbles as coffee beans were ground in what seemed like an unceasing supply. Stuck against the back wall, they were away from wait-staff delivering non-stop dishes but continual flashes of black and white caught Shane's peripheral vision like old black and white movies shuddering through the frames. Tyson must have been as hungry for he didn't pause to slot in the questions Shane knew would be baited hooks seeking information. Shane wasn't going to be caught and reeled in. Between mouthfuls of food, he devoured the coffee so he'd be ready to escape the moment his food was gone. He settled his cutlery side-by-side across the plate seconds after popping the last corner of toast into his mouth.

'I've got to go,' he mumbled around the food as he eased up and squeezed his way around his end of the table, ignoring Tyson's call to wait. His wallet was out and notes extracted before he reached the till. He'd already calculated the bill total and dropped enough notes on the bench in front of the standing woman dedicated to receiving payments. 'Table twenty-three. Keep the change.' He was out the door seconds later, and desperate to get away, power-walked the fifty metres to the lab.

Once in his office, the first thing he did was lay the flat of his hand against the workings of his computer. Not warm enough to have been running while he'd been away, which was good, but it was still only 8.30. In the next thirty minutes a busload of people would be gracing the premises. Those working in the labs would don green protective clothing while the hard-working cogs who kept the company running efficiently by answering phones, opening and distributing mail, running errands and the myriad of other mundane jobs, were sober in dress to maintain the professional status of the business. The most valuable of those was Shelley, who was the most efficient receptionist, cum secretary, cum everything else, he'd ever met. The company would fall apart without her and because she was so efficient everyone kept sweet with her.

Being both a research scientist and a member of the executive, Shane ran the gauntlet of having to change like a chameleon to fit in with either role at a moment's notice. Under the lab finery he wore collared fine cotton shirts and twill trousers. Two ties were looped around a hanger dangling from a hook behind his door. Which one he chose depended on the colour of the shirt of the day. If a more formal look was required there was a multi-flecked sports jacket which would go with most colours, residing in a cupboard. Only when bigwigs came to discuss major contracts, or if Shane was required to attend formal meetings outside, did the coat get an airing.

While waiting for his fellow executives to arrive, Shane flicked through cardboard files from his filing cabinet, deciding which ones weren't so important it wouldn't matter if they were filched. Selecting five suitable candidates he re-labelled them, *Prancer,* and did a more thorough cleansing by pulling out documents which were so obvious it was impossible they had anything to do with this latest project. These he bundled into a new file titled with nothing more than an asterisk. He knew what it meant. It didn't matter if other people didn't.

The four thumb-drives containing Prancer data were replaced by new, unused ones. It took several minutes searching the room before he found a suitable spot to hide what would go into a bank security box before the day was out. He noticed a small gap above the mechanism of the blind shielding the internal window which overlooked the passage and rooms opposite. There might as well have not been a window for the number of times the blind had been raised. The slot was hidden by the narrow pelmet, but the top of his fingers fitted enough to manoeuvre the thumb-drives. Happy they wouldn't be found, he grubbed his fingers down the side of his lab coat, rinsed them and shifted the slats far enough so he could make out which of his targets walked past first. Time to get some answers.

Chapter Six

'Okay, Richo, you want to tell me what's going on?' Shane slammed Steve's office door behind him.

Steve's head jolted upright. He'd been the first of the executives to arrive but Shane had given him ten minutes to settle in before tackling him.

'What do you mean?'

'Don't jerk me around. Mr Security. Why?' Shane yanked the only other chair in Steve's office away from the wall, dislodging a messy pile of magazines, which tumbled to the floor in an even messier heap. He wasn't in the mood to apologise at Steve's raised eyebrow as he swung the now empty chair around and perched on the edge.

'But you knew.' Steve dropped his pen and stacked the papers he'd been working on to one side, with a look daring Shane to do the same with this pile.

'Like hell! Why was I omitted from the discussions?'

'But Bill said you agreed.' Steve seemed to melt into the back of his chair to escape Shane's wrath. The mystified look on his face seemed genuine but Shane's faith in his so-called friends was now tenuous until he could figure things out.

'Agreed to what?'

'Getting Tyson.'

'How could I agree to something I knew nothing about? Why didn't you come to me to discuss it?'

'Honest, I thought you knew. Bill assured me.'

'When was the idea mooted?' Shane was too angry to relax back in his seat. This sensation of feeling as though he was about to explode was something he wasn't used to. This level of anger was new. He was normally an easy-going guy, but now, so much was on the line.

'About a week ago.' A red blush of embarrassment heightened already ruddy cheeks.

'A week? You've known about this an entire week and didn't think to talk to me about it? You were the one who contacted Tyson.'

'Yeah, but…'

'I thought all these types of decisions were supposed to go to executive meetings: executive meaning four of us at the same time.' He shoved four fingers in front of Steve's face as he emphasised the word, adding a name to each finger as he counted.

'Now hang on a minute, I was told not to disturb you while you finalised the details and wrote your report.'

Shane blew his cheeks. Steve was making sense. Shane had been the one to ask for minimal disturbance. Heaving out another breath he scrubbed one hand down his face. His wrath seemed to evaporate along with the carbon dioxide molecules from his breath as he realised it was wrong to take it out on Steve, wrong to make assumptions. Hell, he knew better than to assume anything without basing it on pure proven fact. 'Sorry, but I'm pissed. Tell me one thing, whose idea was it to bring in Tyson?'

'Not sure. I assume it was Bill, could have been Chris but given what happened last year, it's a good idea.'

'Bull! I would never have endorsed bringing in an outsider and you know it.' He hoped his glare gave the right message. 'We were safe with only the four of us knowing.' He paused as things began gelling. An entire week. Someone, or maybe more than one person, had known something was brewing for over a week. More than enough time to pass on information to goodness knows how many people along the chain. Way too much time to organise the late-night visitors and their stage play. Oodles of time to plan a break-in during the meeting when they knew Shane wouldn't be home. But the housebreakers hadn't known about the safe. If Steve was in on something shifty they would have gone straight for the safe. Safe. Tyson had mentioned the safe: info which could have come from only one person. Damn. He searched Steve's face, looking for a twitch of guilt, or shifty eyes or any indication of lying but all he saw was bewilderment.

Unsure what to do, Shane stood and returned the chair to its position against the wall, ignoring the magazines. As he opened the door and left, he paused and twisted his head. Now was the time to drop a bombshell. 'You can pay Tyson off and let him go. It didn't work.' The grin splitting across his face was impossible to contain as he raced along the passage to his own office, ignoring the yelled, 'What? Why?'

It took less time than he'd anticipated. Steve wouldn't have his position as company accountant if he wasn't a smart man. It would take his mathematical brain mere seconds to compute.

'What the hell do you mean?' The words arrived a split second before the body shot through the doorway and hovered. Steve's face had changed from bewildered to something bordering on murderous.

Stunned at the look, Shane took his time to move around the desk, sink into his chair, leaning back with fingers laced behind his head. Why would Steve be so uptight? 'I'm sure I mentioned something about an anomaly yesterday.'

'Anomaly as in irregular quirk?' Steve stepped so close Shane could feel the tension vibrating from his body.

'Anomaly as in two dead rats.' He enjoyed the ways Steve's face screwed up. Now he looked plain mystified as though Shane had taken leave of his senses. Maybe he had and the past two days had been nothing more than a dream. No, more like a nightmare.

'What in the blazes are you talking about?'

'Fighter and Winner died early this morning.'

'Huh?'

It was only then Shane remembered he hadn't told anyone about the names he'd given the two rats, something he'd never done before and didn't endorse. Naming lab rats was a no-no for it indicated attachment, something research scientists couldn't afford to do. But Winner and Fighter had been special. To rid the atmosphere of the simmering tension which felt as though the air was about to explode, he indicated for Steve to sit.

'Pull up a pew. My two rats. They died,' he said as Steve sank down.

'Are we talking about the two survivors?'

'Yes.'

'Why? What happened?'

Shane had thought this through during the early hours. Lying didn't sit well with him but blackmail or theft or whatever it was going on, sat less well. He had little choice but to lie until he figured out who the traitor was. 'When I collated all the results, something didn't add up. I kept getting a tiny glitch here and another somewhere totally unrelated. It didn't make sense. This is what I was going to report at the meeting yesterday morning. When I came in early today to study the relevant samples, I found the two rats dead. They hadn't been gone long for rigor hadn't set in.'

'And this means what – exactly?' A worried frown creased Steve's brow as he leant forward.

'It means I need more time to figure out what went wrong, if anything. It could have been something simple. Perhaps the cancer had taken its toll and they were going to die from the effects in any case. Or maybe the cure was too much for them. They're rats. They're not human sized and don't have an eighty-plus year lifespan. It could mean they were only in remission and the cancer flared up again. I don't know.'

Steve stood and paced in a circle. He paused before spinning one hundred and eighty degrees to face Shane.

'How much time?' The way Steve asked sent up wildly waving red flags.

'I don't know until I've done some dissections, tests and analysis. Why does it matter?'

'Well, err, we'd already begun planning an announcement.'

'Why in hell's name would you do such a thing? We can't afford to go public until we're one hundred percent certain about the efficacy of this drug. It would be professional suicide. If there's the slightest bit of doubt we have to check it out.'

'Hell, I've been working on numbers to see how much it's worth to each of us.'

Shane's eyes slid shut. Money. Each of us. It sounded like Steve was only interested in what he would get out of it. 'Don't you think you're being a bit short-sighted? Even after we announce this it must go through human clinical trials before it even goes on the market. You know how long these trials can take.'

'Yeah, well, but this is the biggest thing we've done. I've been comparing it to other major drug breakthroughs.' Steve grinned. 'This is a multi-million-dollar discovery. We'll be rich men.'

Unbelievable. Money, money, money. All Shane could see was pure unadulterated personal greed. Damn, had he been blind to Steve's personality traits? This attitude was beyond disappointing. Now Steve had shot to the top of the suspicion list. Unable to stomach being in the man's presence a moment longer, Shane stood. 'I've got things to do, tests to run. Would you mind?' He indicated the door.

'Oh, sure.'

Steve was in the passage when a thought shot to the forefront of Shane's mind. 'By the way, whose project did you wangle the money from to pay for Tyson? He wouldn't be cheap.' The question was irrelevant because gut instinct told him the answer. If Tyson had already done background checks on the entire staff, he must have been on the books for longer than twenty-four hours. More like the entire week. For a man with those credentials they were looking at… what… two thousand a day? Which would make it ten grand a week. A snort of disgust escaped. With micro-management there was enough in his grant to finish the project. Take out Mr Security's fee and Shane's budget had already been blown beyond redemption.

Steve turned and his grin was wicked. 'Why, yours of course.'

'Gee thanks.' Shane slammed the door and slumped against the cold metal with his innards feeling like they were being tossed about in a cyclone. Had Steve already spent his share? Made plans for the big holiday? A new luxury car? Sure, the discovery was worth millions, but it was company money, not Steve's. He might be the company money man but to assume how the money would be spent before they'd even gone public was ridiculous. And Steve wasn't the one who had made this discovery. Sure, he worked hard, impossibly hard, working out the figures for projects and tenders for analysis work and the numerous other projects they did. The bread and butter work, which was carried out on the third floor, kept them afloat, enabling the research projects like this one to be viable.

What disturbed Shane the most was how Steve hadn't bothered to ask about the break-in. Was it because he already knew? So much evidence was arrowing straight for Steve and the knowledge didn't sit well.

It took what felt like forever to gain a modicum of composure. He had two more to confront and tests to run: un-necessary tests in the scientific sense for he was certain the drug worked but to buy time, the motions of undergoing further tests were vital.

On a long sucked-in breath, Shane straightened, yanked back his shoulders and opened the door. Which way first? He twisted his head to the left – Chris. No, Bill first. With determined strides he headed right, turned the corner only to be barrelled into by the very man he was looking for. The force caused him to totter backwards and stumble in a bid to regain his balance. Two large hands grabbed his upper arms, but he wasn't sure if it was to steady him or Bill, who also staggered and hit the wall.

'Oops, sorry, mate.' Bill took a step back. 'I was on my way to see you. What's this about you stuffing things up?'

'Excuse me?' It felt as though he had been sucker-punched with the accusation.

Chapter Seven

In disbelief, Shane spun around and raced back to his office where he grabbed the protective clothing he'd worn earlier and dragged them on. As he slammed into his lab, he ignored his name being called, yanked Winner from his cage and laid him on his back on the cold steel which now matched the rat's body temperature. Snatching up a fresh scalpel, he made the first incision. Shane had undertaken so many dissections he could almost do it wearing a blindfold.

'Mate, what are you doing?' A hand grasped his wrist, preventing Shane from making the next cut. He paused, blew out a long breath and slid his eyes shut.

'Dissecting a rat. What does it look like I'm doing?'

'Why?' The hand released its tight grip.

Shane lifted the fingers of his left hand from Winner's shoulders, huffed out a breath and dropped the scalpel.

'Well, since I, how did you put it with such eloquence, stuffed things up, I figured I should unstuff it.' He plonked his backside onto the nearest lab stool, lifted his head and stared at Bill, who at least had the courtesy to look embarrassed.

'Sorry, bad choice of words.'

'I don't think so. I think it's what you believe or why else would you have said it. Look, I don't know what's going on around here, but without me, and the days, months and years I've,' he emphasised the word and pointed to his own chest, 'spent on this, there wouldn't be anything to stuff up.'

'We're in this together, always have been and you know it.' Bill dragged another stool from under the far end of the bench and tried to look relaxed as he settled into it but couldn't quite pull it off. The tension rebounding off the walls wasn't all coming from Shane.

'Together?' The word squeaked out of Shane's mouth. 'If it was together, how come you three discussed bringing in Tyson, then engaged him without including me? Huh?' He stabbed Bill in the ribs. 'Doesn't sound like *together* to me.'

'But you knew.'

'I knew?' His voice rose almost an octave on the two words. 'Did you discuss it with me?'

'Well, no but…'

'When was the meeting? Tell me, for I must have blanked it out of my memory. Remind me. What day did we have an executive meeting with the *four* of us to discuss an executive decision?' Shane stood and paced the entire five steps to the end wall, spun around and stalked back.

'You know we didn't, but Chris assured me you agreed.'

'So now it's Chris. Steve says it was you who discussed it with me. You say it's Chris and what's Chris going to say? That it was Steve? You want to lay a bet?'

'Damn, I don't know but I swear I was certain it had been discussed with you and you had agreed. Now how about sitting and let's see if we can't sort things?'

Shane sat despite wanting to punch someone's lights out. Or maybe the wall, or the bench. He wasn't sure as he'd never physically attacked anything or anyone before, other than the gym equipment with his best friend, Justin, pushing him harder and harder. Somehow, he was sure it would hurt – a lot, but maybe it would release what felt like a thirty thousand volt of charged electricity surging through his body.

'Okay, I'm sitting. Talk.'

'First, what happened at your house?'

At last, someone was concerned enough to ask but he bet it was only because of the fear of Prancer details having been stolen. 'Someone broke in, made a mess. The police took most of the day searching for evidence and I took most of the night to clean up.'

'Anything taken?' By the way the words came out Shane felt sure the question was loaded. How to answer? His mother's voice echoed, 'Truth is always the best.'

'Nothing important and nothing of value.'

'But something?'

'Yes.'

'What?'

'A manuscript.'

'Pardon?'

'My mother is writing our family history. I was editing it. It's the only thing missing.'

'Are you sure? No work material? No reports or results?'

'I'm sure. There was nothing relating to work in my home.' Well, there was. The results of the entire research were locked away in a safe nobody knew about, except Steve and now Tyson, which sucked and worried him.

'But you did take the results home to analyse.'

The depth of the questions was beginning to send alarm bells clanging. Like Steve, all Bill was concerned about was Prancer and Shane bet it revolved around the issue of money. 'What, exactly, are you implying? Yes, I had some results at home but not all. Yes, I did some analysis work in preparation for yesterday's meeting. No, I didn't leave a single thing at home when I came to work yesterday. I had it all with me in my bag. How stupid do you think I am? This is *my* baby, *my* research. I've never left any of my research notes, or results, or details, anywhere where they could be spied on, pinched or anything untoward. You know what this means to me.' Shane stopped short when he realised he was pacing again.

Bill reached out and grasped Shane's arm. 'Calm down, mate, I know all this but it seemed so co-incidental and hell, man, I'm so afraid of things being leaked again. It's the only reason I agreed to this security guy.'

'But I thought it was your idea.'

Bill jerked back as though he'd been shot. 'No way. When I first heard the idea I was dead against it but after thinking about it, the idea seemed logical.'

The shock on Bill's face looked genuine. No-one could feign such a reaction, which was the most reassuring thing Shane had faced in the past two days.

'Then who?'

For a few seconds Bill looked puzzled as though trying to figure out the answer. Or maybe he was figuring out how to answer without incriminating himself. Shane hated how his conscience was seeking damning evidence from each of those whom he'd thought were long term friends; ones he could always rely on.

'You know, I'm not sure. Both Richo and Chris came to me separately to discuss it as though it was a *fait accompli* and inferring you were a part of the equation.' He pointed to the bench and Shane followed his line of sight. The cut he'd made looked more like a jagged tear than a neat incision. Poor Winner didn't deserve this kind of treatment.

'Now tell me about this,' Bill said as he screwed his face.

'What, you queasy?' A grin crept from the corners of Shane's mouth.

'Not really but it doesn't look so good. The rats in this place get treated better than the humans – well until now. Is this one of the rats Richo mentioned?'

'Yes.'

'What happened?'

'He died.'

'Funny man, I can see that, especially now with his guts torn apart. How did he die and why?'

'Which is why I need to do a dissection. To find out.'

'Damn, and this is going to set us back, how long?'

'A week. Maybe more. I need to put every single organ of both rats under the microscope. What happens depends on what I find.'

Bill swore, something he didn't usually do but the same four-letter word had been common in the past couple of days.

'What does it matter how long it takes?' Shane continued. 'We can't make an announcement until there isn't the minutest amount of doubt. You know this, as does everyone else here. We've been working on this for years. The only difference another couple of weeks is going to make is the level of positivity.'

Bill held up his hand. 'I know but we've been planning an announcement. We'll have to put it on hold for a while.'

All Shane could do was to shake his head in disbelief. *We've* been planning. Another thing he'd been left out of. The thought struck; maybe he was asleep in his bed and dreaming. Or maybe he'd been transported to another dimension where he was invisible or was only a paid researcher and not the idiot whose idea this entire company had been way back when he'd been in his final year of study for his Masters' degree, when these other three had been his closest buddies at university: all finalising their respective studies. Shane had mooted the idea. The others had come on board and together they'd nutted out all the pros and cons, gathered together all the financial resources they could lay their hands on and formed a small company. For the first two years they'd all held down well-paying jobs while at the same time throwing every spare hour into building their own company and Shane had worked on his thesis for his Doctorate. They'd started small but the back-breaking hours had paid off. They owned this building. They employed thirty men and women. The company always ran at a profit even after all four of them took out a respectable wage. But now Shane felt as though he didn't belong. Decisions were being made without his input let alone having an inkling about what was being discussed behind his back.

Pausing at the door, Shane grasped the silver knob. 'I know this is a dumb question but who is planning an announcement and why have I been kept out of the loop? You want to tell me what is going on?'

There was a rattle and eardrum splitting screech as Bill leapt from his seat with such force the stool skidded and scraped. 'Pardon, I have no idea what you mean.'

'Oh, come on, planning an announcement. Who?'

'You, me, Steve and Chris.'

The scoffing snort rumbling out of Shane's mouth was not delicate. 'Yeah, right. All four of us. Just like all four of us decided on Tyson.' He yanked the door open. 'Now if you'll excuse me, I've got work to do. And if I don't do it, you and your two scheming cohorts will have nothing to announce.'

'But Shane…'

Shane sucked in a long breath, paused, lifted his head with a definite stare into Bill's eye before pointing to the door. 'Just. Go.'

While going through the motions of dissections for the next three hours, Shane's brain was dissecting and analysing every minute of the past two days. After not coming up with any incriminating clues, he went back over the past few weeks, trying to figure out if he had done something to piss off the other three or if one of them had hinted at something he'd missed. Had there been any innuendo, any sarcastic comment, any sly look which now had meaning? Yes, he'd been busy finalising every detail of his research. Yes, he'd asked for minimal interruption unless it was vital as per normal practice. It was how the company operated in the final stages of any research project, big or small. Whoever was doing the research was granted uninterrupted time to collate every detail for the final report. He'd still gone to regular meetings – well, except for the two he'd had no idea about. Had there been more? Had other decisions been made without his knowledge? Hell, he wasn't sure if he really wanted to know.

When he came to his senses and glanced down at the remains of the two rats spread out on various boards and dishes, he shook his head in disbelief. He'd barely been aware of what he'd been doing but there they were, all laid out in perfect alignment. But now he didn't know what to do with them. There was no need to study any of it but if he disposed of the bits without proper dissections and slide samples, it was more than likely people could ask why.

To re-assure himself, he prepared a slide of tiny sections of each organ and studied them under the microscope. A grin rushed out at the sight of the perfect healthy cells. Not a sign of any cancer in organs which had been riddled with disease six weeks ago. Yes, they were rats but nobody anywhere in the world had been able to come anywhere near these dramatic results. It was Shane's dream that after all the human trials were completed, not a single person would have to go through the agony of dying from pancreatic cancer. And it wasn't only the victims who went through such trauma before succumbing to the insidious disease. His own family had been through hell and back while watching his father deteriorate day by day to skeletal status before passing away from the fatal disease.

After cleaning up, he retrieved the hidden thumb-drives and slipped Prancer files into his laptop computer bag. He had important things to do.

Chapter Eight

'I'm going out for lunch,' Shane called over his shoulder as he reached up to the attendance board and slid his marker to 2pm.

'You're what?'

Shane wasn't surprised at the receptionist's reaction for it was a rare occasion he took the hour he was entitled to for a lunch break. It was even rarer for him to leave the premises for lunch. As he glanced at the board, he noticed Chris's marker indicated he would be absent for the entire afternoon, which prevented the final showdown to finding answers. Was this a deliberate ploy by Chris? There goes his conscience again, playing the bad side. 'Do you know where Chris has gone?'

'Meeting at Anderson Enterprises.'

Shane hovered at Shelley's desk. 'Why? I thought we'd completed the Anderson contract.'

'How am I supposed to know? I'm only the lowly receptionist.'

Shane laughed. 'Who knows more about the comings and goings of this place than anyone.' Especially me, he added in his mind as he about turned and headed for the rear door where he was met by his latest nemesis.

'Going somewhere?' Tyson asked as he stepped in time with Shane, bumping shoulder-to-shoulder as they exited through the door without either budging a centimetre out of the way.

'Lunch,' was all Shane said, hoping his terse tone said enough to put the man off.

'Mind if I join you? There's something I'd like to discuss.'

Shane wheeled towards his car. 'Sorry, but I've got banking business to attend to first, then I'll grab a take-away bite to eat back here.'

Tyson hadn't faltered in his step but paused right slap bang against the driver's door of Shane's car, folding his arms as though he meant business. 'How come you're eating out when you always, without fail, bring your own lunch?'

The glare Shane gave the man was fierce. 'Really, it's nobody's business but mine but since I presume you aren't going to move out of the way until you know every detail of my personal life, picture this - the mess on my kitchen floor yesterday. You know… the porridge of mashed up food my friendly burglars managed to leave behind as a sign of their gratitude. *That* was the contents of my fridge, which is now residing in *that* garbage bin.' He jerked his thumb towards the row of business garbage bins still in perfect alignment along the verge. 'No food means no lunch and I'm hungry. You do the calculations.'

Desperate to get away, he elbowed Tyson out of the way, eased into his car, tossed the computer bag on the passenger seat and started the engine. Tyson only moved when Shane began reversing from the parking bay. When he reached the bank, he paused before alighting. His left hand rubbed over the canvas surface of the bag while he stared at the dark brown brick wall in front of him. Was this the right thing to do? He glanced at the bag. Inside were the relevant files from his office safe and the all-important thumb-drives. Should he keep them hidden or call an executive meeting and lay out all his concerns? Maybe Tyson was there because the other three were genuine in their concerns about a leak. But why hadn't Shane been included? Is Tyson nothing more than a red herring to cover up a sinister plot? If so, who is responsible. So far each of the other executives had blamed one of the others, leaving Shane without a glimmer of a clue.

Shane grasped the bag and pulled it into his lap then with a long huff of breath, relaxed back against the seat. What evidence did he really have implying any skulduggery? First - the probing questions on Monday after he'd called an executive meeting, followed by his late-night visitors. He thought hard. There was nothing about the woman's actions indicating she wasn't telling the truth. Any woman being harassed by a couple of louts would seek a haven until she was sure it was safe to continue her way. Peeking into the room could mean she was being nosy rather than having sinister intent. Even he admitted he'd do the same.

The two men? In the shadows they looked scary but so would anyone late at night, especially when they were wearing dark clothing. What they said could have been true. It is more than possible the woman did break into the man's house. So, did she come back and do the same in Shane's house? Was she the burglar? It sounded plausible, which meant she wouldn't have been after Prancer but would have hoisted his valuables which were in plain sight on his bedside table. Was it a simple case of the importance of the research sending Shane's suspicions into over-drive? Frustrated, he thumped his head against the steering wheel, reeling back again at the responding pain to his forehead. What was his gut telling him?

He snatched the keys from their cocooning slot, shoved the door open and alighted. Gut instinct was screaming at him to hide it all until he knew for sure one way or the other. *Be safe – not sorry*, his mother's voice whispered with one of her never-ending adages he'd spent his life hearing. Too much was at stake to take a risk.

Satisfied he was doing the right thing he strode into the bank where he spent his entire lunch hour securing most of his research in a large safety deposit box. He hadn't thought to bring the contents of the home safe, but they could be added. As he stared at the small silver key, an idea struck. Maybe a different hiding place where he could include this key. Why not a different bank?

By the time he'd purchased a take-away meat and salad roll and driven back to work he was thirty minutes late.

'Two o'clock was half an hour ago,' Shelley said without looking up. The board was something they'd come up with as the company grew. It was an easy way to show who was in or out. It was efficient and worked well, especially when the sharp-eyed Shelley yelled, 'Board or you don't leave,' any time a member of staff got within cooee of either the back or front door without having put their marker against their name.

Shane couldn't hold back his laughter as he detoured to the desk. 'You're complaining about me being a measly half hour late on the only day in at least a year when I've left the premises for lunch?'

She peeked up and grinned. 'Yes, well, you're the boss and they're your rules.'

His laugh echoed around the reception area. 'I'm only one of the bosses and maybe since I am, I can break the rules on a rare occasion. I did indicate I would be out. I can't help it if other people like those at the bank I've been to, aren't as pernickety about time as you.'

'I'm sorry but Mr Tyson has been pestering me about your whereabouts since two. He's driving me nuts.'

He was also driving Shane nuts. 'Let him wait. I'm going to hide in the lunchroom to eat this.' He held up the paper bag. 'If he asks again tell him I'll be in my office at three.'

As the lift door closed, Shane thought he heard Shelley mutter, 'Good luck,' under her breath but with the background whish and gentle thud of the sliding doors, he couldn't be sure so shrugged it off.

The doors hissed open on the third floor and Shane took the three steps across the passage to what was known as the lunchroom. Only one end was graced with a sink, bench and cupboards designed to imitate a small kitchen. Two rectangular tables each had enough seating for eight.

There was a refrigerator to keep food cool and a microwave for the food to be heated. The other three walls were lined with floor to ceiling storage cupboards and in one corner sat a never used cane lounge, a health and safety requirement to house the un-well employee. If one of their workers was ill enough to require a bed, a taxi was called to take them to a medical facility or home, depending on the nature of the illness.

The moment Shane stepped into the room he understood Shelley's smart comment. Will Tyson was sitting in the far corner working on his laptop. Shane paused, wondering whether to stay or lock himself in his office so he could eat in peace.

'About time,' Tyson said without looking up.

Shane laughed and yanked out the chair on the opposite end of Tyson's table. 'Banks these days have fewer tellers, expecting everyone to do their banking on-line. Hence, the queues are longer as is the time one must wait to fix the banking problems which are impossible to do on-line. You were looking for me?'

'You knew that before you left.' Tyson closed the lid down and set the laptop to one side while Shane tore open the paper bag and struggled to find the end of the cling film encasing the lunch he was anxious to eat. Such a simple modern invention, which could be a pain in the rear end at times, he thought as he gave up, shoved his fingernail through the plastic and ripped it away from the bread roll, dislodging half the salad in the process.

'Before you start, there's something which has been eating away at me,' Shane said between popping tiny bits of shredded lettuce and carrot into his mouth.

'What?' Tyson stood and moved around the table, pulling out the chair on the corner next to Shane.

'This is supposed to be hush-hush, so how has your presence been explained, or does the entire staff now know?'

'I'm a business analyst finding ideas to streamline this company to make it even more efficient than it is.'

Shane almost choked on the salad when a shout of laughter burst out. 'That's the best they could come up with?'

'The staff members are buying it.' Tyson said.

'They've probably all got their heads down, buried in their respective jobs, terrified we're struggling financially and they're about to lose their jobs.'

'Not such a bad thing.' There was definite amusement in Tyson's voice.

'Probably not but I bet there are no late lunches, late arrivals, early clocking off or time off for the next few weeks. Now what did you want to see me about?' Shane bit into the roll and began chewing.

'What sort of relationship do you have with the other three owners?'

This time Shane did choke as the mouthful lurched down his throat in one lump. He swallowed hard to get it dislodged, coughed and shook his head with eyes watering. 'Why do you ask?' he managed to squeak out as his lungs sucked in enough air to function as they should.

'I want to know how you all get on.'

Food had lost his interest, so Shane shoved the roll to the middle of the table with his eyes firmly planted on Tyson. 'Is there something I should know about?'

'Maybe but I need to get the picture first.'

It was difficult to figure out where this was going so being frank was probably the best thing to do. 'We've been friends since our final year at university. I met Steve in a business financial management class. We chatted a lot, enjoyed each other's company and it evolved into friendship. He introduced me to Bill, who was a classmate in a different subject. I liked him a lot, we got on well. Bill brought along Chris, who was a bit more difficult to take to. They both studied Business Administration.'

'Did you mingle socially as well?'

'No. We all lived in different suburbs and still do, and we each had part-time jobs in different fields, which kept us busy out of lecture hours. I, personally, didn't have much time to socialise. I worked my way through six years of university, sometimes holding down two part-time jobs. Somehow we formed a friendship at uni.'

'How about now? Do you socialise?'

'Not really, no. Twice a year we have company functions but usually at a restaurant or yacht club or some other hired facility. Bill and Steve are married and hence have their private lives. I mean we are close enough I was invited to their weddings and we have the occasional drink after work, but we don't go to each other's homes for parties or get-togethers. I guess it's because we don't have the same interests. Steve's got a couple of kids, so family time is important to him. Even sporting-wise we have different interests. Bill enjoys rugby, Steve, Aussie rules and Chris, I think, follows the soccer.'

'And you?'

'I'm not a big sport follower. I prefer more arty things: concerts, live theatre, books. I've even dabbled in writing.

I've been dedicating a lot of time to this project and when I take a weekend off, I like to visit Mum and my sisters.'

'I take it you're not close to any of them.'

Shane wasn't sure where this conversation was leading but it was putting the wind up him. 'Business-wise, we're close and I'm probably closest to Steve. Bill comes next but not so close to Chris. All four of us have put a lot into building this company to where it is now. We've been successful and make a better than average living.'

'Do you each get the same income?'

'Of course, why do you ask?' When Shane glanced at the man, he was concerned about the frown marring Tyson's face.

'So why does Richards look like he's a pauper and Hazelby like a multi-millionaire? Why do you receive the same money, when, according to the time sheets, you put in twice as many hours?'

'Do I? I'm the research scientist, it's what I know. Richo is the accountant. He keeps us afloat. Chris is brilliant at finding projects and does the hard yakka on contracts while Bill oversees everything and the personnel, and keeps the machine running smoothly without any major hiccups. We all do what we are trained to do and it works. We're all dedicated to our company. What does it matter who puts in how many hours? It's the nature of our respective roles.' He leant forward and stared at Tyson. 'Why is this important?'

'I think you've had your head stuck over your huge microscope too long. You need to find out more about your partners.'

Shane peered at the man through screwed eyes. 'Are you hinting at something untoward?'

Tyson stood and returned to his original chair where he sat and re-opened his laptop. 'A strong suggestion. By the way, I'm not privy to exactly what it is you have been working on.'

'You're not?' Shane was staggered by this admission.

'No, Richards told me you have made an exciting breakthrough which has to be kept from your competitors at all costs until you are ready to make an announcement. I was told about the leakage of a previous product your company developed but which was stolen. Hence, my presence here. To ensure it doesn't happen again.' He shut down the computer and slipped it into a bag he retrieved from the floor. 'Think about what I said,' he added as he headed for the door.

'Is it so important?' Shane asked as he rose and tossed his uneaten lunch in the bin. With his innards re-tied in knots once again, the thought of food made him feel bilious.

'I think so.' Tyson left, leaving Shane bewildered and more than worried.

Chapter Nine

In one sense it was relaxing to be walking the supermarket aisles. Now he was away from the office, Shane could breathe but with the number of people transferring food items from shelves to trolleys it felt as though the entire suburb had made it a life's commitment to shop in this place at this time. To make it worse, the shelf packers couldn't keep up with the shelf raiders. The spot which usually held his preferred natural yoghurt with all the right microbes for good gut health had been as empty as the Todd River in Alice Springs. For the next few days he would be eating a poor substitute filled with sugar because it was the only brand left. What remained in the pre-packaged salad mixes looked as though they'd been there for a week. All the fresh packets were nestled in other people's trolleys while Shane's held the best raw ingredients he could find after them having already been picked over.

Taking a final glance into his trolley, Shane figured he had enough to last until the weekend. He was desperate to escape the crush. A long sigh escaped when he reached the checkouts where there was a snaking queue at each, so he tagged onto the end of what looked to be the shortest. After shuffling along a few paces, he discovered he was at the self-checkout section. He counted the number of machines and made a count of the patrons ahead of him. Thank goodness he'd be next in line to at least one of them.

His eyes lingered on the woman on the end when a twinge of recognition hit his grey matter. His midnight visitor had just slotted her credit card into the machine. Time to get some answers. Leaving his trolley where it was, he zigzagged between customers and jutting trolleys, ending up behind the woman. A quick scan of the monitor told her to *Please Remove Card,* so Shane reached over her shoulder and did exactly as instructed.

'Hey, that's mine!' was yelled in his ear as he turned the card over and read the name.

'You!' A fist thumped into his chest.

'Yes, me, Miss Jessica M. Simmonds. The man whose house you broke into.' He held the card out between two fingers.

'I did no such thing and you know it.' She snatched the card from his fingers and shoved his shoulder with hers before scrabbling to sort her shopping.

'You trespassed.'

'I was hiding and you were no gentleman by threatening to call the police, forcing me to leave while those thugs were still in your street.'

To prove he did have some gentlemanly skills he lifted the woman's last two bags from the counter and nestled them with utmost care into her trolley. 'You peeked into my window.'

A sucked-in sound escaped the woman's lips at the same time she turned bright red.

'Hey, you, move your trolley!' was shouted in a tone so unpleasant there was a sudden silence and all eyes turned his way. Shane glanced around in time to see his shopping come hurtling towards Jessica. To prevent imminent injury, he stepped around her, gasping out a four-letter word as the lower bar cracked across his shin.

'Serves you right,' she whispered then had the temerity to giggle.

'Can we talk?' Shane asked as he grabbed the handle of her trolley to prevent her from leaving. 'Please,' he added when she paused.

'Why? I don't like you. You were mean.'

'Sorry if you think me mean but I was being cautious. Justified caution I might add.' With one hand still gripping her handle, Shane began scanning his shopping but getting the items into bags was a nightmare. He paused and eyed the woman. 'Please. I need as much information about those two men as I can get.'

'Why?' Thank goodness she eased off her stance. Then surprise, surprise she began bagging his groceries.

'Thanks Miss Jessica. M. Simmonds.' He grinned as he kept scanning.

'Why?' she asked again.

'The police are looking for them and my description was too scant. You might be able to describe them better.' As an excuse it was weak. He was more interested in the woman since she was his number one suspect but at least she was still here and doing a darn sight better job of packing than he could.

After paying, Shane pushed his trolley outside and smiled when he heard her following. An elderly couple vacated a wooden bench so he steered towards it. 'Let's sit here for a minute.'

Jessica hesitated, glanced around, shrugged her shoulders and eased down as close to the end of the slats as she could without falling off the end.

'I'm not going to attack you,' Shane said as he perched on the other end.

'I don't trust you.' It was kind of cute the way her chin lifted in defiance.

'And you think I should trust you after you sneaked a peek into my house in the middle of the night?'

'Sorry but…'

'You couldn't resist.' Shane laughed at the look on her face when her head shot around to stare at him. 'You want to know something?' he added at her rising blush of guilt. 'In similar circumstances I would have done the same.'

'You would?' A shy grin crept out.

'Now what can you tell me about the two men? What happened Monday night and did you break into his house?'

'No!' came out so loud, other shoppers stopped and gawked.

'Tell me what happened,' he said much softer as he reached out with one hand to still the shake in her arm.

'Most evenings I go either jogging or power-walking. Monday night I was walking down your street but was in the next block. Those two guys came from the opposite direction. I ignored them until they crossed to my side of the road. As they neared, the taller man, the one you spoke to, began talking smutty things like, *what have we here, a good lay, looks hot to me, how about licking my…* you know.' Her eyes darted away. It amused him to see her look so embarrassed but now he understood her desperation to hide. If it was true.

'Even when I crossed the road he followed me while the other one remained on his side. I didn't trust them, you know, the things they said, the way they stalked me, so I ran, jerking to the centre of the road to get past them. Thank, God I'm fitter than them. By the time I got near your place I was far enough ahead I thought I had a chance to hide. I raced into your neighbour's property but they had those fences and gates blocking off their back area. The humungous sign saying *Rottweiler* put me off… what are you grinning about?'

'Rocky, the Rottweiler passed away a month before Christmas and was replaced by a Chihuahua.'

'A Chihuahua? You've got to be kidding me. So, I scrambled over your side fence to escape the vicious itty-bitty Chihuahua and hid on your veranda. Your light was on, so I assumed someone was home. I would have yelled out if they'd got close to finding me.'

'Why didn't you?'

'Why do you think? I didn't know you. You could have been worse than them. I mean your yard is like a jungle, so I figured you weren't the nicest person.'

'Because of my yard?' He scoffed. 'Maybe I'm too busy to maintain my yard to your impeccable standards.' He turned back to her and edged closer, amused when she glanced at the narrowing space before looking back at him. There was still a good thirty-centimetre gap when he stilled. He knew he needed to spend more time in the garden, but he didn't think it had reached jungle status. It got mowed every month, well, maybe sometimes it was six weeks and most of the shrubs needed a damn good haircut. 'Will you think better of me if I tell you I'm fussy about the inside? I like everything to be clean.'

'Not from what I saw. Oops, sorry.' Redness rose up her cheeks again.

'You don't hold back, do you?' Shane managed to gasp out as he stood and grabbed his trolley. 'I feel I need to redeem myself. I'm a respectable scientist who has never and will never harm a woman. My mother brought me up to respect women, not that I had much choice when I was the only male in the house. My two older sisters would never stop hounding me if I showed disrespect to a woman. So next time you need somewhere safe, feel free to knock on my door.'

Poor Jessica looked distraught. She stumbled to her feet. 'I'm sorry, but before you go, why do the police want to know about those two men?'

'My house was ransacked the next morning. I gave them your description as well as theirs. Now I can pass on your name. Maybe you should visit them first to give your version of events.' Shane strode away, enjoying the muttered insults being thrown at him. Being called a bastard and beast in the same five minutes was a record for him, but at this moment he probably deserved it.

By the time he reached home and unpacked his groceries, hunger pangs had begun stabbing. The easiest and quickest meal was to grill a steak. A glass of wine would have gone down well but he had places to go. Having munched down the steak and a side-salad, and with dishes cleaned, he dipped into the shower and was out almost as soon as he hopped in. He was about to open the door leading into the garage when he paused, mid-stride, turned and backtracked.

It had been a risk leaving the remains of his research locked in the safe for the day, but it was more of a risk to carry it around with him. Thoughts of car accidents, or even a carjacking, centred in his brain. Who knew what measures his adversaries would take to steal Prancer? Assuming it was what the burglar was after and if they returned for a second try, the first place they would look was in one of the rooms they hadn't searched before. But surely they would realise he wouldn't leave any information lying around after the first attempt. He leant against the passage wall, thinking – where could he hide it until he could get to the bank? And it would be a different bank. He had accounts in three different financial institutions, living up to another of his mother's common adages about every single delicate egg getting crushed if they were in the one place. Stupid really, how he lived by those sayings, especially since nowadays, they were considered trite but hey – this one made a lot of sense and money-wise, after all the building society and bank disasters, it was wise to spread one's savings and investments in different platforms.

As he thought, he glanced around trying to figure out a halfway decent place to hide the research. He caught sight of the manhole. Why not? There were layers of dust-laden insulation up there. If he was careful, he could hide it without disturbing too much dust and leaving a trail to the hiding spot. Add in rodent droppings and the possum he had ousted a few months back had probably left his calling card as well, which could deter possible thieves from searching.

It took less than fifteen minutes to empty the safe, wrap the contents over and over in a large garbage bag, use a chair to hoist his body into the roof space and hide the bag under the insulation in the hardest place to reach. There hadn't even been room for him to lift his head. Stretched flat along the beams and rafters he hid the packet at the end of arm's length adding a scattering of rat poison around to deter any rodent eating the paperwork. It was hard enough putting it there so anyone who found it probably deserved it as a reward. He didn't like to think about retrieving it as he brushed dirt and unmentionables from his clothes. It was a useless exercise, so he stripped off trousers and shirt and dumped them in a bucket of water to soak in disinfectant.

A sweater was added to his clean outfit in case the evening turned chilly. It was supposed to be autumn, but summer had decided it would linger a little longer although the nights were getting a bit crisp. One hand grabbed the scrap of paper with Steve's address, from the hall table, while the other snatched up keys. To save time hunting the house number and street name, Shane punched the details into his mobile phone and set it in the hands-free cradle. It wasn't often he got lost, but Steve lived in the less familiar northern suburbs, which had expanded at an alarming rate over the past couple of years, to the extent he didn't know what some of the newer suburbs were called.

It seemed most commuters were safe home enjoying the evening meal for traffic was light, making it a quick drive across the city to follow the freeway north. Forty-five minutes later he followed directions on the screen and turned into Steve's street. As he pulled into a coloured concrete driveway, Tyson's words came back to him and he wondered if there was a sinister reason why Shane had never been invited to the Richards' home. There had been several invites to Bill's place before he'd married, all which Shane had accepted and enjoyed the events. But since the stuck-up Lisa had arrived on the scene, the invitations had ceased but Shane hadn't minded for he didn't really like the woman. Earlier in the piece, prior to marriages, Shane had the guys around for barbecues a couple of times, but once Steve had married the far more amenable Grace, those weekend get-togethers had gone by the wayside. It was pity really. Maybe he should invite them all and re-instate the habit.

After killing the engine, Shane sat and studied the building in front of him. A modern brick and tile house took up most of the tiny block, leaving little room for a garden apart from a two-metre strip of lawn fringed by garden beds filled with myriad shades of green. Steve had moved here about five years ago when the first child had arrived. They'd needed more room for a growing family, but they'd certainly skimped on any playing area. A poor excuse for a porch protected the recessed front door, which stood to the side of a garage, barely large enough to squeeze in two cars, leaving little room to store all those objects a person didn't want in the house. Where on earth would Steve store tools, garden implements, the mower and bikes? To the right of the door was a room Shane presumed was the master bedroom. He knew the rough layout of these narrow fronted but long homes for there wasn't much leeway for an architect to make on these blocks of 500sqm or less. There was no way Shane could live like this, after growing up in a country town where there was plenty of room to breathe. It was one of the reasons he'd bought an older home to renovate. It sat in the middle of three quarters of an acre with mature shrubs and trees bordering the rear and side boundaries. He'd chosen the house because it sits in a tree-lined street filled with classic older homes. Many had been renovated to bring them back to life. Most had modern interiors, much as he was in the process of doing, and revitalised exteriors maintaining the classic Australiana look. One day, when there was more free time, he planned to modernise the garden but for the moment it was adequate, especially with the large covered patio across the entire back wall of the house.

Focussing back on the mundane front door of this dreary modern build, he figured it was time to face the lion in his den. A huff of breath for courage and Shane eased from the car, pressed the remote locking device and strode along the entire metre of paved footpath. His knock on the door went unanswered but someone was home for the television was blaring and voices hummed in the background. He knocked louder. Footsteps echoed, followed by the rattle of keys being turned. The main door opened to reveal a diminutive woman standing shadowed by the security screen. There was a sucked in breath of surprise.

'Shane, what are you doing here?' The tone was far from friendly.

'Hi, Grace, is Steve in?'

'Oh, err… um… he's bathing Chloe. What do you want?'

It rankled when there was no move to unlock the screen door and the sharp tone was not how he remembered Grace. He recalled a shy, quietly spoken but always friendly Grace. 'I'd like to discuss something with Steve. Would I be able to come in and wait for the bathing duties to finish?'

'It's not a duty, it's a pleasure,' Grace snapped.

Shane was stunned. 'I didn't mean to offend. I apologise if it sounded as if I was. I know I don't have kids yet but when I do, I would regard spending as much time with them as the duty of being a good parent; a very pleasant duty.' This felt like a weird conversation and he wasn't sure how to continue. 'So, is it all right if I come in?'

'Err, um… I'll get him to phone you.'

And then she closed the door.

He waited. And waited. Until eventually he walked down the path, bewildered and confused.

Once home, he headed straight for the kitchen, yanked a bottle of red wine from the rack above the fridge and poured a large glass to the brim. It was too full to carry to the den, so he bent and slurped a good mouthful before retreating to his favourite chair where he sat back and closed his eyes.

What the hell was going on? He couldn't recall, ever, being given the cold shoulder by anyone. Certainly, Grace had never spoken to him with such venom before. It had only been three months since the last office party two weeks before Christmas and the conversation with Grace that night had been amiable with a fair amount of laughter. Had he said anything untoward? It was hard recalling the conversation, but no way had he been disrespectful or rude or… what? No, there had been no negativity, no insults, no put-downs. He wasn't like that and nor was Grace – until now.

His mobile phone rang, interrupting deep thoughts. A glance at the number told him it was Steve.

'Shane here.'

'Shane, you called around. Why? You never come to my place.'

Was that condemnation? 'Probably because I've never been invited.' A telling silence followed.

'So why did you come tonight?' The quieter voice was less confrontational.

'It's no longer important. I have my answer, loud and clear. Have a great evening.' Shane hung up, switched off the phone and stormed to bed, wondering what in hell's name was going on?

Chapter Ten

Spending time roaming the labs and chatting with the scientists and technicians about their respective projects was a pleasant way to spend the morning. This time it was also a fact-finding mission to ensure he knew what was going on.

So far Shane hadn't discovered any projects he hadn't been aware of, but he had confirmed one thing: the contract with Anderson Enterprises had indeed come to a satisfactory conclusion two weeks ago. Now, while he chatted and offered suggestions, half his mind was churning over what Chris had been doing yesterday – if he had been at Andersons at all. And he was away from the office again this morning, finalising a new contract, or so he had been informed by Shelley Thompson. Chris being out was normal; half his time was spent chasing contracts, meeting with the cock-a-doodle-doos of companies issuing the contracts, to gain signatures and hand out copies of signed documents.

Catching sight of Tyson, Shane farewelled the group testing water quality for the government and chased after the man. 'Tyson, hold up a second.' He fell into step alongside him.

'You actually want to talk to me for a change?'

'No need for the sarcasm. You're here. I was riled about the way you got here.'

Tyson stopped and turned towards Shane. 'I understand and I'm sorry. It was a bit of a shock for me when I figured you hadn't known but maybe it's a good thing in one sense. Here, let's go in here so we can be a bit more private.' Tyson opened the door to a small office. Shane followed, noticing the desk, two chairs, computer, a pile of books and another of files which hadn't been there a week ago.

'I see you've made yourself at home.'

'I had to set up somewhere to make my story appear legit. Sit.' Tyson pulled out a chair, which Shane recognised as being one from the lunchroom. Tyson slipped around the other side of the desk and settled into a far more comfortable leather office chair, obviously filched from one of the conference rooms, but Shane had done the same because they were so comfortable.

Unease settled in his stomach as Shane sat. 'I feel like the recalcitrant child who has been hauled into the principal's office to explain my misdemeanour.'

Tyson laughed as he settled back into his seat with his hands clasped behind his head. 'I'd say you would be the last person in this building I would chastise, which is why

I said it was a good thing; it let's you off the hook. From what I've discovered so far, someone is trying to screw you. Exactly how important is this discovery of yours?'

'Damn.' Shane jerked upright and perched on the edge of his seat before dropping his forearms onto the desk. 'I get the same feeling, but I don't know who.'

'The importance. Give me a clue, something I can work on.' Tyson leant forwards and mirrored Shane's stance. If he reached a bit further, they would be finger-to-finger.

'On a scale of one to ten – ten.'

'I take it ten means money.'

'Lots of money.'

'How many figures? Six?'

'More like seven, possibly eight. Maybe nine.'

'Hell!'

'Exactly, so you now know why I was irate when you were at Tuesday's meeting. We'd made a pact to ensure only the four of us knew anything about what I was working on. For them to bring in another person, well to me it was traitorous.'

'So, you think one of them is after...' Tyson flicked a dismissive hand in the air, 'whatever it is. Hell, can we at least give it a code name?'

Shane plonked back into the chair. How well could he trust this man? He had the credentials but was he working for whomever? No, give nothing away. 'Okay, let's call it... how about...' he glanced around the room and noticed a red flashing light on the phone. 'Red, we'll call it Red.'

'I can work with that. Now, what made you suspicious?'

'Probably seeing you after the goings on of the night before followed by my house being burgled. Far too many co-incidents all at once only a few days after telling the guys I'd succeeded, which seemed to generate an unusual spate of inquisitive probing questions from each of them. Those questions were the first things to send my nerves on edge.'

'Who do you suspect?'

Shane laughed. 'Now you are asking *the* million-dollar question. Steve is top of the list right now. Chris comes second because he's been suspiciously scarce since the meeting. If it's Bill, he deserves an Oscar award for acting but I can't dismiss him. It could be all three in cahoots but I don't think so.'

'What about a different person apart from the three.'

'It would mean one of them has double crossed me and blabbed.'

'But none of them could have broken into your house. They were all here.'

'This means an accomplice or maybe more than one. This is what I wanted to talk to you about.' Shane searched his trousers pocket, pulled out a folded piece of paper and slid it across the desk. 'Find out all you can about this woman.'

Tyson opened it out and read the contents. 'Jessica Simmonds.' He glanced up. 'Who is she and why her?'

'She's the woman on my veranda late Monday night.'

Tyson sat back with a stunned look on his face. 'And how did you manage to get these details?'

'I ran into her in the shopping centre.'

'Which doesn't explain the credit card number.'

'Yes, well it happened to be poking out of the pay machine.'

Tyson laughed as he shook his head. 'And you remembered the numbers?'

'Not all of it. It's the same type of credit card as mine so must have the same first set of digits. It's almost impossible to forget the 0010.'

'And the other four?'

'There were five in my family, now there are four, one male and three females -5413. Easy.' Shane stood. 'Now I must go. I'd appreciate any info on this woman and she must live somewhere close to my house as she shops in the same centre and was within her nightly power-walking regime.'

'If you ever want a change in career, I could use a man with your talents. By the way, here's my card. I've written my private mobile number on it. Don't be afraid to call me any time, day or night, if you feel threatened. Whoever is after Red, won't much care how they get it.'

Shane paused in the doorway. 'Probably true but if they kill me they've wasted their time for I'm the only person who knows the details of Red.'

'Your computer?'

'Clean, same with my laptop and home computer.'

'Smart man. I'll get onto this now.'

Shane left, hoping to be able to lock himself in his office until Chris returned. His hopes were dashed when he spied Steve propping up the wall opposite Shane's office door. Steve was studying the screen of his mobile, so Shane turned to escape but as Steve lifted the phone to his ear, he glanced up and straightened.

'Where have you been? I've been looking for you. You won't answer your phone and you didn't put your marker on the board.'

Shane's hackles shot up at the aggressive accusations. He ticked off one finger. 'First, my marker is on the board as me being present because I've been here since 7.30.' He held up another finger. 'Second, as per normal, I've been working all morning in the labs, with the groups, which is exactly what I'm employed to do.' Another finger joined the other two. 'Third, my mobile phone is in there,' he indicated his office door, 'where it won't disturb me while I'm concentrating on project details. And fourth, I don't appreciate your aggressive tone. What in hell's name have I ever done to you to warrant this animosity?'

'What's going on?'

Shane sighed at Bill's voice. He turned and leant against the wall. 'I wish I knew,' he rasped out on another sigh.

'You two never argue so what's the problem?' Bill glanced between the two men.

'Ask him,' Shane indicated towards Steve, 'for I honestly don't have a clue what's got up his backside.' He glanced at Steve whose face wore an angry frown.

'Maybe we should step inside your office so we don't disturb the entire building,' said Bill as he nudged Shane towards the door at the same time he grasped Steve's shoulder and tugged him away from the wall. The door closed with an echoing snick.

'Now what's the problem? Steve?' Bill asked as he pulled out the spare chair and shoved Steve into it. Shane moved around the desk and sank into his own chair, reclined back and popped his feet onto the desk giving the impression of the nonchalance he certainly wasn't feeling. This was going to be interesting.

'Steve?' Bill asked again after a lengthy silence.

'I don't know. Shane came around to see me last night.'

'And that's a problem? Why?' asked an amazed looking Bill.

'He didn't stay and when I rang him later, he hung up on me.'

'Why don't you tell him the rest of the story?' Shane asked, fighting to stay calm.

'What do you mean?' Steve straightened.

'I knock on your door and the response I received from Grace was so cold it was at least minus fifty degrees Celsius. She shut the door in my face when I asked if I could come in to speak to you. Like I said on the phone, the answer was loud and clear. I can't recall ever having said or done anything untoward to upset either of you. If I did, why didn't you say something so I could apologise?'

'You don't understand,' Steve stuttered as his face did an amazing thing. There was a red rush of either anger or embarrassment racing up his neck while his cheeks paled to a scary white.

Unable to maintain his nonchalant pose, Shane removed his feet and leant forward. 'You're right, I don't have a clue about why you are so angry with me. My house gets ransacked and you don't show a skerrick of concern about it. All you did was to get on your high horse about the delay in Prancer. To top it off, all three of you make decisions behind my back without even giving me a hint about what you are planning. Don't you think it's me who should be a tad angry? And I am. I'm right royally pissed but I don't go around treating you all with the contempt I was shown last night.' He centred his attention on Bill. 'I went to Steve's place to discuss all this with him. And while you two are here, I won't be in first thing tomorrow. The glaziers are coming to repair the smashed window.' He pointed to Steve. 'You know; the one you couldn't care less about. Bill, here, at least showed he cared about my welfare by asking about the break-in.'

'Shane!' Bill admonished.

Shane huffed out a breath. 'I know, I'm sorry but this has been a hell of a week. I need time out. I think I'll spend the weekend away, catching up with friends. It might ease the tension in me a bit.'

'But what about Prancer? And the tests? Surely you should be completing the tests.' Steve yelled as he stood and shouldered Bill out of the way.

All Shane could do was stare at the simmering man who looked as though he wanted to tear Shane apart. Stunned, he turned to Bill, who looked equally as shocked. 'This is what I mean. At the moment Steve doesn't give a damn about anything other than Prancer.' Shane stood and headed for the door where he turned. 'My only question is why? Maybe you two should think about the answer. Now if you'll excuse me, I'm going out for lunch. I need fresh air and to get away from this increasing tension.' He turned and stormed through the building, ignoring Shelley's standard admonition about the board. Stuff the lot of them.

Chapter Eleven

Three hours later Shane returned to the office feeling far more relaxed. Lunch had been a grease and salt-laden takeaway hamburger and chips chased down with at least ten teaspoons of sugar in flavoured water sold in the guise of healthy fruit juice. He'd savoured every crumb and sip, especially as he'd been lolling on the grassy banks of the Swan River, soaking up the sun. To make it even more pleasant, not a soul had interrupted his peace. Black swans and various varieties of other waterfowl had graced the waters, swimming and ducking in search of yummy morsels to fill their bellies. Birds had calmed his ire by flitting about while singing in syncopated harmony as the last of the summer cicadas chirruped their strident sounds. He'd done his best to clear his head so he could simply appreciate and enjoy.

Once inside, Shane made a deliberate detour to the board and made a show of tut-tutting as he lifted off his magnetised marker and slapped it back exactly where it had been with a resounding thwack. He veered towards Shelley's desk and grinned at her before stepping into the elevator where his agitation returned like a tsunami.

Chris was in, which meant Shane had no choice but to confront the last of the three if there was any hope of finding answers.

The walk to Chris's door was far less enthusiastic while he scrabbled for a way to handle this with any subtlety. What he wanted was to jump in with accusations and questions but figured all it would do was to put Chris on the defensive. He knocked but didn't wait for a response, instead barging in, determined to study Chris's reactions for any signs of guilt.

'Shane, hi.' Chris looked him straight in the eye and sort of smiled. 'I've been meaning to catch up with you, but this new contract stole all my time. Sit.'

'What contract?' Shane tugged a chair from the wall and placed it at an angle so he could sit in comfort with legs stretched out. He wanted to appear relaxed even though he was anything but.

'Anderson Enterprises were so pleased with the way we handled the last project, they offered us a new one. We signed and sealed it this morning. A quarter of a million dollars.'

Well there goes all Shane's suspicions blown away in a puff of nothingness. 'Doing what?'

'The same as before but twice the amount. Apparently, the previous project was a test for our company. We passed with flying colours.'

'What team will be doing the project and how long is it going to take?'

'I thought the same team would be a good idea and it will be for six months. It was Jacqui's group wasn't it? Are they free?'

'Yes. They do have another project from the boring company, testing water samples from a new bore field but it wouldn't be too hard passing the project to Callam's team. Six months is great. Email me a copy of the contract so I can study the details.'

'Already done. Now what happened at your place? You charged out of here so fast I couldn't ask.'

Shane couldn't believe this conversation - it was so normal and nothing like what he'd expected. 'Some punk, or maybe more than one, broke in and had fun tipping the place before police arrived.'

'Anything broken?' Chris lolled back in his seat looking so much at ease, Shane wondered if it was an act even though he looked and acted like the normal everyday Chris Evans.

'Only the laundry window.'

'Anything taken?' His left hand had picked up a pen and was tapping on the desk in a rhythmic staccato. Were they nerves?

'A pile of scrap paper.'

'Excuse me?' The pen dropped and Chris straightened. 'Why would anyone steal scrap paper?'

'At a guess I'd say they grabbed it at the sound of sirens, thinking it was something important. It looked like a pile of printed notes.'

'Nothing to do with Prancer? You were working on results at home, weren't you?'

Were they leading questions or was Chris doing his best to cover up his involvement? It was hard to tell but his left hand was again tapping at a furious rate on the desk. 'I'm sure the rough draft of Mum's family history had nothing about Prancer in it. Mum knows nothing about it.'

'I can't believe you haven't told her what you were working on, given the way your father died.'

'She's known for years how my aim was to find a cure. She knows I've been working on it between other projects but ever since we made the pact to keep it secret, I've abided by my promise. I'm not an idiot and I'm not a traitor. This is my baby. No way am I going to be responsible for someone stealing ten years of research.' Shane sat back studying Chris for reactions. He was looking down at his still stabbing hand. It took about thirty telling seconds of silence before Chris lifted his eyes.

'Steve seemed upset about a setback. What happened?' Chris finally asked.

Ha, now we were getting down to the nitty-gritty. 'The two surviving rats died.'

'So, the formula didn't work.'

Was this a statement or a leading question? Shane wasn't sure but it was certainly probing but hadn't he prodded and poked all morning, seeking some clue to see if other things weren't going on behind his back. He shouldn't have these doubts and hated how these suspicions lived with him every second. 'It worked.'

The stabbing ceased and Chris straightened, looking much more alert.

'The rats were cured but now they're dead. More tests are needed to find out why. I've done dissections, made up slides of samples from the organs and frozen the body parts. Now I need time to study everything in detail to work out why.'

'If they were cured, why does it matter why they died?'

'Well it would be a fat lot of good if the cure killed the patient. It would ruin all of us if we claimed to have a cure, yet all the patients dropped dead.'

A whispered curse slipped from Chris's mouth. 'How long are you going to need? I mean it *does* work.'

'Didn't I tell you it works, less than a minute ago? Now there's something I need to know.'

Chris leant forwards. 'What?'

'Tyson. Whose idea was it to bring him in and why wasn't I in on the discussion and decisions? You must have known I would never agree to it. Whose idea was it to not talk to me about it?' Chris didn't blush but a muscle tightened against his jaw and his stare was fixated on the pen.

'It was Steve's idea…'

'Unbelievable!' Shane shook his head in disbelief. 'And of course, I knew about it. Right?'

'Well, yes, of course, what's wrong with you?'

Shane laughed; he couldn't help it. The laughter gurgled unbidden upwards, exploded and kept coming until his eyes watered. Somewhere in the background he heard Chris ask if he was okay. He was laughing so much he couldn't formulate an answer but he was far from okay. He was bewildered and more certain now there was a planned conspiracy to steal Prancer. Still chuckling at the absurdity of the situation, Shane stood, made his excuses and staggered to his own office where he locked the door to seek solace in his personal laboratory.

He sat for a while cogitating the day's discussions before a few conclusions came to him. To ensure his actions weren't suspicious he needed to behave in his usual manner. An ironic laugh slipped out at this thought for so far, his actions today had been anything but normal, apart from the round of discussions with the teams. So, he needed to get back on track or at least appear to be on track.

First, he rang Carol. Tomorrow was Friday, the night they usually dined out somewhere a bit swanky. It was a great relief when the chat they had was the most normal thing to have happened since Miss Jessica Simmonds had lobbed onto his front veranda.

Date made, he rang his workout buddy, Justin, and invited him over for drinks this evening to hand over the cricket club minutes since he planned to be away over the weekend and wouldn't be able to give them to him at the gym early Saturday morning as arranged. Working out wasn't his favourite past-time. In fact, he had to force himself to go but with the hours he spent in a laboratory, sitting staring into an eyepiece of a microscope, it was a necessary few hours of torture, which Justin seemed to enjoy inflicting on him, if he wanted to remain fit and healthy. Once he began his routine, he didn't mind so much. It was forcing his body to get out of bed before seven on a Saturday morning which was the hard bit. A couple more hours snuggled under the doona catching up on sleep was far preferable.

A phone call to his mother and sisters ensured they would be around during the weekend and lightened his mood to a level he was feeling like the Shane Douglas he knew. While he was at it, he added Tyson's number to his call list. Calls made, he settled down to fabricating a few files containing reports and analysis data of Prancer misinformation, dropping in a couple of formulae which looked impressive but were nothing more than common household products. In particular, he liked the one when vinegar and bi-carbonate soda are combined so he included it. These he saved under the name PR. Anyone searching his computer would assume it was short for Prancer. It was fun sifting through old projects for analysis sheets, graphs and notes on microscopic studies, printing them off and shoving them in files which he placed right at the back of his filing cabinet under the same heading. Put together it resulted in utter nonsense. To the untrained eye, the pages looked authentic and would take someone trained in the field a few days to discover they'd been had. He didn't bother making false thumb-drives. There was little point. If someone broke into his office, they'd search the computer first, download relevant files and while waiting, search the filing cabinet. Besides, there were no thumb-drives with Prancer labels among the stack in a long set of narrow shelves he had constructed for the specific purpose of storing saved project files and he didn't have time.

By the time he left for home, Shane felt rejuvenated, especially after he'd rigged both the computer and filing cabinet with a fine filament, which would snap should either be opened or moved.

At home two hours later, Shane padded down the passage to open the door to Justin Doyle. They settled at the kitchen table, Shane's favourite place for entertaining. It always felt homely and it was the way he'd designed the room when he'd renovated two years ago. Thanks to knocking down a wall between what was a shoe-box-sized kitchen and a large formal dining room, he now had a fantastic space with a large extendable table at one end. To him, formal dining rooms were a thing of the past and not often used. A large functional island separated the two areas, giving plenty of both storage and bench space to the ultra-modern kitchen with top-of-the-range gadgets. It was a place he enjoyed working in.

Justin and he always got on well and tonight didn't pan out any different as they caught up and exchanged friendly banter over a couple of drinks. It felt so normal after the past few days of turmoil. Since he was driving, Justin stretched out two stubbies of low alcohol beer and a mug of coffee while Shane preferred wine chased down with black tea. After an hour of relaxed normality, they got down to the reason for the visit and went over the AGM minutes before both scrawling their signatures at the bottom. Justin stood to leave.

'May I use your bathroom before I go?' Justin said as he popped his mug on the bench.

'Sure, you know where it is.' Shane waved him away, collected the empty bottles and placed them on the end of the island ready to go into the recycling bin in the morning. He rinsed out the glasses and mugs in hot water and set them on the draining board before wiping down the sink and bench.

'Psst, Shane, come here.'

Shane spun around at the harsh whisper. 'What…'

'Shh.' Justin put a finger to his lips as he beckoned Shane over with his other hand.

'What's the matter? Why are we whispering?' Shane said against Justin's ear. Justin didn't respond but instead grasped Shane's elbow and tugged him towards the bathroom. Shane reached up to switch on the light, but a hand stopped him. Mystified, Shane followed the line of Justin's held out arm and pointed finger. He jerked to a standstill when he spied two shadowy figures huddled against the back fence, half hidden behind one of those scraggly shrubs he always promised himself he would trim back – one day.

From this distance it was hard to make out any definite features other than two people sitting on the ground with bent knees and… did they have binoculars? In the darkness it was doubtful Shane would be seen but any sudden movement might give them away, so he backed out slowly, tugging Justin after him. Once in the passage he leant against the wall, mystified as to why the guys were still there if Justin had used the toilet. Surely, they'd seen him. He asked the question.

'I didn't turn on the light. I could see well enough from the kitchen light. And I didn't flush yet. Thought the noise might alert them. Who are they?'

'You think I know who is lurking in my back yard?' but he had an idea. It occurred to him the trespassers wouldn't be seen from the kitchen, but it was possible the two strangers had reconnoitred the property and see him and Justin at the table. What were they doing just sitting there? Were they waiting? Damn, maybe they were waiting for Justin to leave. 'Okay, I have a feeling they're waiting for you to go. It's probably the same guys who broke in Tuesday morning.'

'What do they want?'

'I don't know,' Shane lied. 'They only managed to search three rooms before the police arrived. Maybe they want to see what else I've got.'

'Is anything missing?'

'No.'

'So, what have you got hidden away that nobody knows about. Sorry – they,' he pointed outside, 'must know or they wouldn't be there.'

'Believe me there's nothing here except the normal stuff everybody has. They searched my bedroom last time but left the jewellery, coins and small items and apart from my sound system, which they didn't touch, I've got nothing of much value.'

'So, what do you want to do? We could go out there and scare them off.'

'Or we could set a trap for them.'

'How? Why?' Justin crept back to the bathroom door and took another peek around the door. 'They're still there. Haven't moved.'

Shane touched his arm. 'Let's go back to the kitchen. They probably saw us chatting at the table and assume we're still there. Let them think they haven't been spotted.'

Back in the kitchen, Shane crossed close to the window so he would be noticed if his trespassers were watching for movement. Both men settled in the chairs they'd used before. 'Have you got any sort of weapon in your car?' Shane asked as he reached for his mobile phone.

'You mean a gun or something – no way?'

Shane laughed. 'No, some sort of waddy or something heavy you can wield or do some damage with. I'm going to call a work colleague who may be able to give me an idea what to do.' He searched for Tyson's number; thankful he'd added it to his call list after a fair amount of misgiving.

It took so many rings for Tyson to answer, Shane was about to hang up when he heard a deep voice grumble, 'Tyson here.'

'Will…'

'You're actually using my first name. What have I done to deserve this?' Laughter cackled down the line.

'Funny man, Tyson, but I have a problem.'

'Spill it, my friend.'

Friend? He was expanding things a bit but right now Shane would get on bended knee and grovel. 'I have a friend here…'

'The lovely Carol?'

'How did you… never mind. No. This so-called best friend of mine makes sure I torture myself at the gym every week. We were catching up over a couple of drinks. I do have friends you know.'

Laughter echoed as response. Shane couldn't figure out why he detested this man at the same time he was beginning to take to him.

'Now what is the problem, Shane?'

'It's not a problem yet but I have a feeling it's going to be a serious problem as soon as Justin leaves. There are two… I'm assuming men, hunkered down behind a bush against my back fence.'

'I'm on my way.'

'Hang on, I have an idea. If they're waiting, maybe they're after me.' A shudder snaked all the way down his spine. 'They know where my bedroom is. Well, I assume it's the same house-breakers.' The revving of an engine startled him, and he glanced around before realising the sound was coming from the phone. Tyson was indeed on his way.

'Go on, I'm listening. It'll take me about forty-five minutes, less if I'm game enough to test the speed limits.'

'I'm going to turn my bedroom light off last, so they'll think I've gone to bed. But I'll sneak into another room, armed with whatever I can find. The window directly behind my garage is where I'll be. I'll unlock it after I'm sure they're inside.' Did he say that? Damn but he was an idiot. This could be the dumbest thing he'd ever done.

'Don't put yourself in danger, my friend, get out.'

'I want to catch these bastards, find out who they're working for. Me running will achieve nothing,' except maybe his life, 'and they need me alive – remember?'

'Is there any Red stuff at your place?'

'No, well yes but it's not in the house and is well hidden.' Now he was sorry he hadn't made the time to take it to the bank. It was almost impossible to find unless they burnt the house down. A shiver raced across his shoulders at the thought. Arson wasn't something he'd contemplated. Good job there was a copy already in safe keeping. 'I'll phone if they disappear.' Shane hung up.

'What's going on? Needing you alive doesn't sound like you don't know why those two guys are sitting out there.'

Damn he'd forgotten about Justin and he'd said too much. 'Yes, I *think* I know what they want but I can't discuss it. Work ethics won't allow me. I'm sure you understand since you work for the inner circle of the government.'

'Are you in danger? I can stay.'

'Maybe, but without me, they've got nothing so I don't think I'll come to any harm and you can help…'

'How?' Justin interrupted as he leant forwards looking eager.

'By leaving.'

'Huh, no way.'

'If you're here they won't come closer. I need you to leave, but park around the corner and call the police. Insist on no sirens or lights. I presume those two out there will wait about thirty minutes to ensure I'm asleep. I'm going to let them break in. Tyson should be here by then.'

'Who's Tyson?'

'A top security guy we've employed. His size alone should scare those two out there.'

'I'm not sitting around the corner waiting for you to be beaten or worse.' Justin kept pacing but paused bent over the table with outstretched arms every time he said something.

'I'm not asking you to. Give it fifteen minutes before you walk back. But don't come to the house. Hide across the road. Make sure you come running if there's shouting or whatever. In fact, I'll bring your number up on my mobile and have it ready to ring in case I need you in a hurry.' While he spoke Shane slipped his phone from his shirt pocket, swept down the list of numbers until he found Justin's and brought the number to the screen. All he needed was to press the call button. 'But don't get in Tyson's way. Let him come in. You can't miss him.'

'Big guy.'

'Huge guy. I'd say six feet four with shoulders…' Shane stretched out his arms full width. 'Now have you got a weapon of some sort?'

'Cricket bat do?'

'Brilliant. Now go. Let's get this rolling.' And it was the last thing he wanted to do. This was so ridiculous. He was asking for trouble – serious trouble.

Justin moved to the door and paused. 'Are you sure? We could still chase them off.'

No, he damn well wasn't sure. In fact, it was the stupidest idea he'd ever had. 'I'm sure. I'll walk you outside as I'd normally do. We'll say goodbye loud enough for them to hear.' Shane waved a hand in the general direction of the back fence.

He winced at Justin's farewell. It was loud enough to waken close neighbours. Shuddering at the volume, he turned and paused before sucking in a long breath for courage as he hurried to the door. Getting ambushed out here wasn't such a brilliant idea. None of this was a brilliant idea. It was bordering on suicidal.

After closing the front door, but leaving the deadlocks unlocked, Shane returned to the kitchen, removed all the sharp knives from the block near the stove and hid all but one in the bottom of the freezer. It was a crazy thing to do but they were weapons: ones which could be used against him. The largest went with him into his bedroom and sat within easy reach while he carried out his before bed ablutions in the en-suite after he'd dropped the blind over the window, guessing it was a normal action but since this bathroom was at the rear of his home it wasn't something he usually did. Tense nerves and innards which had tied themselves into tight knots, accompanied him. As he switched off the last light, he estimated Tyson should arrive about the same time the two trespassers made a move. There was no certainty. Shane was going by gut instinct based on what he would do in the same situation, but this could all go pear-shaped within seconds.

He was about to sneak down the hall when an idea came. Turning back, he mounded a dressing gown and spare pillow under the doona and stood back to check if it looked sort of like a body in the bed. He shivered; body was not the best word choice. Satisfied with the result, he scarpered on tiptoe, glancing through the family bathroom window as he paused in the doorway.

Damn, they'd gone. Where are they? He didn't dare go closer for fear of being seen. The fourth bedroom, tucked in the back corner of the house, was rarely used. It contained the obligatory bed, a double, which his nieces shared when they came to the city with his sister. An ironing board was in its permanent state of being set up for any last-minute touch up of a shirt. It stood against the far wall, filling in the only spare space. A tiny bedside table sat each side of the bedhead while the capacious wardrobe was built in. It was the smallest room in the house but still larger than a lot of bedrooms he'd seen in modern houses. Renovating this room was about seventy-nine on his list of things to do.

Not having a clue what to do next, Shane took care in peeking through the edge of the curtain. Seeing no unusual shadows or any movement, he turned the key in the window lock and slid the catch to the open position, wincing at the slight screech of the rarely used mechanism, adding an oiling to his *to do* list. All he could do now was sit and wait so he perched his backside on the bed and blew out a breath of tension.

Chapter Twelve

The seconds felt like minutes and the minutes like hours. With ears attuned to the silence, waiting for the slightest of tell-tale sounds, Shane barely moved. Cramp began setting in, so he stretched one leg at a time, his spine, followed by head twists to ease the cricks in his neck. Next, he worked on arm muscles – out and in, flex and ease. He slid off the bed and squatted on his haunches. Up and down he pushed to get blood flowing and sinews loosened.

A soft *squawk* was followed by silence. Ten seconds later there was a low and long *squeak*. A *scrape* followed another period of silence.

Shane stood, lifted the knife from the bed, crept to the side of the window and ever so slowly, edged the end of the curtain outwards, far enough to enable him to see the outline of a man standing as though pinned against the wall next to the boarded-up laundry window. Now he understood the sounds. Entry was being gained by removing the boards. It was a smart move. Prising off the boards made less noise than breaking another pane of glass or whacking on dead bolts which he had on all external doors.

The thrum of an engine stilled not only Shane but also the one man he could see. It might have felt like an hour since Justin left but it had been less than thirty minutes. There was no way the car nearing the house was Tyson's. Shane prayed it wasn't Justin returning by car.

It was amazing how the *whish* of rubber against bitumen was so predominant when your brain was centred on the single sound. An arc of light lit up the air, the trees, the bushes and fence towards the front of the property. It disappeared as fast as it came leaving everything in profound darkness until retinas adjusted and shapes could be discerned again. The rumbling engine faded to a hum leaving the world in silence until normal night-time noises emerged once again.

The man outside moved a step away from the wall. He was handed a board which he leant against the wall. The ever so slow squawks and scrapes continued until the next board was removed and placed against the first one on an angle. It was ridiculous the way Shane's mind was telling the man out there why he should be laying the boards flat on the ground. One accidental knock against the growing mound of wood and an almighty racket would follow.

There goes the sixth and final board. The other man, about the same size as the first, came into view, cupping his hands to make a foothold. Shane sought recognition. Neither man was tall enough to be Chris or Bill nor paunchy enough to be Steve. Were they the two men from Monday night? It was impossible to tell but he thought there had been a greater difference in height before.

A muffled *oomph* and the remaining man ducked while two legs wriggled in the air before vanishing with a *thud*. A bag appeared and was held up towards the window. Two arms reached out and grabbed the bag. Another bag followed seconds later. What was in those bags? Wild imagination visualised a heap of implements which could be used to muffle and restrain. Maybe cable-ties, a rope, a gag. Shane shuddered at the picture of syringes and sedatives and what they could use to subdue a six-foot man who was going to fight back like Muhammad Ali to escape. Damn but he was an idiot even being here. Whose dumb idea was this?

A few seconds later the same two arms appeared again and the second man was hoisted up and in. Listening for sounds was not hard for the quieter the two men tried to be, the louder they were. One bad thing for burglars who wanted to rob older houses was the floorboards. No matter how well-maintained they were, the boards creaked. Shane's were in top condition. The first thing he'd done when he bought the 40s built home was to rip out the old carpets and have the pristine jarrah floorboards re-nailed, sanded and sealed. It looked magnificent but was now guiding him to the whereabouts of his burglars.

To ensure he didn't make the same mistake, Shane toed off his sneakers and crept to the door in socks. He put his ear to the wood of the door but this time the age of the house went against him. Doors in the 40s were built to last, from the same solid hardwood and didn't transmit much noise; a good thing when living in the house but not so good in this type of situation. They weren't hollow-core modern doors which were flimsy and nowhere near as soundproof.

A sudden muffled creak came from the other side of the house: his bedroom, he guessed, which opened onto the veranda via a set of jarrah-framed, glass panelled French doors.

Taking utmost care, Shane grasped the contoured brass doorknob and turned it until he heard the inner barrel snick and release. With knife held high, he inched the door open a fraction and peeked through the crack.

The small passage was clear. His held breath huffed out as he took a tentative step, sliding his socked foot as close to the wall as he could fit for there was less movement of floorboards closer to the walls.

Step by slow step, he crept along the passage, past the laundry to the corner of the larger main passage, to the edge of the now wide-open bedroom door where he paused before peeking.

Something was wrong. Why was it still so quiet? Why hadn't they discovered he wasn't in his bed? Were they even in the bedroom?

Shane glanced up and down the main passage. Still clear. He dared a peek around the door's edge. He could make out only one man who wasn't taking things out of the bag to subdue Shane but was filling it with every single item on the bedside table and drawers. Clock radio had gone. Book was gone. Dress jewellery, pens, coins and everything else – all gone.

Shane spun around at the sound of heavy breathing and brandished the knife ready to defend himself.

The huge shadow racing down the passage could only be one person but how he could move with such stealth was beyond belief and why hadn't he heard Tyson clambering through the window? Shane held up one finger and pointed to his bedroom. At the second finger, he waved his hand towards the front rooms. Tyson nodded and slid against the far passage wall as he edged past the bedroom door, sneaking a quick glance inside. Shane couldn't believe the man dared to shove his hand inside the door and switch on the light before he took off.

The intruder spun around, saw Shane, glanced at the lump in the bed before shooting another stunned look at Shane. Before Shane could even think about reacting, the man hurled the bag towards the French doors. Whatever was inside the bag was either very heavy or sharp for the bag went straight through. The resultant sound of smashing glass was accompanied by a yell from Tyson and scuffling noises.

'Pete, run!' was yelled as Shane's man bolted over the bed, put his hands up to protect his head and barged through the still falling glass shards, creating a racket loud enough to awaken nearby neighbours.

A few seconds later there was a sharp crack which sounded like gunfire followed immediately by a squeal, *oomph* and a *thud*.

'Justin!' Shane yelled as he turned and raced towards the front door. He didn't dare risk going through the sharp pieces of still hanging glass to be torn to ribbons. He was almost at the front door when he slammed into what felt like a brick wall.

'Hold up, Shane,' rattled in shuddering eardrums. He looked around, stunned to see Tyson had a hold on the man who had fled outside.

'How did you get him so quick?' Shane glanced at the still locked front door then remembered Justin. 'Justin's out there. I think he's been shot,' he added as he fumbled in his haste to turn knobs and unlock the screen door. Man, it was all very well securing a house with all these locks but trying to get out in a hurry was a nightmare. At last the doors were open and Shane shot out, leapt off the veranda and raced around the side of the house where he pulled up short.

Justin was sitting on top of the second man with a cricket bat pressing the man's shoulders into the ground.

'What the …' was all Shane could get out as he stared at the man on the ground. Didn't Tyson already have him? He turned at the sound of a scuffle and saw Tyson frog-marching the man from the bedroom, along the path. Completely baffled, Shane strode over to Justin. 'Are you all right? I heard a shot.'

Justin grinned. 'Not a shot unless you call me using this man's head as a cricket ball.'

The man under Justin wasn't moving. 'Is he dead?' asked Shane.

'No, well I don't think so. He's probably a bit woozy with a nasty headache. I scored a six.' Justin rose and turned the man over whose arms flopped to the ground. There was no struggle left in him.

Shane stared at the man's face and swung his eyes back at the man with Tyson's arm wrapped around his shoulders. 'Well I'll be damned,' he spluttered. 'They're twins — identical twins.' And they didn't look anything like the two men from Monday night, although he couldn't be sure for he hadn't had a clear view of the second man. These two had to be in their forties. And the clothes; there was no smart leather jacket or black jeans. The twin on the ground wore grey baggy track pants which had seen better days and a dark hoodie, while his brother's blue jeans were equally tatty and teamed with a similar hooded sweater.

To add to the cacophony of the night, sirens sounded moments before red and blue strobe lights lit up the street. 'I thought I asked for no lights or sirens,' Shane said to Justin.

'That's what I told them.'

Shane sighed in resignation. Now the whole flaming neighbourhood would be pouring out of doors in various states of dress and undress and he wasn't wrong. Within a minute the path on both sides of the road held small groups of gawkers, all mumbling among themselves and of course they all had to take photos with the ever-present mobile phones.

It took almost an hour for burglars to be shoved into a paddy wagon, statements to be made to explain what they were all doing there and how each man had been involved. Shane tried retrieving his belongings but was told in no uncertain terms they all had to be bagged, photographed and fingerprinted etcetera as evidence. He would get them all back sometime soon. He bet the *sometime* was the predominate word. After sending Justin home to his wife, another two hours had passed before he and Tyson had removed what felt like millions of glass fragments, scrounged around to find enough scraps of wood to cover the holes and hammered untold nails into his beautiful jarrah window and door frames. It was going to take an entire bucket of wood filler to fill in the holes.

'It would be easier to replace the frames,' said Tyson as they sank into kitchen chairs with a glass of wine each.

'You're probably right.' Feeling something prick in his head, Shane grubbed the fingers of one hand through his hair, dislodging bits from the garden, including a black ant which he dropped to the table and slammed his fist down to squash it.

'Poor ant.' Tyson grinned before sipping his wine.

'I'm too tired to care and it bit me.' Shane used a leaf from his hair to scrape up the mashed ant. He swept the bits into his palm with the side of his other hand. After dropping them into the bin he washed his hands and moved back to the table, leant back and let loose with a loud yawn.

'Can I doss down here for what's left of the night?' asked Tyson as he set his empty glass to one side.

Shane hesitated.

'You don't like me, do you?' Tyson asked.

'It's not that I don't like you, I kind of do, but the way this whole thing has evolved has severely dented my trust levels.'

'I understand but I could give you several pages of references from high-ranking federal and local officers who will vouch for my integrity. I'm on your side, which reminds me. Miss Jessica Michelle Simmonds is 28. She's a specialist physical education teacher at a local school. There are no black marks against her name, not even a parking ticket. She's a former state athletic champion and I'm certain she is not involved in anything underhand. There is absolutely nothing leading her to any kind of relationship to anyone in your company. She did report being hassled by two men to the police. She's clean. I'm sure.'

Shane sighed as he sat back and drained his glass. 'I guess we now have one to tick off the list.' He smiled. 'I bet her specialty was high jump.'

'What makes you say that?'

'She's taller than average with long legs and she vaulted my back fence with ease and grace. I couldn't get over the way she did.'

'You're half right. She does heptathlon. Now what do you think about the twins?'

'I don't want to think about them at all. I guess now they're caught I won't have any more problems.'

Tyson began running a damp finger around the rim of his glass, setting up a high-pitched humming. When the noise began irritating him, Shane yanked the glass away. 'Okay, I'm biting, why did you bring the twins up?'

'I'm sure you still have a problem.'

'Why?' Shane collected both glasses and moved to the sink where he rinsed them under steaming water.

'Think of the difference between tonight's burglary and the last one. On Tuesday nothing was taken but the place was searched indicating the trespassers were looking for a special item. Tonight, the one in your room was stuffing into a bag, anything which might get them a couple of dollars at a pawn shop. What puzzles me is how they didn't even care you were in the house, but, at a guess, I think these two are used to getting in, taking what they can as quick as possible before getting out. I'd say they are habitual burglars used to raiding houses with the owners asleep in their beds. But, and here's why they are still a big problem. The other twin was being a lot more careful, flicking through and scanning pages in the drawers of your desk. He was the one looking for a particular item. His bag was empty of any small items they could flog and there are a few pieces of value in that particular room. The guy wasn't interested. The police are going to report back to me on their background and known associates and it's the associates I'm really interested in. The information could lead us to the one person responsible for wanting your research.'

A roar of anger and frustration swelled up inside Shane. He wanted to let it out but held it back. 'That's all I need. So, I'm back to square one, which leaves me with a bit of a dilemma. How safe is my house going to be when I visit my mother and sisters over the weekend? I really don't want to come back to find my home torn apart.'

'I can doss here for a few days. But right now which bed can I use? I'm buggered.'

'You're not getting mine. You'll have to curl up in the guest room. At least it's a queen bed. You already know where the bathroom is,' he added after the long groan from Tyson, who obviously didn't relish folding his huge frame on such a small mattress. The width wouldn't be a problem but the length would. 'There are clean towels and face washers in the cupboard under the sink. Goodnight.'

Chapter Thirteen

'Where's the dishwasher?'

Shane popped the last corner of toast into his mouth and twisted around to see a bemused looking Tyson standing in the kitchen with both hands holding dirty breakfast dishes. This was going to be interesting to see how the man reacts. 'I don't have one.'

'Excuse me?' The poor man almost dropped the dishes as he spun around to stare at Shane in disbelief. 'You've got this fabulous kitchen full of the best money can buy and you don't have a dishwasher?'

'No.'

'Why? Everyone these days has a dishwasher.'

'Not quite everyone.' Shane couldn't hold back his grin. This was not the first time his lack of this modern appliance had caused stunned disbelief.

'Please explain?' Tyson finally settled the dishes on the sink.

'Because I know what lives in them, under and behind those bright clean looking steel boxes. Have you ever seen inside the hoses and workings of a dishwasher?'

A loud groan rumbled from Tyson's mouth. 'Do I want to know?'

'Probably not. One of my uni papers was a report on what grew in the hidden recesses of these fabulous machines which theoretically save time but in reality, don't. Think of the time it takes to scrape, rinse off and stack the dishes in the trays. Add around an hour for the cycle followed by unpacking and putting away the dishes. It takes me two minutes to wash the meagre number of dishes I have at each meal. It would take a week for me to fill the machine: a week of festering food. My exercise was to take samples from one hundred machines and grow the cultures. The hardest thing was finding a hundred households who would let me loose in their kitchens with a screwdriver and specimen jars.' Shane collected his own dishes and carried them to the kitchen.

'Why would that be so hard?'

'What deterred most was the idea their machines were harbouring a pile of nasties which gave the impression I would think the owners weren't hygienic. I had to resort to my mother and sisters sweet talking their friends and co-workers into allowing me in their kitchens under the pretext I would fail my degree if I didn't get this project done. Still they had to beg and cajole.'

'What was the result?'

Shane laughed. 'I don't have a dishwasher, nor do my mother or sisters. I grew some interesting cultures. Some of the Petri dishes looked like multi-coloured jungles if you take into consideration the size of a microbe. It took me weeks to count the numbers and variety of micro-organisms. Some were unexpected leading me to think there are a few families out there who eat really weird food or put odd things in their dishwashers.' Shane began washing the dishes under flowing hot water.

'Like what?'

'Shoes.'

'You have to be kidding. Why would…? Never mind. The picture I'm seeing in my mind isn't boding well for my dishwasher. Why aren't you using detergent?'

'Because there's no grease.'

'Huh?' Tyson lifted a plate and was about to wipe it dry with a tea towel when Shane snatched it away, rinsed it again and put it back on the draining board.

'It's healthier to let the dishes air dry. Tea towels add germs to the plate when you wipe them over. And detergent is there to break down grease and fats not to kill germs, which it doesn't. It's the hot water which kills the germs. I could go into detail about exactly what chemicals are used to make detergent…'

'Please don't,' Tyson growled while Shane laughed and decided to take it a bit further.

'And I could describe how much the tiny little critters love dish washing sponges – especially after they've been left residing in the bottom of the sink, wallowing in moisture for a day.' It was hard keeping a straight face at the sounds of disgust coming from Tyson.

'You obsessive about this or something?' Tyson asked.

'Not at all. A lot of micro-organisms are good for you. But after studying them my entire adult life, I know a lot about their favourite breeding grounds and what each is useful for or the opposite. Some are very nasty little critters. There's every chance the more modern dishwashers are built better, but I'm still not prepared to find out.' Shane wiped down the sink with an open weave super-wipe he used instead of sponges. These could be tossed in the washing machine and soaked in bleach. Finally, he placed a clean tea towel over the dishes.

'I thought you said a tea towel wasn't good.' Tyson pointed to the offending article.

'No, what I said was when you use one to dry the dishes you merely transfer germs from towel to dishes and smear them over the surface. A clean towel over the top prevents air-borne germs from settling. Nothing is perfect. You can't prevent all germs from landing on anything and our bodies depend on a certain number of organisms to operate properly. Certain micro-organisms are essential for good gut health. I keep the nasty ones limited by avoiding their breeding grounds.'

'And now I've had a lesson in Microbiology 101, I'm off. I need to get home to find clean clothes. I'll see you at work.'

'Not for a while. The glaziers are coming to replace the laundry window. I need to be here. Now they'll have to come back to fix the door.' Shane sighed as he put away the breakfast items. 'My insurance company is going to love me.'

Tyson laughed as he left. 'At least you'll get your stolen items back. Tell them it could have been a lot worse,' echoed down the passage.

While waiting for the glazier, Shane crawled into the ceiling cavity to retrieve the research, deciding to return them to the safe until he left. A visit to a second bank was on the morning's agenda as a priority.

It was almost time for lunch before Shane managed to reach the office, where the first thing he did was check for broken filaments. Relief surged when all were intact. It was not only pleasing to know a work buddy hadn't been snooping but it felt like ten tonnes of pressure had been removed from the atmosphere. Maybe he was being over-cautious, he thought as he plonked into the chair and spun towards the desk. Maybe this entire thing was a figment of his imagination. Jessica Simmonds was exactly as she claimed, a scared woman seeking refuge from danger and Shane had repaid her by shooting her to the top of his suspect list: an imaginary suspect list for he had no proof of anything. Didn't he base his entire career on proven fact?

Then there was Steve. No doubt there was something wrong with the man but what proof did he have that Steve was trying to *steal* Prancer? Yes, he was interested in the money it would bring but steal it for himself alone? Nobody would ever believe it was Steve's research for he was an accountant not a scientist. Damn, but he should have thought of this before. He thumped his head on the desk twice for stupidity before straightening on a definite thought: all was not well on the Steve front and he wouldn't take the man off his list of suspects until he figured what was wrong.

His thoughts turned to Bill and Chris. The conversations he'd had with both appeared normal. Yes, they probed about Prancer, but they had a right to those questions. Sure, the company would survive without the money Prancer would bring in but the money they received would boost the coffers to a level they wouldn't have to work so hard to get contracts. Instead, they could put all their energy into building the company to a standard where everyone would be seeking them out to carry out various research projects instead of the other way around. The company's credibility would skyrocket.

He ate his cheese and salad sandwich while trawling through emails, deleting those irrelevant pieces of twaddle some people seemed to find sick pleasure in forwarding. Who had time to read them? Only half were important. Some he answered while others he printed off and placed in the *To Do* tray. Most were from fellow workers seeking verification of facts or checking on procedure. To him, it was a normal part of his role and of the day's work, which sometimes took a lot of his precious time. But he'd rather do things the right way from the start than waste twice as much time re-doing it because correct procedure hadn't been followed.

A knock at the door brought relief. He rubbed a hand along tight neck muscles as he spun around to see Tyson opening the door.

'You got a minute?' Tyson asked as he walked in, giving the room a claustrophobic feel. Even though he was only four inches taller than Shane he seemed to take up so much space.

'Sure, I need a break from the mundane. What's the problem?'

Tyson settled a hip on the edge of the desk. 'You need to sack this man.' A file was flung onto the desk with a splat. It skidded as it spun and ended up next to the keyboard.

Shane glanced at the name. 'Nathan Boyd. Why? He's a junior on one of the teams. I've not heard any complaints about him. I was talking to him yesterday and he seemed to know what he was doing.' Shane flicked the file open and leafed through the pages. It contained Boyd's CV, copies of his qualifications and references. His job application form and notes Chris had made at the interview drew the file to a close.

The desk creaked as Tyson leant over and flicked through the pages, drawing out five, which he spread on the desk. One finger stabbed at a certificate. 'Fake.' His finger moved to the next certificate. 'Same with this one.' He tapped each reference. 'Fake, fake, fake. These people don't exist.'

Stunned, Shane stared at the other man's face. 'Are you sure? We always ring numbers to verify references. Chris and Bill would have phoned these people.'

'They might have rung these numbers and probably received answers but none of these numbers are those of the companies named on each reference, I've contacted all these companies. Nathan Boyd, if it's his real name, has never worked for any of these.'

Shane swore under his breath before lifting each sheet and examining the words. 'So, what do we do?'

'You sack him.'

'I realise that but this guy's only been with us for a few months.' He turned to Tyson. 'What if he's a plant?'

'Which is why I've brought it to you.'

'And I guess I'm supposed to be the bunny who takes this to the other three to confront them by asking questions. Thanks a million.'

'No it's not what I intended. Who sits in on these interviews?'

'It depends on what the job is for. Usually it's Chris and Bill. Sometimes it will be only one of them. I get called in if there's a technical scientific requirement, Steve, if it has financial relevance.'

'Were you in on this one?'

'No and yes. I wasn't at the interview but was shown the certificates and information in the references to see if they fitted the requirements.' He thumbed to interview notes. 'This is Chris's handwriting, so he was present.'

'Was Bill?'

'I don't know. He could have been. Only one takes notes. We don't record who is present at each interview but maybe we should.'

'Might be a good idea from now on.'

Shane dropped his head into his hands as a shudder wound its way down his spine. What if this guy was a spy from another company? What did they want? Were they having a general look to see what we are working on or could they have got wind of Prancer and are the ones creating havoc with his life? Damn, damn, damn. He lifted his head.

'He's a spy, isn't he?' he muttered aloud.

'Possible and there are two scenarios here.'

'Only two?' Shane twisted his head towards Tyson.

'Two probables. One, he's from an outside company and snooping or two, one of your guys brought him in as a red herring so if there are any suspicions they can be directed to this poor sap.'

'Which means Chris, Bill or Steve has blabbed and there's a third scenario. He's here to do the actual snooping on Red.'

'Yes, and any or all of the executive could be in on this. This interview could have been a set up.'

A groan worked its way from Shane's gut, all the way up and released on a long breath. 'I don't know what to do about this.'

'Sack the man. You don't need any explanation other than his certificates are fake.'

'He could be useful for getting information about who is responsible.' Shane swung back in his chair and plopped his feet on the desk, smirking as the soles brushed dust on Tyson's otherwise immaculate tan trousers. The man knew how to dress.

'If you start asking questions and he's guilty, he's going to clam up like his lips have been super-glued together. If you call him out on his fraud, no-one, including Boyd, will know of your suspicions which means we're free to keep investigating. I can have a man keep tabs on him to find out where he goes.'

'This,' Shane turned the folder over and pointed to the name printed on the cover, 'isn't going to be his real name.'

'More than likely but I can do some research to find out.'

'I can't fire him without going to the others.'

'No, but all you have to do is call an executive meeting with Boyd present. Call him out on his duplicity in front of the other three. Tell them I found it when I was doing my investigation, which is what I was employed to do. I came to you because you were first on the team I met after I found the truth. We can pretend I didn't come to you until early Monday morning, hence the reason you called the meeting. We'll watch for the reactions from the others.'

'Okay, when do you want to do this?'

'Monday. It will give me the weekend to have my man trail Boyd. I'll have him followed from the time he leaves here tonight. Monday morning, after you've been here about half an hour, call an exec meeting for later in the day. Say 4pm.

'Done. Man, I hope this is the end of this madness,' Shane said as he removed his feet.

Tyson collected the papers and shoved them back into the file. 'So, do I but I have serious doubts. I'll keep these until the meeting.'

'Just dandy,' Shane whispered to Tyson's back as he left. He relaxed back while thinking about Nathan Boyd and his role. He was a junior researcher on a team of four. When learning the ropes, these juniors did the menial tasks. Until they proved themselves, they were nothing more than lab assistants. But still they had to have some experience. They had to know names of solutions and chemicals and tools and instruments. They had to know and understand chemical processes. If he had been inept, the team leader would have lodged a complaint. There was only one way to find out for himself: he would have to spend another afternoon working with the teams. They would think it odd

– two days in a row but maybe he could tell them he was at a loose end and needed something to do. His derisive laugh echoed from the walls as he headed for the third-floor labs. Shane Douglas was never at a loose end. He had more work waiting for him than he wanted to think about. There was a pile of emails to start with to which he'd promised answers by the end of the day. Ah, it was the excuse he would give. He was coming to see what the problems were and answering in person.

Chapter Fourteen

Shane relaxed back into the upholstered dining chair, which was far more comfortable than most he'd sat in at various restaurants. He was so looking forward to this evening where he could forget about work and the problems of this past week. Thanks to Carol's message to say she had been held up at work and would meet him here, he was early because he didn't have to pick her up. The restaurant wasn't new to him; he'd been here before but it had been renovated in the past six months. Now it was more… cosy was the word which came to mind. At the same time it still felt classy, for which it had a reputation. He prayed the same chef was cooking for the food had been both delicious and impressive on their previous visit. For a minute he wondered why they hadn't been back in the past six months but both he and Carol enjoyed trying different eateries and there were hundreds to sample around the city and suburbs, especially along the coast and riverside. They gave each dining establishment their personal ranking, crossing anything less than three stars off the list. Three or four stars deserved another chance to go to the top while five stars were definite repeats. This one had earned four stars so maybe with the update it might gain an extra tick of approval and they would grace the premises with their attendance more often.

While sipping on the obligatory iced water, Shane studied the room to figure out the differences. The chandelier-type lights had been replaced with dimmed recessed ceiling lights. Wall sconces now held tiny LED globes directed downwards to light up the tables with enough light for diners to see what they were eating without being intrusive. More important, Shane could read all the words on the menu. He'd been to a couple of restaurants where it was so dark, the words were indecipherable and he hadn't been back. Both those places had been crossed of the list before they'd even tasted the food, for ambiance was of equal importance in ratings.

It felt like there was more room now, so Shane studied the layout. It also had changed with fewer table settings, giving the place a sense of intimacy. The word boded well. Maybe it was a precursor for the night. Hmm, it would have to be at Carol's place because Tyson's presence at Shane's house put a dampener on any thoughts of intimacy in his bedroom, with only a wood-framed wall covered in plasterboard between the two. Oh, yes, the comments from Tyson would not be subtle, or pleasant.

Carol was almost upon him before Shane spotted her. He stood to greet her, planting a kiss on her cheek at the same time as giving her a loose hug. To do more in public would earn him a scornful remark since Carol disliked public displays of affection, something he'd learned early on, but he'd never figured out why and had never been game to ask.

'Hi, you look good.'

'Don't lie, I've come straight from work.' She tempered the words with a smile as he pulled out her chair.

'I'm not lying. You always look good in blue. It highlights the colour of your eyes.'

Silence ensued until they were both settled with Carol's ever-present capacious bag tucked against the wall, under the table. He had no idea what she kept in her bags but from the outside they always looked to be stuffed and he knew the many different bags she owned were expensive and fashion statements as well as being functional. But they were nowhere near as pretentious as those outlandish bags, Bill's wife carried around. Lisa's were garish and huge. As he filled Carol's water glass from the carafe, he eyed her, taking in the thick straight hair, cut longer at the sides than at the back: a style which suited her round face. 'Why do you think I was lying to you?'

'To make me feel good and I appreciate it. It's one of the things I like about you; you never put me down.'

'Well, thank you but I don't understand why you think I'd want to put you down. I admire you. You are an attractive woman and I don't mean only in the physical sense. I like everything about you.' He paused, noticing the flush of pinkness spreading across her face. It amused him the way she fanned the heat with her menu but when she took too much time replacing it with precision, it hinted at deliberately taking time. When she finally looked up her face had turned serious, causing his heart rate to rise.

'How come, if you think blue suits me, why did you say my yellow dress looked good?'

'The one you wore to the cocktail party?' A strange, tense feeling ran through him. He knew which one it was and now he was in a bit of a pickle.

'Yes, but I'm surprised you remember what I wore.'

'Sweet, Carol, I always take note of what you are wearing. As for your outfit, you asked me if I liked the dress. The dress was fine – classic and elegant. It was perfect for the occasion.' He hoped it was enough but the look in her eye told him different. The increased tension gripped him, bunching the muscles behind his neck as well as those in the gut area.

'A very tactful answer. Now tell me the truth, how did I look in my yellow dress?'

Now he had a problem. 'How big a hole would you like me to dig for myself?'

'That bad, eh?'

'Honey, you want me to be absolutely honest?'

'Yes.' The look of determination on her face wasn't boding well for a pleasant evening.

'Fine, as I said, blue suits you, as do most colours you wear. The yellow wasn't so good...' he held up his hand as she leant forwards with a grim tight mouth, 'please let me finish. Yellow seems to sap your complexion. Two people asked me if you were not feeling well and one... I don't know how to say this...'

'Straight out will be best.' Carol's arms had crossed and her back was rigid.

'One man asked me if congratulations were in order.'

'Congratulations… for what?'

Thank goodness the expression had altered to one of surprise. 'I asked the same question. He wanted to know if you were suffering from morning sickness and was I responsible.'

'Excuse me?'

'Those exact same words were my response.' His heart and every other organ in his body were jammed somewhere very uncomfortable. Somehow, his lungs had forgotten how to breathe as he watched her eyes change from utter surprise to anger then… was she grinning? He exhaled, the held breath hissing between clenched teeth.

'I saw a photo of me taken that night,' she laughed, which completely perplexed him. 'I have to agree with you. I've given the dress to charity.'

Now he was the one sitting back with the stunned look on his face. 'Well, hell,' was all he could think of to say.

'Next time I look so awful, I'd appreciate your honesty before we arrive at the function so I can change my outfit.'

'Okay, but I doubt you'll buy a yellow outfit again so I think I might be safe.' He hoped it would be so. No way did he ever want to be in the position of telling a woman she looked awful. Once was enough. Growing up in a house full of women, he'd learnt at an early age to be tactful after informing his sister she looked like a butternut pumpkin when she wore a dress of similar shape. It puffed out from the waist, looking like a doughnut until it reached mid-thigh where it was held against her legs with an elasticised hem. After his sister had fled in tears, his mother had taken him aside to explain the art of tact after agreeing with him that Shona looked ghastly. It had been a hard concept to grasp at twelve, because essentially, he'd been told to tell a lie, after all the years of it being drilled into him to always be honest.

'It's the only time I haven't liked you in an outfit.' He grabbed the menu and held it out to her. 'Let's see if the food here is as good as I remember. What takes your fancy?' He read every darn word to give himself time to recuperate, before giving his choice to the patient waitress, who hovered at his side a tad too long. He felt the silent disapproval of his tardiness in deciding but too bad, he was the customer and was giving the new menu the consideration he hoped it deserved.

After the less than pleasant start to the evening, Shane kept the conversation to safe topics. Discussion of the food took precedence after the first bite of his Thai flavoured prawn entrée. Each of the five pieces was plump, cooked to perfection and delicious.

'Try this.' He held out his fork with the last half of a prawn speared on the end. It was something they often did when they ordered different dishes. It felt good when her warm hand wrapped around his fingers as she guided the fork to her mouth and the morsel of white flesh disappeared delicately between glossy pink lips.

'Mm this is good; I wish I'd ordered prawns now. Do you want to taste mine?'

Shane eyed the small mounds of flesh hidden under a coating of gold crispy crumbs and shuddered. He wasn't normally squeamish, but the mere thought of eating lamb's brains brought a picture of recently dissected rat's innards to mind. Their intestines were about the same size and appearance.

'No thanks, I'll stick to seafood tonight.'

The pan-seared barramundi with crispy skin was better than he'd remembered. After relishing the last piece, he set his knife and fork together on the plate and slid it to one side before leaning back in the chair to watch Carol while she finished the last two forkfuls of her seafood linguine. 'Did you enjoy your meal?' Shane asked as the waitress removed the two plates and handed each a sweets menu.

'Very much so, I think the food here is better than before.' She lifted her glass of white wine and took a sip. 'How are things at work?'

Shane threw his head back and exhaled. The last thing he wanted to talk about was work. Carol had stilled, peeking over the rim of her glass. It was ridiculous the way he now saw every look, every word, as a sign of nosiness into Prancer. He had to get a grip so forced his body to relax, took a sip of wine, swilled it around his mouth and swallowed. 'Work is work. Today was much the same as any day.'

'Have the police caught your burglar yet?'

'No, not yet. In fact, I've heard nothing from them. Maybe I should phone them on Monday, but they did say they would get back to me if they had anything to report.' He didn't know why, but he didn't want to mention the second break-in. Which was strange. There had never been any hesitation in discussing anything with Carol before, although she didn't know about Prancer. After last year's leak, he had never brought up the subject with any outsider, but he had discussed other projects he worked on.

'Now, how about you, anything interesting happening at work?

'Um, no, which is why I've handed in my notice.'

Shane reeled backwards against the chair, so hard it slammed against the wall. To say he was gob-smacked was an understatement. 'You're resigning? But you love your job.' And it was only last week she had been gushing about a new project her team had been given.

The blush racing up her cheeks didn't disguise the way she looked everywhere but at him, causing all the hairs on his body to stand to attention. Alarm bells were ringing, very loud and very clear. What had gone wrong when she had nothing but glowing comments only seven days ago.

'Loved but lately I feel like I'm in a rut so I'm searching for another position in a different company. I might even take some time off to go on a holiday: overseas maybe or go east.'

'Hang on a minute, are you sure I'm dining with the Carol Maguire I've been dating for the past year? That Carol doesn't do holidays. A week at a time at the most, she informed me more than once.' Both times had been when he had suggested they go away together, once for a long weekend and the other for their annual leave. She had been adamant about never taking so much time off in one hit, citing being far too busy at work. One hand swept through his hair and down his face as his head shook from side-to-side in disbelief. 'Where did this come from? If I hadn't asked, were you going to tell me?'

There was a long pause, sending a cold feeling of dread settling on his shoulders. There was no doubt she was baulking.

'Nothing is settled…' There was something telling about the long pause and stricken look on her face. It appeared she was scrambling for the right words to say; words, he guessed, which were not telling the entire truth and he felt damned guilty for thinking in such a way.

'It's just feelings I've had lately. To begin with it was only the occasional sense of frustration when something didn't go to plan at work. I thought… I thought… maybe I was coming down with something or maybe my iron levels were low. It built up into something more and I struggled to find the impetus to go to work each day.'

'You had a health check?' he asked, simply as something to ask for he didn't believe her, especially the way she rambled and with the pauses but it was her body language which was telling him far more than she probably intended. Never before had she intimated things weren't hunky-dory at work. In fact he couldn't recall one single occasion when she wasn't glowing about work, in particular – last week.

'Umm… err…yes. Blood test and liver function test were both normal.' Her dessert spoon was being jiggled up and down in a nervous twitch.

'You haven't answered my question.'

'Which question?' The way she said it and the pink flush rising on her neck told him she was being evasive. She knew damn well which question and he knew damn well something weird was going on.

'When were you going to tell me?' He tried for the nonchalant look, sitting back in the seat on a slight angle, one hand rested on the white linen tablecloth while the other was in his lap, clenched tight because his gut was sending him alarm bells, but Carol couldn't see it.

'I'm telling you now.'

Shane didn't know whether to leave it alone or take it further for he was certain she hadn't intended to spill this information tonight.

'Yet you've been feeling restless for how long? Months? But you've not said anything. Why? And where does it leave us?' He flicked his hand between the two of them.

'Nothing has changed. These are only thoughts. I haven't made any definite plans. I may not do anything.'

Words were coming out of her mouth, but Shane could tell by the rapid fire, along with the intensified redness of her complexion and the eyes not being able to focus on him, they were words hiding the truth. Everything had changed and he didn't like the *definite* plans. To him it indicated there were plans in place: ones he hadn't been included in for if they included him she would have made suggestions prior to this evening. He got the feeling their relationship wasn't anywhere near as permanent as he'd believed, but he sat there, barely listening while he tried hard to keep calm, when inside he was exploding. Two days ago he'd thought his world had tipped upside down; now it was in free-fall, spinning out of control. Now he understood her behaviour on Tuesday night. Now he knew why she wouldn't stay the night and his earlier thoughts of a night of hot sex had been so off the mark it was ridiculous.

'Say something.'

The loud demand brought him back. 'Exactly what, would you like me to say? I'm stunned?' He paused, waiting. She said nothing. 'Well, I'm stunned,' he finally said to break the silence. 'What has shocked me the most is why you never mentioned any of this to me before and why you are now planning a holiday alone when you have always refused to even consider spending a holiday with me. Now I must ask myself why?'

Sitting back, he waited for a response but again got nothing but a stricken face which couldn't look at him eye-to-eye.

'I honestly thought we were closer.'

Carol reddened with further tightening of the lips.

'I believed we were close enough we could discuss what was troubling us. But now it's obvious you didn't have the same belief for not once have you mentioned any unhappiness about your job and I'm damn sure you wouldn't have said anything tonight if I hadn't asked. I thought we trusted each other to know what we spoke about in private remained private.'

Her eyes flicked to one side.

'I thought we were so close, neither of us was afraid to open up to the other, to listen with compassion and offer suggestions.' A surge of anger threatened to overwhelm him when she kept her head turned but he held it back as he stood, withdrew several large notes from his wallet to pay for the meal and dropped more than enough on the table. She must have heard for she finally turned her head back, glanced at him, at the money and him again with a frown forming.

'What are you doing?'

'Leaving.'

'Why?'

'I thought we were so close we would always be honest with each other.' He paused, noting the guilt sweep across her expressive face; a face, he bet, revealing much more than she intended.

'I now know I was wrong,' he muttered as he yanked his jacket from the back of the chair and left her sitting there with her mouth agape.

It was a damn good job she had her own car and he bet it had been a deliberate ploy so she had an excuse to not spend the night with him. He'd never been angry with her before, never had a need to be. As he stormed to his car, he tried to figure out why he was so angry. It wasn't because Carol felt the need to change jobs, or to have a holiday. He could understand both of those because he'd been in the same position himself. Take this weekend. He was going south because he was in desperate need of a break after months of too many long hours spent finalising his research.

When he reached the car, he yanked the door open, folded his length into the seat and dropped his head on the steering wheel with his arms hugging each other around the top, still sorting things in his mind until clarity arrived. It was the evasiveness and the lying and finally realising after all these months of dating, how Carol didn't have the same trust in him as he had for her. 'Damn it!' He thumped a clenched fist on the steering wheel as he flung back against the seat.

It took a while before the simmering anger settled to a level where he thought he could drive home safely.

Chapter Fifteen

It felt weird sneaking around his own home but Shane wanted to get on the road early. Sleep had been elusive, with snatches here and there, between bouts of being wide awake with a churning mind which refused to let him relax enough to fall into the deep sleep he needed. Being unconscious would have been welcome, but he refused to take chemical knock-out drops to gain such a state. Now, weariness gripped him as he spooned muesli into his mouth between sips of the strongest coffee he could tolerate. He had a two-hour drive, so he needed to be alert and stay awake when, now, his body was begging for sleep.

He tried not to think about last night, but the events kept crowding into his grey matter in bright technicolour.

'Why are you up so early? It's Saturday.'

Shane spun his head around at Tyson's gruff voice and raised his eyebrows at the jockey shorts hanging low on the man's hips. 'Sorry, I didn't mean to wake you. I want to spend as much time as possible with the family.'

'You look like a train wreck, my friend.' Tyson moved to the coffee machine and poured what was left in the carafe into a mug he took from the rack next to it. He took a sip, swallowed then gagged. 'Hell, man that's so strong it's beyond bitter.'

Shane laughed and slugged down the rest of his own coffee, refusing to show any sign of disgust at the ghastly taste. It was so bad he felt the need to choke but held it back. 'I've got a two-hour drive, so I need to be alert.'

'Alert! This poison will keep you awake and buzzing on a high for the entire two days.' Tyson emptied the coffee down the sink, filled the mug with water and rinsed his mouth out several times. 'How was dinner?'

This was why Shane had wanted to sneak out before Tyson woke. How was he supposed to answer? The last thing he wanted was to discuss the disintegration of a relationship he now realised he had wanted to be permanent. Answer the exact question, you fool, Tyson only asked how the meal was, not the evening. 'Dinner was delicious; the chef excelled. By the way, in case you feel the urge to search my house, the safe is in the wardrobe in the room you're using. It is open and empty. There is not a trace of my research on this property.'

'You still don't trust me, do you?' Tyson pulled out the chair opposite Shane and sat.

'My level of trust right now is at an all time low.' To escape further scrutiny, Shane began stacking his breakfast dishes, but a large hand grasped his wrist.

'I take it the date didn't go so well. You were home too early, especially when I expected you to spend the night with the lovely Carol.'

Shane told Tyson what he could do with himself as he wrestled his arm free. 'Yes, Carol is beautiful and you're welcome to her.'

Tyson sat back. 'That bad, huh, but I'm not interested. My fiancée would not be impressed and I'd never risk losing her. Holly is a keeper, one of the best. Do you want to talk about it?'

'No.' Shane stood, gathered his plates and washed them; ignoring Tyson despite knowing he was being stared at: he could feel the scrutiny stabbing into his back. It was a relief when Tyson had the good sense to keep his mouth shut and his thoughts to himself.

'Young Boyd went straight home from work and didn't go out or meet up with anyone last night. The address he gave for your records is where he lives now but he only moved into the rented unit two weeks before he began work with you. It's a three-month lease with an option to renew after each three months. There is no trace of him prior to his application for work. I'll have a man keep tabs on him all weekend.'

Shane leant against the sink and huffed out a long breath, willing his frustration to go with it. 'Sorry, I don't usually get so uptight, but this past week has been so screwed up…'

'I know and I understand. I think the weekend with your family will do you good. Relax, have fun and forget about work. I promise I'll keep things safe here and remember, I'm on your side.'

'How did your fiancée take you not being available for the weekend? You should have told me about her.'

'Have no fear we're catching up today and probably all night. Holly was working last night.' Tyson grinned. 'I hope you have no objection to her staying with me.'

'Not at all, go for it. Feel free to use any food in the fridge and pantry and there's wine up there.' He pointed to the rack over the fridge. 'I'll be back in time for dinner tomorrow night.' Desperate to escape, Shane turned, strode to the passage and picked up his overnight bag in one hand and laptop computer in the other and left, determined to do exactly as Tyson said: forget about work and enjoy the family.

An hour later, Shane had discovered how switching off a brain which was determined to work in over-drive, was not going to happen. Obeying the speed signs, he slowed to drift through Pinjarra, studying the buildings, the people on the pathway going about their Saturday morning business, the cars and anything else he could focus on. He preferred this drive than the newer freeway for it was far more picturesque and had more small towns to break up the boredom.

His concentration was so intent he didn't notice the elderly man stepping onto the crosswalk until he was almost upon him. He slammed on the brakes and swung the steering wheel away from the man, missing him by less than a metre. The car juddered to a halt, leaving a stench of burning rubber wafting in a haze of black smoke.

Another squeal of brakes was followed by shouts. Shaken, he glanced into the rear-vision mirror to see the car which had been following him down the highway for the past thirty minutes, jolt to a stop, almost on his boot. Shane waited for the crunch of metal hitting metal, but the only sounds were bystanders venting their thoughts on his less than exemplary driving skills. Expecting the driver to get out and berate him, Shane opened the door and staggered to feet which didn't want to hold him upright. But the car reversed away, swung around him and sped off. The driver's head was at such an angle Shane couldn't make out whether it was a man or woman.

'Idiot!' was spewed at him from the pathway while the man he'd almost killed, just stood there, looking stunned and pale.

'I'm so sorry,' Shane said as he neared the man and grasped his elbow. 'Are you okay?' It was a dumb question for the man, who had to be at least in his eighties, was the same white as Shane's lab rats and trembling so much he looked as though he would tumble to the ground.

'I'm fine, son,' the man quivered out.

The poor man was far from fine so Shane assisted him across the road and settled him on a bench outside the nearest building. 'Sit there while I park my car. I'll come right back.'

A wrinkled hand reached out and patted his arm. 'I'll be all right, my boy. You go on your way.' Blue knobbly veins pulsed under the almost translucent skin marred by dark age-spots and two yellowing bruises. Being called *son* and *my boy*, did something to Shane's insides to the extent he couldn't breathe. The last time he'd been called *son* by a man was only hours before his father died. Sucking in a breath, Shane placed his hand over the top of the old man's and squeezed gently.

'Sir, I'll be back. Maybe I can buy you morning tea.'

'Sounds nice, thank you. I'll wait here to see if my heart still works.' The grin was weak but was there. Shane wondered if it was forced to give them both a warm fuzzy to chase away the surge of adrenalin.

Knowing the man was still shaken, Shane raced back to his car, drove to the nearest exit and parked outside the Dome café. He jogged back to the gentleman who looked so still, another surge of adrenalin topped up what was already spurting through his veins. Had the man died from shock? He paused mid-stride, searching for some sign of the man breathing. He almost jumped out of his skin when the man looked up and smiled. His own heart began beating double time as he neared the man. It was only when he dropped to his haunches he noticed the frayed edges of immaculately pressed trousers and the white button re-attached in red cotton to the threadbare but pure white shirt.

'Sir, it would be an honour to share morning tea with you. Let's go in here and see what takes your fancy.' He was rewarded by a warm smile, which he returned, but frowned when a tear appeared in the corner of the man's eye.

'I'd like that, son.'

The single tear nearly did Shane in. Emotion welled, threatening to choke him. It reminded him of another single tear: in his father's eye the day he passed away almost twenty-three years ago. On that unforgettable day the family knew the end was near and each of them spent time alone with his father to say their farewells. At ten, Shane understood to a certain extent what dying meant but didn't have the maturity to really grasp the fact Dad would never be there again nor the extent of the pain and grief he would go through. At the time, Shane didn't know what to do or say so he listened to his father gasp out his last two sentences. "I love you, son. Look out for Mum and the girls." Then a single tear had appeared. Suffocating with emotion, Shane had managed to plant a kiss on his father's cheek before finding enough breath to choke out, "I'll love you forever, Dad." Overwhelmed, he fled from the room bawling his eyes out. It was the last time he'd seen the man he had looked up to and adored.

'Son, son, are you all right?' Somewhere in the background Shane heard a voice and momentarily thought it was his father's. A hand shook him back to the here and now. He shivered, lifted his head and focussed on the wrinkled features of the man in front of him.

'Sorry, for a moment there, you reminded me of my father.'

'How's that? He would be much younger than me.'

'The look on your face. It was the same look Dad had moments before he died from cancer when I was ten.'

'I'm sorry for your loss. It must have been a tough time for you, especially when so young. Every boy needs a father.'

A wrinkled hand hugged Shane's arm with a strength he hadn't thought the man could still have, but it felt so damn good. His heart tweaked as he slid his eyes shut. Heavens, but he missed his dad. He shuddered then remembered where he was.

'Let's get inside.' When it was an obvious effort for the old man to rise from the wooden bench, Shane offered his elbow, which was grasped and tightly held while the man hauled his frail body upright. They remained linked together until they found a vacant seat inside, where Shane assisted the man to sit. He took a seat opposite, withdrew two menus from the box holder, handing one across the table. 'What would you like Mr…?'

'Daniels but call me Jim.'

'My mother would spank my hide if she heard me calling someone from an older generation by their first name.'

'Ah, a well brought up lad. It's a pity such courtesies are lacking these days. The young'uns now seem to have little respect or aren't taught many manners. But I insist. Calling me Mr Daniels makes me feel as though I'm back in the classroom, teaching, and it has been too many years.'

'You were a teacher?'

'High school – science.'

Shane smiled. 'Ah, a man after my own heart. There's a reason we met. I'm a research scientist… micro-biology but chemistry was my favourite subject at school.' Shane pointed to the menu. 'Now choose and I will order.'

The next sixty minutes were a delight listening to Jim Daniels relating stories about the less well-behaved students and humorous disasters of his career. Shane let the man ramble as Jim polished off a plate full of scrambled eggs and bacon on two slices of buttered toast while Shane dismissed his one coffee a day habit and relished a far more enjoyable version than the one he'd forced down earlier.

When Jim hobbled and limped his way to the bathroom, Shane glanced around and caught a glimpse of his car through the window, jolting when he noticed a man dressed in black, peering through the car windows while tugging on the door handle. What looked like a screwdriver was held in one hand. Shane shot from the chair and raced for the nearest door. 'Hey, you, what do you think you are doing?' he yelled as he flung the door open.

When the would-be car thief glanced up, there was something familiar about him which twigged Shane's sub-conscious but despite wracking his brain he didn't know who the man was or where he'd seen him. Before he could get down the two steps, the car thief turned and ran. Shane raced after him, but the fugitive scrambled into a car which must have been idling for it immediately reversed, slammed to a halt, turned ninety degrees after which he sped away with a loud squeal of rubber burning against bitumen.

Recognition hit. It was the same car which had followed him down the highway and almost rear-ended him. He noted which way it turned onto the highway – the same way Shane had intended going. Gut instinct told him the driver would wait further along the road for Shane to appear. He didn't know why but he was certain this car was following him for a reason and there was only one logical reason he could think of.

Returning inside, Shane paused at the sight of Jim slurping the last of his spearmint milkshake. Shane couldn't help but smile at the scene of an ancient man enjoying the drink with a child's zeal. 'Jim, I have to go.'

'What a pity, but I understand. Can I say one thing?'

'Sure, what is it?'

'My dear Jeannie and I were never fortunate enough to have children. A case of mumps when I was a young man destroyed any chance but we didn't find out until we'd tried for several years. They didn't have IVF back in those days, so all our students became our children. But if I'd had a son, I think I would have liked him to be just like you.'

A solid lump of emotion threatened to choke Shane. 'That's the nicest compliment I've ever received. It has been my pleasure to meet you.' He took out his wallet, withdrew a business card and placed it in front of the other man. 'If you ever want someone to talk to, please, don't be afraid to phone me, any time, even if it's the middle of the night and you're feeling lonely. I'd love to hear more of your stories. Farewell, my friend.'

'Thank you for listening to an old man. Not many do.' That single tear showed its face again, tugging hard at Shane's heartstrings. He bent and gave the man a hug, instinct telling him the poor guy was lonely. He wished he could stay and listen some more but all he could do was grip one hand in farewell.

'I enjoyed our chat. Thank you for your time and God bless.' Without looking back, he strode outside, folded his tall frame into the driver's seat and drove a short distance back the way he'd come. Instead of turning right, he turned left which would take him cross-country to Mandurah, where he would join Forrest Highway before turning south to Australind. If his pursuers knew where he was headed, they wouldn't have been tailing him. Too bad they weren't aware he'd grown up in this beautiful corner of the earth and knew all these back roads very well.

All the way, he couldn't help but think of Jim Daniels and his father. Today, he missed Dad more than ever and he was damn glad he was on his way to spend time with the rest of his family.

Chapter Sixteen

How he loved it here. Even though Australind was now a suburb of the City of Bunbury and had a fair population, it was still a laid-back beauty spot, which, to date, hadn't suffered an influx of tourists, like many other south-west towns had. What could be better than sitting on the lawn at the water's edge, legs stretched out, soaking up the sun and scenery and appreciating life? He loved watching the calm waters of the estuary undulate under different lights, whether it was the full reflection of the sun, the moon and stars or the dappled shadows of a cloudy, windswept day. He loved hearing the water lapping against the sand and the squeals and laughter of not only his nieces and nephew but of all the children who spent hours at the water's edge. As a child he'd loved the same things the kids were doing now: fishing, swimming, sailing and exploring.

There was nothing better than dropping the clothes to reveal bathers, run full pelt into the water and lift the legs into your chest, landing in the water curled up like a bomb to see who could make the biggest splash. There were the walks along the beach first thing in the morning, turning over stranded jellyfish so they would fry and harden in the sun, searching under stinking seaweed for some new treasure and dragging home gnarled pieces of driftwood which had been bleached white by the months floating on the ocean.

He'd learnt to swim here and honed his abilities until he could swim like the seals which sometimes paid a visit. As his eyes focussed on a man and a young boy fishing, memories surged of him, with his dad.

'What are you doing, sitting over here all by yourself?' His mother dropped to the grass beside him, mimicking his position, legs stretched out and leaning back on her arms.

'Catching my breath after the soccer match, those kids are getting too big and too cunning.'

'You love it and so do they.'

'Yes, but three guys on one team against two women and four kids is a bit unfair.' It warmed his heart to hear his mother laugh.

'It's good having you home.'

'I love coming back but you know how busy I've been.'

'I know.'

'Do you remember the last time we brought Dad down here?' It had been about three weeks before he'd died. There had been a break in the wintry conditions. On the second sunny day in a row, they'd bundled his father's skeletal frame in warm clothes, settled him in a wheelchair and the four of them had wheeled him across the road and over the lawn to the beginning of the sand. Their steering hadn't been great, especially when the wheels sank a bit and skewed them off course. They'd all doubled up in laughter, even Dad had been able to break out in a grin. With Dad's husky instructions, they'd thrown in baited fishing lines and handed one to him, who had been too weak to pull in the fish he'd managed to snare. The three whiting they'd caught had been a decent size, so they'd cooked them for dinner with Mum baking an entire large bag of frozen chips to compensate for the lack of fish. It had been a fun day: the last they'd had as a complete family.

A hand settled on his thigh. 'Dad cried that night. They started off as happy tears. He told me it was one of the best days of his life but we both cried sad tears when he started talking about the things he'd miss. He was sorry he'd never see you three grow up into adults, see you all graduate, walk the girls down the aisle or enjoy the grandkids.'

'You never told me these things.' Shane put his hand over his mother's as his heart made an uncomfortable tumble turn.

'You were too young at the time and later, when you were older, it became a private memory I held close.'

'I bet he also told you to meet someone else and enjoy a full life.' Shane rolled onto his side to watch her face.

'He did and I've been on the occasional date but when you know what it's like to have the best, it's hard to settle for anything less and your dad was the very best. I'm happy and I do have a social life. It might have been different if I hadn't had you three but you filled my life. You're a lot like him, you know, in looks and nature. I wish you would marry. You were keen on Carol, so I had hopes there.'

'You and me both.' He rolled over further onto his stomach and began picking at the lawn. 'But Carol wasn't so keen. I have a feeling I won't be seeing her again after last night.'

'What happened last night?'

'It's crazy really but things she said, the way she acted, I got the feeling she was saying goodbye. I still can't put my finger on what exactly was wrong, but she seemed evasive and was hiding something. I lost patience and walked out on her. After this past week I'm kind of spooked about people doing sneaky things behind my back.'

'How's the research going?'

He twisted over to eye his mother. 'How do you know I'm still working on it?'

She laughed. 'Because I know you. You'll never give up. It means so much – probably too much.'

'What do you mean?'

'Your dad's death has affected your entire life. All through high school you chose subjects needed to get you into the university course you wanted. You swatted hard ensuring you passed with distinctions. You were even researching every detail you could find on pancreatic cancer before you even got to uni. You probably knew everything about the disease, about treatments, about death rates, about causes and all other research. If Dad had lived, I wonder what other career you would have had.'

'Mum, I enjoy my work. I was always going to study science and so you are the first to know, my research is finished.'

She sat up and swung her legs around. 'What do you mean?'

He grinned. 'What do you think I mean?'

There was no movement, no sound except for his mother's face which frowned before her eyes widened and mouth gaped. 'You've done it, haven't you? You've found a cure.'

Only when she was almost bursting for breath did he let loose with a grin. 'Yes…' was all he managed to get out before she hurled herself at him and hugged him tight.

'Dear, God, I don't believe it. Really, truly, honestly?'

Shane laughed as he disentangled their arms, rose and reached down to haul her up. 'Yes, really, truly, honestly. That's what I was doing earlier. I was on-line filling out the patent application in my name.'

'You're going it alone and not in the company name? Why?' She scrambled upright.

'First, this is my research and mine alone. Not a single other person has had any input. Yes, I've carried out the research on company premises but I own a quarter of the property and have put thousands of unpaid hours into this. Third and this is the most important, only four people knew how close I was to succeeding.'

'You kept it from us. Why?' Mum looked hurt and he couldn't blame her.

'After last year's theft of a breakthrough, we four executives made a pact to keep any further important results under wraps. We swore to confidentiality but now at least one of those is trying to steal my formula. None of the other three have science credentials so it would be easy to discredit any claim they make but like last time, they could sell it off to a big pharmaceutical company. I can always add the company name later if I'm proved wrong but right now the vital thing is to get my research patented.'

'Are you sure it works?'

'Yes, but even though the product still has to undergo human trials it can be patented. It's normal process for new medical treatments.'

'What's going to happen when the other three find out you have gone behind their backs?'

'By the time they find out, I hope I've discovered who the traitor is. Hopefully, the others will understand why I've done what I'm doing. After last year's debacle where we lost a couple of million dollars through stolen research I'm sure the only person upset by the way I'm doing this will be the culprit. Anyone not guilty will appreciate my actions. Well, that's my reasoning and over the past week I've thought long and hard about this. I've tossed pros and cons around so much it has addled my brain. To me, number one priority is to get my research patented.'

'Now you've explained it, I agree but surely now it's patented you have nothing to worry about.'

'The patent application is in but it takes time for them to let me know if it's been accepted and give me a patent pending.'

His mobile phone ringing was an intrusion he didn't appreciate. Flipping it from his pocket, his thumb hovered over the off button until he noticed the number. Tyson wouldn't ring unless it was important. He slid his finger across the screen and held the phone to his ear. 'I recall you telling me to forget about work.'

'And I *don't* recall you telling me I'd have to spend the entire day entertaining your visitors.'

Shane jerked upright. 'What visitors? I wasn't expecting anyone.'

'The first one arrived an hour after you left. The glazier has fixed your bedroom door.'

'On a Saturday?'

'The insurance company insisted it was a safety issue since the dopey duo gained access through your previous break-in. I guess they didn't want a third claim. While they were here, Jessica Simmonds arrived, looking for you.'

'Why? What did she want?'

'She has information about the two men from Monday night but refused to tell me. Like you, she doesn't trust me. I'm getting a complex about this lack of trust. She left a phone number for you to ring. An hour later Steve's wife knocked on the door.'

'Grace! This I can't believe. She gave me nothing but a freezing cold shoulder when I visited the other night.' Stunned, Shane walked away, not wanting to upset his mother. So far he had glossed over the facts, only mentioning he needed another print-out of her manuscript. Worrying Mum wasn't about to happen.

'Again, I wasn't trustworthy enough to be given any details but she's asked you to contact her on her mobile and stressed you don't call Steve or the land-line.'

A sudden hefty punch to the solar plexus wouldn't have shocked Shane as much as this had. Words defied him.

'Are you still there?' he heard through the fug in his brain.

'Yes, I'm confused. Is that all?'

'Sorry, no. Now I have Carol badgering me to tell her where you are.'

'Carol? Why? What the hell does she want?' But he knew. She was probably upset with him for walking out on her but hell, she deserved it.

'From what I can make out from her ramblings, an apology, but she's insistent I tell her *exactly*, her words, where you are. Which is why I'm ringing. Do you want me to tell her? I might warn you she'll probably drive down there and spoil your weekend. She's not in the best of moods. I'd describe her as an irate hornet ready to sink in her nasty sting.'

An apology. Maybe she deserved one but he deserved one as well. 'No don't tell her.' All he heard was a long groan and a sigh, followed by silence. A muttered curse followed: one which, as a kid, would have earned Shane a session with a cake of soap washing the filth from his mouth.

'I have a feeling she's not going to accept no as an answer and I'm the one who will be wearing the consequences,' Tyson finally ground out.

Despite Tyson's anguish, Shane couldn't help but grin but he couldn't figure out why Carol was so upset. 'I take it Carol isn't in hearing distance. I hope you haven't let her loose in my house.' Pictures of his belongings being flung in all directions were galloping through his brain.

'No, I'm outside. Holly is making her a cup of coffee but Carol didn't believe me when I said you weren't at home and stalked through every room looking for you.'

Shane laughed. 'I really don't understand why she's so angry. It's not like her. I paid for the meal and she had her own car, so I didn't leave her in a pickle but she's the one who dropped a few bombshells about her sneaky little secrets. See if you can't get her to disclose where, when and for how long her planned holiday is.'

'I take it you aren't included in this holiday.'

'You're a smart man.'

'So, what do you want me to tell her about your whereabouts?'

Shane thought. If he said nothing she might think to come here. She'd been before so knew where all his family lived although it had only been a one-day visit and they hadn't stayed the night. He'd told Bill and Steve he would be visiting friends and there was every chance she would ask them if she didn't get an answer. Friends… friends… friends… what friend could he mention who was far enough away Carol wouldn't lob on their doorstep? A picture of his latest friend came to him. 'Tell anyone who asks that I'm catching up with an old science buddy who lives in a country town.' It was as truthful as he could get. Jim Daniels was old and had a scientific background and Shane had met with him, so he wasn't exactly lying. 'She's never met him if she happens to ask who it is.'

'And what country town do I mention, because I'm certain she'll nag me until I say?'

Shane wracked his brain. Pinjarra was too close and an easy drive from the city. Once there she would search for his car and probably think to come here. Not south: it was too close for comfort. There weren't many big centres to the north unless one went to Geraldton which was too far for him to have gone for only an overnight stay. Which left east. Narrogin was large and not an easy distance. Carol wouldn't go so far when he was due home tomorrow. She'd wait.

'Try Narrogin.'

Tyson laughed. 'Sneaky and done. Your other visitors know not to expect a call until at least tomorrow night. Even though your house is now secure I'll wait here until you return. It feels a bit like having a hot weekend away.'

After hanging up, Shane turned off his mobile phone in case Carol called. Being out of reach was a much better idea.

Chapter Seventeen

The sun had weakened, having fought its way through grey broken cloud which was galloping across the sky. Wind gusts tugged at branches, stripping autumn leaves from their anchors and swirling them across the lawn, road and footpath, leaving them in red and orange hued bunches wherever they got caught. The waves in the bay raced each other to see which could reach the shore first. In their haste they tangled with each other, leaving white foam and scum tossed every which way.

Inside, it was still warm. The chilled breeze hadn't yet found a way through tiny cracks to hunt out the warmth still lingering from last night's open fire. Pausing from his reading, Shane eyed the increasing tempest outside. This was the first time in months he'd been able to give the Sunday paper more than a cursory glance. He even had time to solve the Sudoku and all but two of the cryptic crossword clues. These last two had him stumped but he figured the solutions would come to him in the middle of the night, as answers to problems were prone to do. He wasn't sure why this was so. Maybe it might have something to do with the brain having a chance to rest from the millions of processes it underwent each day. What was even more amazing was being able to catch up on a few hours of sleep, not fully awakening until almost nine. He couldn't remember when he'd last had the chance to sleep so late. Probably the last time he visited home.

A brunch at his sister's boutique winery had filled his belly to an uncomfortable level; he was still digesting the ploughman style smorgasbord he'd enjoyed with the entire family. He was not only sated but content and at peace with the world. He should have made the time to return to the family fold more often. He would in the future especially now he would have more free time.

A long sigh escaped when his mobile phone played its familiar tune, regretting switching it back on earlier. The only reason he glanced at the number calling was in case it was Tyson. The number was unfamiliar and wasn't from the metropolitan area: the code indicated the call was from the southwest, so he answered by giving his name.

'Son, help me.'

Shane shot to attention while trying to figure out who the wavering voice belonged to. 'Who is this?'

A gasp, a pause then, 'Jim…' was followed by a loud *thunk* as though the receiver had been dropped.

'Jim is that you?' A long weak groan was the only response before a scary silence. With the phone still held against his ear, Shane raced to the kitchen calling his mother, before figuring she wouldn't be able to do a darn thing. He hesitated, wondering what the best course of action would be. Police: he needed to call the police.

'Shane, what is it?' his mother called as she hurried in with a blue folder clutched against her chest.

'It's the old man I told you about. He rang me for help but now I can't get a response from him. You've got a south-west phone book?' She nodded as she reached over and pulled a cupboard door open.

'In here.'

'Can you find the number for the Pinjarra police?' Between talking to his mother and trying to get a response from Jim, Shane raced to the childhood bedroom he always used when he came home and shoved clothes into his overnight bag. It was a struggle to zip it up one-handed, so he left it gaping.

'Here's the number.' His mother held out a scrap of paper.

'Can you dial on your mobile?' Shane called Jim's name again and paused when he heard another brief whispered plea for help. 'Jim, Jim, can you hear me?' Silence was his only answer. Dropping the phone on the desk, he closed his laptop which he'd been working on earlier and packed it up along with all its bits and pieces. After zipping up the bag he glanced around for any item he'd missed.

'Here I've got the station on the phone.' His mother handed him her mobile phone. While Shane talked, he moved his two bags, one at a time, to the front door. It was only a slight sense of relief when the officer he spoke to knew who Jim Daniels was and where he lived.

'An address, I'm on my way but I need his address,' Shane demanded as he scrabbled around in the dish on the hall table for something to write with and a scrap of paper. He found a blunt pencil and frowned. With no time to spare he had no choice but to chew splinters of wood from around the edge of the lead until he had enough to scrawl the few words on the back of a shopping docket. A bright blue file appeared before his eyes as he tossed the pencil back into the bowl.

'I printed this off early this morning,' his mother said. 'I know you've been busy so there's no hurry.'

Shane slid the manuscript under his left arm and lifted both bags from the floor. 'Sorry I'm leaving like this but I want to make sure the old man is okay. He sounded desperate. Give me two weeks. After we've got everything sorted I'll have more free time.' He leant forwards and pecked his mother's cheek. 'Love you, Mum.'

She opened the door and stepped out behind him as he charged across the veranda and down the two steps. 'Ring me. Let me know what happens,' she called after him.

Shane lifted his right arm in salute, yanked the car door open, tossed the computer bag onto the passenger seat, hid it under the much larger clothes bag and popped the manuscript into the opening before sliding into the driver's seat. With desperation eating, he wasted no time in driving off.

The back roads were almost traffic free, yet Shane had to force himself not to speed. To keep his mind off what was waiting for him in Pinjarra, he listened to the inane banter of a talkback radio programme, making it a three-way chit-chat by yelling his opinions on what was said for the next eighty minutes.

The gloom seemed to lighten the further he went inland but it wouldn't be long before the cold front coming from the south-west would catch up with him again. The forecaster had predicted rain before nightfall in the city. Once back in Pinjarra, it took Shane longer than he liked to recall and figure out the verbal instructions the sergeant had given him over the phone. When he thought he'd found the street he checked the name he'd scrawled, slowed at the corner and turned right into a street shaded by mature trees, which reminded him of the street where he lived. A crowd of vehicles flashing red and blue strobe lights told him exactly where he needed to be. As he neared, he noticed one vehicle was an ambulance standing with its rear doors hanging open. Shane climbed out of his car and jogged through the melee of vehicles and onlookers to the rear of the ambulance but it was empty. Spinning around, he raced up the brick-paved pathway towards the house.

A uniformed officer approached him. 'Mr Douglas?'

Shane nodded, reaching out a handshake. 'How's Mr Daniels?'

The officer's face faltered before forming a deep frown. 'What's it to you?'

Taken aback, Shane dropped his unshaken hand and shivered inwardly. 'Jim rang me, I rang you guys.'

'Why?'

'He begged me for help.'

'Why didn't you?'

'Didn't I what?'

'Help him.'

'I came as soon as I could. It's quite a distance between here and Australind.' There was a long pause with a cold feeling settling in his gut. He took in the well-cared-for wooden house. An old rocking chair stood still to one side of the veranda. By the hollowed out soft cushions and the tossed aside rug, he figured it was used often. It would catch the early morning sun and be a cool spot to relax on a hot summer's day. His head swam while for an instant, he pictured the laughing face of the frail 92-year-old he'd taken to with such ease.

'Can I see him?' Shane asked.

'No. This is a crime scene.'

'Excuse me?' Shane recoiled. 'Why a crime scene?'

'The house is upside down, ransacked. Jimmy was beaten… badly. He died from his injuries.'

A roar of anger swelled up inside Shane. Why? Why would anyone do this to a man who was so obviously frail? A hand of frustration grubbed through his hair and down his face. More than likely because he was so frail and an easy target: too weak to fight back.

'Have you known Jimmy long?' the officer asked.

'No, I only met him yesterday.'

'Is that so? I need to know your movements for the last twenty-four hours.' A notebook came out of the officer's shirt pocket followed by a pen which was clicked open and poised over the pad. 'Name and address please.'

Dumbfounded, Shane stared at the man. 'You think I did this? You must be kidding me and you know my name. You used it when I arrived. I gave my details over the phone.' Shane didn't miss the slight blush rise up the already ruddy cheeks of the officer who could do with more than a few hours in a gym. 'I've just driven from Australind. Mr Daniels was alive less than ninety minutes ago when he rang me asking for help.'

'Why did he ring you?'

'I have no idea but he wouldn't have done so if I had been the one to hurt him, would he?'

'And your movements?' The pen had stopped moving and rested on the spot where the last word had been written.

This was unbelievable but Shane figured compliance would save time. 'I stayed at my mother's house, had brunch this morning with my entire family, dinner last night with my sister, her husband and two daughters. Afternoon tea yesterday was a picnic on the foreshore, again with the entire family. You want verification? Call my brother-in-law. He's a lawyer based in Bunbury.'

The officer held up his hands and tried to look stern but couldn't quite carry it off. Instead he looked pompous, giving Shane the feeling this officer was maybe the overzealous type. He was acting as though his word meant it was so, without searching for facts before passing judgement.

'No need to get uppity. I'm only doing my job. Nobody around here would harm old Jimmy. He's an institution in Pinjarra. You're a stranger in town who befriends an old helpless man so I ask myself why? Now give me your details.'

There was a lot Shane wanted to say. How come Jim was so lonely and desperate for someone to talk to if he was so well liked? How come Jim rang Shane for help and not the local police, a neighbour or some other town resident? But he thought it was better to keep his thoughts to himself or he might end up in handcuffs. Miffed his word wasn't good enough, he huffed out a frustrated sigh. Nobody here knew him, or his background and the officer was, as he'd indicated, only doing his job so Shane did as he was asked, adding all that had happened the previous morning in minute details until the officer raised an eyebrow.

'Enough,' he said but he was still scribbling as though trying to get all Shane had said, onto the paper. Shane suppressed a grin at the frantic writing. The report this man wrote out would make interesting reading for there was no way it would be verbatim, and he wasn't about to sign a statement which wasn't word for word true.

'I'd like to add that your poke at me about being a stranger in town, therefore I am guilty, is so ridiculous it is laughable.'

The writing ceased again and one eyebrow rose so high it seemed an impossibility of nature. 'How so? It seems logical to me.'

'The Southwest Highway runs through the centre of this town. Thousands of people pass through each day, many of them calling in for a pit-stop. Hence there are hundreds of strangers in town every day. Any one of them could have perpetrated this abhorrent crime, even the low-life who was trying to break into my car yesterday morning.'

'What low-life?'

'If I knew I'd tell you. The staff at the Dome cafe saw him.'

A plop of cold water smacked against his hand, followed immediately by another and another. Shane glanced up. The cold front had moved quicker than he'd anticipated. Within seconds the singular plops turned into a steady tattoo. 'Since there's nothing I can do here, I'll continue on my way home.' He retrieved a business card from his wallet and held it out. 'I'd appreciate it if you could let me know the outcome and funeral arrangements.' He turned to go, shuddering at the small groups of gawkers standing in front yards and among emergency vehicles. There had to be forty people standing there, many with mobile phones held to their eyes.

'Now wait a minute,' was barked at him.

Shane twisted his head.

'I haven't given you permission to leave.' The tone was not only demanding but offensive.

Shane stared at the man's eyes, dropped his glare to the hand hovering over what looked to be a stun gun then locked back onto his eyes with a stare so powerful the officer seemed not to be able to look away. His heart was thundering but he forced his body to remain still. 'I'm sure I've already said I gave my details over the phone to whoever in your station took my call. You wouldn't even be here or know about Mr Daniel's predicament if I hadn't rung you and if you took the time to turn my card over,' he made an issue of jabbing a finger in the direction of the card, 'you would see all my details written there in plain English. I don't appreciate being falsely accused of a heinous crime because you jump to conclusions without a single shred of evidence and know nothing about me. Good day.'

The moment the officer glanced down at the card, Shane spun around and wove his way to his car, petrified every second he would find out exactly what it felt like to be zapped by a stun gun. He was surprised he managed to get seated and the motor started without an electric current stopping him dead in his tracks. He leaned out to pull the door shut and noticed the officer heading in his direction.

'You're a doctor?' the man asked in a far more conciliatory tone as he stopped only a metre away. 'We could use you inside.'

A cynical laugh escaped Shane's mouth. 'PhD not medicine.' He paused as something came to mind. 'You demanded I give you my details, yet you failed to give me yours. I understand an officer of the law is obliged to give his name and rank either verbally or by showing his ID card before questioning a suspect.'

Bright red heat rushed up the man's neck and face. 'Sergeant Bob Molloy.'

'I'll remember your name when I write a report on the way you have treated me like a criminal,' Shane said as he sent the man a supercilious grin before yanking on the door. It was difficult figuring out if he was plain angry or more deep-seated emotions were making him feel like he wanted to punch something. Instead he yanked on the door and slammed it to release some of his angst but it didn't do any good for tension still simmered. It took quite a bit of manoeuvring to turn among the five emergency vehicles and macabre onlookers who refused to budge a single centimetre from their individual bird's-eye view of proceedings before he was able to drive off.

Windscreen wipers fought a furious battle against the relentless sheet of water bucketing from the skies until he was halfway back to Perth. It was as though the heavens were pouring out their grief for the callous loss of life of such a genteel elderly man. For barely knowing the man, it was ridiculous the way Jim's death affected him. The pain settled deep into his gut. Maybe it was because the old man reminded Shane so much of his dad. For much of the way, Shane's thoughts mirrored the atmosphere. It beggared belief how any person could have such little regard or respect for a fellow human being.

Chapter Eighteen

The place looked deserted as Shane brought his car to a standstill in the driveway of his home. Tyson's car was missing, unless he'd locked it in the garage, which would have been sensible. Switching off the engine he turned to find the handle of his overnight bag.

When he noticed the emptiness of the gaping opening, his hand stalled. The blue file wasn't where he was sure he'd dropped it. As he swore under his breath he reached over and slid his fingers down both sides of the seat. Not feeling the file, he reached under as far as he could. Still unable to find it, he twisted to search behind the seats, scrabbled around both sides with his hands, patting around with outspread fingers. Still nothing, so he unclipped the seat belt, climbed from the car and opened the rear door for a more thorough search. He lodged his body across the back seat and dropped his head into the foot-well to search under both seats, finding nothing but a two-dollar coin and a dusty ball-point pen.

A long huff of frustration escaped as scrambled brain cells aligned and he wriggled upright. How could he have not noticed the manuscript was missing since Pinjarra? Probably because he was concentrating on the death of an old man. The missing file meant one thing: one of the onlookers had stolen it. A whole heap of unsavoury thoughts tumbled through his head with only one conclusion: Shane Douglas was to blame for the death of Jim Daniels.

Dear God. His head dropped into his hands. This was so unbelievable. Why? A sensation of severe queasiness enveloped him.

Suddenly he remembered his laptop and scrambled from the rear seat, shot around to the passenger side of the car, yanked open the door and lifted the clothes bag. The sigh of relief whistled through clenched teeth when it was still there, hidden well under the floppy side of the much bigger overnight bag. So, the thief must have made a quick grab thinking the file held the research. He supposed it had been thick enough with over three hundred pages of printed notes, giving the impression it looked important and he bet a month's pay it was the same man from the day before: the one who had attempted to break into his car. Logic told him it was also the person responsible for Jim's death, which didn't ease his own sense of stabbing guilt one iota. If Shane hadn't spent time with the elderly man, Jim wouldn't have been the object of such a grisly attack. It had been a dumb move to leave his car unlocked while he spoke to the police but hell, the last thing on his mind at the time was thinking someone would steal his mother's manuscript – again. And now he had to ask her for another copy, which was a minor consideration if he considered the ghastly result of the entire exercise. How was he going to forgive himself?

Gutted, Shane hoisted the two bags from the seat and headed for the front door, pausing only long enough to ensure the car was locked by tugging on a handle.

Once inside he settled both bags on the floor inside his bedroom, spun around and headed for the kitchen where he spied a sheet of paper torn from a notebook. He picked it up to read that Tyson had gone to investigate a break-in at the office. Oh, hell, what now?

Tyson would be back at four. He glanced at his watch. Already after. There was a list of phone numbers and names of his visitors. Not being able to summon up the guts to ring anyone, he veered towards the fridge where he scanned the contents before grabbing cheese, tomato, cabanossi and sliced gherkins. As he juggled the items into his arms, he spied two half-filled tubs of dip, which he hadn't purchased so added them to the pile. Once he had everything laid out on the granite bench, he figured he'd better do something with them although a glance at his watch told him it was too late for afternoon tea and too early for the evening meal. His shoulders rose with a frustrated sigh before they slumped as he huffed out the remaining air from his lungs. What the heck, it would do as a snack and he could add sliced fruit, some nuts and fresh salad if a more substantial meal was needed.

Shane was slicing cheese when he heard the front door open, followed by footsteps. He winced at the thought of what the next few minutes would reveal. For some reason he couldn't figure out why, he was glad Tyson was here. Somewhere along the line he'd come to trust the man and he did like him, more than he dared to admit.

Tyson appeared in the doorway. 'How was your weekend?' he asked as he strode towards the bench.

'It was awesome up until the time I murdered a man.'

The silence was deafening as Tyson straightened from pulling out a stool. He stood stock still, his eyes in an unblinking stare.

'You want to run that by me again?' Tyson finally said after a good thirty seconds. This time he managed to get the stool away from the bench and settled directly opposite Shane.

Shane blew out his cheeks as he dropped the knife and rested his hands on the edge of the bench with stretched out arms before relating the details.

'You're not responsible for this man's death,' Tyson said as he reached over and gave Shane's forearm a friendly grasp. 'The person responsible is the man who did it.'

'But if I hadn't stopped to chat to Jim I wouldn't have been seen talking to him. Whoever did this must have thought we were friends. I gave old Jim a business card so he could call me if he ever felt lonely. They might have thought it was something else, something more important. I don't know but because of me this poor old guy was brutally beaten to death. I feel guilty as hell.'

'As far as I can see, you gave a lonely older citizen the time of day and an hour of friendship. Sounds to me it was more than any of the locals did. He wouldn't have rung you for help if he hadn't taken to you. Now, are we going to just look at this pile of food? Let's fill our plates and sit at the table and I think we need something stronger than tea or coffee to drink.'

The warm fuzzy feeling of friendship felt good. Shane forced a grin as he finished chopping and dicing while Tyson collected plates and cutlery, opened a bottle of red wine and filled two glasses. Tyson sat against the wall while Shane settled opposite at the table. He took a sip of wine, swilled it around in his mouth, taking the time to appreciate the mellow warmth before swallowing and sitting back. He eyed Tyson. 'What happened at the office?'

'Ah.' Tyson settled his glass on the table and ran his finger around the rim. 'I told you we would have young Boyd tailed over the weekend.'

Shane nodded as tension tightened across his shoulder blades. This was not going to be good.

'Well it paid off. He turned up at work around two this afternoon. My man who was following, called because he had no way of getting into your building to see what Boyd was up to. When I arrived, Boyd had been inside for around thirty minutes. I deliberately made a lot of noise as I entered, to see how the man would react. I presume he wasn't supposed to be there?' Tyson shot Shane a questioning look.

'No, we don't have any projects running at the moment requiring twenty-four-hour attendance and being a junior, Nathan would never be the one to do observation work.'

'That's what I thought and using the fire escape to get in ran up a red alert to start with.'

'Excuse me!'

'Apparently he used a key to get in the fire escape…'

'The fire escape! Why would… hell, no need to answer. Only a handful of employees need to work after hours. They are given a back-door key and the code, which we change bi-weekly. Only someone with less than honest intentions would use the fire escape but where would he get a key from? Nobody has one.'

'Who knows but we'll attempt to find out. I searched the bottom floor first but found nothing untoward. Next, I went via the elevator to the third level, because Boyd is stationed there. I couldn't find him so entered the stairwell in time to hear running footsteps. The door at the bottom opened and closed before I had a chance to descend. I was told Boyd had parked around the corner about a block down, so I ran to the nearest rear window and saw him hightailing it towards his car. He had what looked like a file in one hand. It appeared to be one of those buff coloured envelope type manila folders. I'd say, from its bulk, it contained a fair swag of papers.

'Since we already suspected *someone*,' he indicated the stressed word with air quotation marks, 'was after Red, I rushed down to the second floor. The photocopier on level two was hot so had recently been used. Your personal computer in your office was also hot to touch and your metal filing cabinet had been jemmied open but not shut properly as hastily put back papers were all skew-whiff and jammed the drawer. I assume young Boyd heard me and didn't have enough time to get the paperwork he was copying, back into their correct place. You might want to check first thing in the morning. I'm sure you'll know exactly what is out of place.'

Even though Shane had kind of expected this, hell, he'd even set things up, it still rankled. The only good thing about the situation was now he had proof about his suspicions and he wasn't imagining things. But with this knowledge he had a major problem. He glanced at Tyson.

'If Nathan was at the office at two this afternoon, it isn't possible he was the person responsible for Jim's death because I received Jim's phone call not long after two and *that* particular culprit was still there when I arrived at Jim's house.

'Why do you think this?' asked Tyson.

'Because a file was stolen from my car while I was speaking to the police officer.'

Tyson leant forward, a serious frown creasing his brow. 'What kind of file? Please don't tell me it was important.'

It was a struggle to keep a straight face. Shane fought a losing battle when a grin broke out. 'Whoever it was now has another copy of my mother's family story.'

A shout of laughter from Tyson echoed around the room. 'Seriously?'

'Seriously. And if Nathan stole what I think he stole, he now has two files of mumbo-jumbo consisting of random pages of results and reports from a weird combination of projects, many years old and none of which are important. Together they look impressive. It will take a layman hours and hours to figure out they've been had. If Nathan takes it to a skilled researcher, he'll be ridiculed, especially when they figure out the couple of impressive looking formulae I included.'

'What about the stuff on your computer?' asked Tyson.

'First, my computer is password protected with a new password last thing Friday, so it would take some time to log on. An I.T. whizz would probably be able to do it given time. Second, half an hour would only give Nathan time to search for and download what he'd think are relevant files. A forensic computer specialist would be able to search for the real files, which I have already copied and erased. Once again, I set up a few false leads. If Nathan spent so long photocopying, he wouldn't have had time to get into the computer.' Even though he now trusted Tyson, Shane didn't think it wise to reveal how he'd already set the patenting process in motion, at least not until the patent was registered.

'By the way,' Tyson interrupted, 'Carol is leaving in ten days for South America: Rio De Janeiro to be exact. No return ticket yet.'

A wave of anger swept over him as Shane glanced at Tyson. His mouth was gritted in a fine line as though he was the guilty one.

'Holly noticed a travel document poking out of Carol's handbag. When she went to the bathroom, Holly snuck a peek.'

It was a shock to feel the depth of hurt which settled in his innards. The pain in the chest region as his heart contracted was something he hadn't experienced since his father's death. Until he could sort things with Carol it was something he didn't wish to discuss, especially with a complete stranger, so to deflect the heat from his failed relationship, Shane crossed the room, filled the electric kettle, switched it on, reached up to take out mugs, coffee, tea, sugar, milk and set everything in a line along the bench.

'And you don't want to talk about it,' said Tyson.

'No.'

Chapter Nineteen

'What are you doing?'

Shane swore as he levitated from the floor and spun around. 'Jeeze, you scared me half to death,' he said while willing his heart to slow to a less thunderous pace. Standing, he eyed the woman leaning over the reception counter, wondering if she was plain mystified at his behaviour or mad at him for poking through her cupboards and drawers, although technically, he owned the furniture and everything contained in each recess.

'Doesn't explain what you are doing,' Shelley said as she straightened and plonked her handbag right slap bang on the desk in front of him.

'I'm looking for a key.'

'Why? You have a full set of keys to this place.' Shelley rounded the counter and shouldered him out of the way before tugging her chair into its rightful place, snapping shut the bottom drawer he'd been caught rummaging through, with an authority which gave definite vibes she was indeed irate with him. It amused him when she fingered everything on her desk as though checking every single item was where it should be.

'Not quite all,' Shane said as he hoisted one hip onto the end of Shelley's long working space.

Shelley turned towards him with a frown forming across her brow.' I don't understand. Have you lost one of your keys?'

'No, I'm looking for a key which unlocks the fire escape.'

'Uh, why? The fire door opens from the inside without a key, hence the reason why it's called a fire escape.'

'Funny, Shelley. I know all this but I'm looking for the key which opens it from the outside.'

'Why? We have both front and back doors which we all use to get in and out.'

'My, we do have a sense of humour this morning.' Shane quirked an eyebrow in Shelley's direction. 'There still has to be a key since there's a keyhole and none of my keys fit said hole so, since you are the amazing woman who knows where everything is around here, I figured you know where it is.'

'You could have asked.' Shelley removed a plastic tub full of what appeared to be leftovers from last night's dinner. It looked far more appetising than the sandwich he usually managed to slap together each morning and despite the secure plastic lid, a delicious aroma escaped, tantalising his gastric juices to growl in anticipation. Grinning at him, she dropped the container into a drawer and stowed her small tote bag behind a box of photocopying paper in the bottom shelf of the stationery cupboard. It was a great hiding place which was needed after a spate of thefts in nearby businesses where thieves had wandered in and noted where workers' bags resided. They returned later with an accomplice who distracted the employee while handbags were hoisted.

'You weren't here to ask,' Shane quipped.

Hands went to hips as Shelley jutted out her chin. 'Are you inferring I'm late?'

Shane grinned. 'Heaven forbid, I wouldn't dare. I don't recall you ever being late and I'm not having a go at you. I'm looking for the whereabouts of a key.'

'Why?'

A long sigh slid out as Shane wondered how much he could or should tell her. Hell, if there was anyone in this building he trusted above everyone else it was Shelley Thompson. 'Because yesterday afternoon someone was seen entering this building via the fire escape.'

The statement had an effect which could never be staged. Shelley's jaw dropped and her eyes widened in an instant. 'You're joking!'

'Unfortunately, I'm not. So, do you know where the key is and I'd appreciate it if you could keep this little morsel to yourself until after the executive meeting this afternoon.

'Um, yes, but I don't recall notice of a meeting having been issued.'

'You haven't issued it yet. I've emailed you the details. Now, key?'

'Oh, yes, follow me.'

Shane followed, along the passage, past the two larger conference rooms which were rarely used and to him were a waste of space. Well, maybe one of them was, for on the rare occasion they had a meeting with the entire staff, they all managed to fit into Conference Room One. When Shelley turned right, he followed until she paused at the locked door of the supplies room, which was tucked behind one of the conference rooms. It was vast for it needed to hold a large variety of scientific implements and materials.

'Was anything taken?' she asked over her shoulder as she slid a key, which seemed to appear from nowhere, into the lock.

'Papers from the filing cabinet in my office were copied.'

The ensuing silence was deafening. It was as though the world had instantly stopped on its axis. There was no movement, nor sound, not even the soft huff of a breath. When the key dropped to the ground with a loud tinkle the world jerked back to life. Shelley spun around.

'Something weird is going on isn't it?' Shelley paused as her eyes rested on his. 'Will Tyson isn't here for the reasons we've been told, is he?' There was another hesitant pause before her eyes flicked away. 'Sorry, it's none of my business but things haven't felt right this past week. You've had words with all three execs, which is unusual for you never lose your cool and you've always got on so well. Also, you've been taking time out during the day, the atmosphere has been tense around here and now someone has broken in.' Shelley bent to retrieve the key. She straightened slowly before facing Shane. 'Is there anything I can do?'

'Trust you to be so observant. I can't say much yet but this week is probably going to be the same. The best way you can help is to do what you always do but let me know if you feel something or someone is out of kilter.'

'Someone other than you?' Shelley said with a wry a grin before she turned back around and opened the door.

Shane laughed. He guessed he'd been behaving different but hell, his life had been skewed. 'Yes, and for your information, I'm going out for lunch again today.'

'Ooh, hot date?'

'I wish. No, a meeting I wish I didn't have to have.'

The room was as immaculate as it always looked and Shane wouldn't have thought anything was out of place until he spied Shelley going rigid. She pointed to a glaring empty space on the keyboard which held a full set of master keys – minus two. He guessed one was the master key to his own office. She didn't have to say a word and he could understand why she would be put out for she was the only person allowed in this room. Supply requests go to her. She fills out the orders and has someone deliver them to whoever requested them. Shelley kept tabs on every item which went in or out and was super-efficient in maintaining up-to-date records of all stock. It was a system worked out several years back after complaints of the storeroom being left in an unholy mess and people being too lazy to mark off what they took. The resultant chaos meant they kept running out of important items and having an oversupply of obsolete junk. Items were ordered when they didn't need to be because someone couldn't find what they required in the jumble. It had taken weeks of sorting, counting, re-stocking and tabulating every single item to restore order. With the fastidious Shelley now in charge of the stock room, there had never been a problem since. Everyone in authority kept sweet with Shelley because she was one of those perfect employees who would be impossible to replace.

'No,' Shelley replied as she glanced around the room as though searching to see if anything else was out of place.

'Who has keys to this room?'

'You four execs and me. No-one else.'

A four-letter word slipped out, causing Shelley's eyebrows to lift in shock. It was rare for Shane to swear in front of women and now he'd done it twice in the space of ten minutes. 'Sorry, my foul language was uncalled for. You have your key and I have mine, which leaves three other people.'

'You think one of the other execs took the keys? But why? They don't need another key to get in and why would they want to break in through the fire escape?' A shudder rippled across her shoulders. 'Something bad is going on isn't it?'

Shane sighed as one hand grubbed through his hair. 'Look, I'd appreciate it if you kept all this to yourself. But can you keep an eye on the passage and let me know who comes this way? Nobody should since you are the only one allowed in here.'

'Sure thing but now I've got the heebie-jeebies. I'm going to be jumping at shadows.'

'You're in no danger, but I think we have a mole working here. Remember the stolen project last year?'

'You think it's the same person?'

'Not sure but it appears so. I'm working on it.'

'Hence why Will Tyson is here, I guess.'

'Keep it to yourself. Let's go. I've got a host of tasks to complete today.'

Back in his office, Shane stared at the now tidy pile of papers he'd un-jammed from the top drawer of his filing cabinet. The sight created a grin. Good luck to the thief. Deep down he hoped whoever was behind this, tried to sell or patent the formulae. He slid the aligned papers back into two files and settled both into the rear of the drawer. The bin would probably be the best place for it now they'd been copied. He hesitated, pulled them halfway out again, paused but shoved them back in. Better to leave them, just in case.

Next job on his list was to phone Carol. He hadn't been in the mood last night: hadn't wanted the confrontation, especially after the cloak and dagger type call to Grace. When she'd answered, her voice had dropped to a whisper telling him to hang on a minute. While waiting, he'd heard mumbles followed by footsteps and the opening and closing of a door. "I need to meet with you in private," had been her opening words, which had rendered him speechless. He was even more stunned when she suggested a time and place. Lunch today was at an eatery he'd never heard of, in the city.

Using the office landline, Shane dialled Carol's work number. It took several rings before he heard the *click* of the receiver being lifted.

'Hello,' he heard in an unfamiliar voice, or maybe Carol had a cold.

'Carol?'

'Err, no, Carol no longer works here, I'm the new team administrator.'

'Excuse me?'

'Who is this?'

'Jim,' popped unbidden out of his mouth. He winced at the memory. It was the first name which came to mind and he couldn't figure out why he hadn't used his own name. 'Jim Thompson,' slipped out, causing him to cringe at the use of Shelley's surname. What the hell was wrong with him? 'Carol never said she was leaving. When did she leave?' Shaken by the news, Shane hunched forwards. Tension thrummed through him as he scrambled to think logically. Saying stupid things wasn't going to get him the details he should already know. Most people in her office knew him and of their relationship. Admitting he didn't know these details would surely clam up this person.

'Friday was her last day. Are you one of her customers? I thought we had informed all her clients of her dis… um… leaving.'

Shane's breath caught. Was she going to say dismissal? Was Carol fired? Was that why she'd never said anything? Was she too embarrassed? Why would she be dismissed? What did she do? Maybe it was a redundancy. Yes, it had to be. Carol was a loyal, hardworking woman. But now he had to think of something logical to say.

'No, an associate gave me her name and number as someone who might be able to help me with a PR problem.'

'Maybe I can help you.'

Now he was in a pickle. Serves him right for lying. How did he wangle his way out of this? 'I need to discuss this with my boss. I've got your number so I can get back to you. To whom am I speaking so I know who to ask for?'

He jotted down the familiar name and hung up. Sarah James had been an underling, two steps down from Carol, who had been head of her team. He sank back into his chair and swore.

'Well, that was colourful.'

Shane's head shot up to see Tyson standing in the doorway. 'Knocking would be appreciated.'

The man had the temerity to grin. 'I knocked. You didn't hear. Who were you abusing?' Tyson didn't wait for an invitation to enter. Instead he stepped in, shut the door and settled into the chair opposite Shane as though he owned the place.

'None of your business,' Shane snapped, earning himself a pair of raised eyebrows. 'What can I do for you?'

'My, we are in a foul mood this morning. I've come to make an appearance to verify the story we made up, informing you about Boyd this morning. What time is the meeting?'

'Four. I'm going to invite Nathan on the pretext of having a three-month review of his position but since we rarely do this, I won't ask him until about ten minutes before, so he won't have time to ask questions of his co-workers. I'll butter him up with praise; mention this as an opportunity to raise any concerns or questions.'

'Sounds logical. Have you checked your computer?'

'Yes. I can't find any evidence of access being gained. I tried the last five passwords I'd used but none would open it.'

'How often do you change your password?'

'Weekly but on different days so there's no pattern. I've been doing it this way since my research was looking promising but I've deleted everything pertaining to… err… Red.'

'How do you remember each password? Do you write them down?'

'No, I have a system. It's not hard for me to remember but I'm not telling you.'

Tyson's hands went up in submission. 'I'm not asking. Have the others agreed to the meeting?'

'They'll be there regardless of what they've got on. My message was, *I've got results,* only it's not the results they'll be expecting. You'll be there?'

'Wouldn't miss it.'

Chapter Twenty

It wasn't hard to spot Grace Richards in the café for she sat huddled in the far corner as though she wanted to be inconspicuous, but her attempt at anonymity made her presence even more obvious. Arms crossed tight over her chest, scrunched up her bright red jacket. Nervous eyes flicked around the room, giving the impression she was on the lookout for an axe-murderer, sending Shane's nerves into over-drive. He was almost upon her when he spied the stroller shoved out of sight. A sleeping young girl lay in it, propped up by a comfy looking cushion. As he neared, something about the child drew his eyes as though they were magnets. He wanted to drag them away but found it impossible for the girl wasn't asleep but had turned her head and now stared back at him from an ethereal face, fringed by ebony curls. She was the most beautiful child he'd ever seen. His eyes dropped and heart stalled at the way distorted stiff fingers poking from a fleecy jacket, jerked to a stuttered wave. Hell, why hadn't Steve said anything?

Dragging his eyes away and up he focussed on Grace who must have noticed his staring for her mouth was thin and tight. He couldn't be sure if it was in anger or embarrassment but his agitation levels shot up a few more notches.

'How are you, Grace?' he said as he pulled out a chair opposite but again eyed the girl and reached towards her. Unsure how Grace would react and terrified he was doing the wrong thing he settled his hand over both of those of the girl and smiled at her. 'This must be Chloe. She's beautiful.' He was rewarded by a wide grin and a pair of blue eyes which sparkled at him.

'I had to bring her. I'm sorry.' The whispered words sounded both haunted and apologetic at the same time. Leaving his hand where it was, Shane turned his head and eyed Grace whose face told him she wasn't angry but more terrified. Now he understood why, in the past few years, Grace always wore a haunted look.

'Why are you sorry?'

Grace's eyes dropped. 'Because... because... it's not easy.'

Shane reached across the table with his other hand, grasped Grace's wrist and gave it a comforting squeeze. 'Grace, I had no idea young Chloe here has a disability but being born with parts which don't work so well doesn't alter the fact your daughter is still a beautiful human being. Why didn't Steve, or you, tell us about her?'

'He… we…' she straightened and her face relaxed. 'I can't believe you accept her condition with such ease.'

'Why wouldn't I? Who, among us is perfect? We all have faults and quirks. And what is her condition?'

'Um… cerebral palsy.'

'And her brain works fine,' Shane added as he turned back towards Chloe and smiled at her again. 'You are such a beauty,' he said and was rewarded by another heart-stopping grin. He turned back to Grace. 'There are different levels of disability in cerebral palsy. How is Chloe affected?'

With her jaw dropped, Grace's face was an easy read, her expression now of disbelief. 'You must be the only person I've met since she was diagnosed, who is so open… not afraid to discuss Chloe's disability. Most people clam up and turn away, embarrassed or disgusted.'

'I doubt they would be disgusted but maybe they don't know what to say or are afraid of how you would react if they said anything. A friend of my sister has a child with Down's syndrome. They discuss it openly. Young Jackson tells everyone he meets about his condition as though he is proud of having the extra chromosome. It breaks the ice and negates the embarrassment. He is a fantastic kid and I can tell by the way Chloe reacts that she is also a great kid. Can she walk?'

'Um, not yet but with Botox treatment and splints, along with intense physiotherapy, the specialist is sure she will be able to in time. She has a medium disability, mainly to her left side but she crawls relatively well.'

All those medical bills would be expensive, Shane thought. Steve and Grace needed money – a lot of money and what better way to get it than sell Prancer to some overseas pharmaceutical company. Maybe he'd found the culprit from the previous theft. The thoughts left a bitter taste. 'Now you said you needed to talk to me in person. Why are we here?'

'Steve said I should apologise to you for the other night so I'm apologising.'

But her eyes weren't apologetic for they looked downright angry and her tone was insincere. What also didn't make much sense was why Grace wanted privacy without Steve knowing, especially if it was him who told her to do this. 'So, you're only apologising because Steve insisted?' A weak nod was her only answer. 'Sorry, but your apology isn't accepted for it's not from your heart.'

Grace's eyes shot past him over his shoulder with an expression of disbelief accompanied by reddening cheeks. Her eyes changed to anger as they settled on him with a fierceness which jolted him. 'I'm not sorry for it's all your fault.'

It took several seconds before he could think of something sensible to say. 'What exactly, is my fault?'

Grace looked as though she was firing up. She leant forwards and thumped a closed fist on the table, causing the obligatory salt, pepper and sugar containers to rattle in protest. 'All the extra hours Steve has to work, the serious cut in pay. You have some discovery you won't reveal, which could make the company solvent again letting everything go back to normal.'

What in hell's name was she spouting on about? What extra hours? What pay cut? The company was insolvent? While his mind scrambled to make sense of what he'd heard, Shane couldn't move. It was as though his entire body had been super-glued to the wood and vinyl of the chair. He wanted to explode, to rant but a prickle of common sense tickled his brain cells into a *don't panic* mode. It took strong willpower to force tightened muscles to relax as logical thoughts began forming. He needed to find out why Steve had told her any of these lies before saying a thing to Grace. Something weird was wrong here, but how to respond to her claims?

'I can't stay for lunch.' He stood, took out his wallet and dropped a fifty dollar note onto the table. 'Stay and enjoy lunch on me. I'll get back to you within a week with some explanations.' He hoped but couldn't be certain he would be able to.

Unsure of what else he could say, Shane turned away before turning back to squat in front of Chloe. The girl didn't deserve to be ignored so he tickled her in the ribs and enjoyed the resultant gurgle of giggles. Tilting his head, he glanced at Grace. 'Never feel guilty or be ashamed to show off your beautiful daughter.' Shane stood and strode away, satisfied with the look of surprise on Grace's face but beyond disgruntled with her revelations.

The heavy traffic on Shane's trip back to work was fortunate because it forced him to concentrate on manoeuvring through the congestion instead of labouring on Grace's outburst. Continuing deluges of rain chased spurts of sunshine away as the storm front began breaking up, leaving behind large puddles where road drains couldn't cope and had backed up. It made the roads slippery and for some obscure reason a few drivers turned as manic as the weather, creating havoc when their driving skills didn't allow for the conditions.

A long sigh of relief escaped as he finally pulled into his designated parking spot with car unscathed. After turning off the engine he sat back in the seat, staring at the grey concrete wall. The colour mirrored his mood: grey and depressing. So many weird things were happening all at once. Carol loses her job; Nathan breaks in to steal Prancer and now Steve spouts a pack of lies to his wife. Were they related? It distressed him far more than he expected to put Steve way ahead on the suspicion list and he had no idea how to go about confronting the man on what he'd heard. At the tap on the window, he spun his head sideways to see the belted trousers of Tyson. The hips moved backwards and lowered as Tyson dropped into a crouch.

'Are you going to sit there all day?' came muffled through the shut glass.

In response, Shane shoved the door open, terrified of asking a simple question in case the answer was yet more bad news. 'Do you want me for something?'

Tyson stood and stepped towards the front of the car to allow Shane room to alight. 'Only some news on the dopey duo,' he said to Shane's backside as Shane reached in to retrieve the laptop, which he was now too afraid to let out of his sight. Even though there were no longer any Prancer details contained on the hard-drive, only he knew this, so it was a hot target, but he really didn't want to go through the process of purchasing a new one, downloading and uploading and all the other tasks one needed to set up a new computer despite doing a back-up each day.

They walked side-by-side, only parting company to get through doors before coming together like magnets. 'Please let it be good news?' Shane muttered as he slid his marker on the staff board to *In*.

'They weren't responsible for the first break-in or at least one of them wasn't,' Tyson said as he held open the elevator door for Shane to pass through first. 'Peter and Paul Dickerson are petty criminals with a long history dating back to young teenagers. Not the best of a home life as kids. Dad scarpered when they were young. A series of men were in and out of the house, one was a paedophile, another physically abusive. Unfortunately, these men left their mark. Paul is a sex offender, released from jail only hours before the break-in. His brother came the same day to pick him up but there are no details of where he came from. They weren't forthcoming with a home address so could be homeless, which could be significant. Both are now back in jail and have begged to not be released but won't say why. Usually, when such a thing happens, it's because they're afraid of retribution. At a guess, I'd say Peter was contracted by heavies to find evidence of your research.' Tyson stood against the wall while Shane unlocked his office door. They both moved inside and pulled the door shut behind them.

'Just my luck to be targeted twice in less than week,' Shane said as he sank into his office chair. A derisive laugh escaped. 'My days are getting better and better.'

Tyson plonked into the chair opposite Shane, the chair emitting a groan in protest. 'Sounds like something else has happened. How was lunch?'

Again, Shane was caught off guard. He hadn't told anyone about his meeting with Grace. 'What do you mean?'

'I was looking for you to tell you about the twins. Shelley said you had a luncheon meeting.'

A tentative laugh escaped Shane's lips and rippled around the enclosed space. 'Lunch was non-existent. I left before we got to order.'

'A bit of a habit of yours.'

This time a loud laugh bubbled out. Shane couldn't hold it back. 'Yes, well, I couldn't stay. It appears my dinner guests are in cahoots to see who can shock me the most. Today's guest won.'

'More shocking than Carol? Tell all.' There was a challenge in Tyson's voice.

'Not yet. I want to surprise everyone at the meeting this afternoon. It will be interesting to see how they all react.'

Chapter Twenty-One

Determined to be early so he could pick the ideal spot to see each person's body language, Shane headed for the conference room the very second he got off the internal phone to Nathan Boyd. He'd left it as late as possible to inform Boyd of the meeting so there was little time for the man to discuss things with his team-mates. No doubt they would tell him how a three-month review was not standard procedure. In fact he could only think of once before when they'd had to review an employee's performance.

Early as he was, Tyson was earlier, already ensconced in an armed, leather chair at the far end of the small circular table. When setting up these rooms, they hadn't been miserly with luxury, ensuring seats were of the best quality, especially in the comfort stakes, for meetings were often long and experience from university days had taught them all how uncomfortable some seats could get after sitting in them for hours on end.

Before selecting a seat, Shane walked around the room, studying the position each would sit. A groan rumbled out when he realised Tyson already had the best spot. Tyson's wry grin told Shane the dratted man had been on the same thought level.

'I'll observe while you do the talking,' Tyson said. 'I'd suggest taking the seat under the window. You won't be looking into the glare.'

'Good idea. I've decided not to mention yesterday's search of my office.'

Tyson frowned and opened his mouth but before he could utter a word Steve arrived, followed by Bill. As Shane sat, Tyson slid a black vinyl file towards him. Shane shot a quick glance at Tyson before opening the file far enough to see what it contained, nodding when he recognised the top paper: Nathan Boyd's so-called credentials.

'So, you have good news for us,' said Bill as he opened out a notebook and removed a pen from his shirt pocket. There was a gleam in his eye which Shane didn't like, but maybe it was simple anticipation. Now he was certain he knew the culprit, he had to stop seeing every nuance, word or glance as suspicious and a sign of guilt.

'We'll wait until everyone is here,' Shane said as he moved to the door and peeked around the edge. Chris had just turned into the passage and Nathan was stepping out of the elevator at the far end. Good, timing was perfect. Shane allowed Chris to pass but waited for Nathan, holding him up until everyone inside the room was settled and chatting turned to mumbles. Stunned silence ensued the moment Nathan stepped into the open doorway.

'What…?' came from Steve at the same time Chris shot from his chair.

'Gentlemen,' Shane said as he pulled out the chair next to his and motioned for Nathan to sit while he remained standing. 'Since Nathan is a newcomer, I've asked him here to see how he's finding the position and if he has any concerns.' He had to hold back his grin at Nathan's audible sigh of relief. No doubt he'd been on tenterhooks wondering if he'd been seen the day before. Well, let him think he's safe; it will make a more dramatic revelation. When everyone was seated, Shane moved to the left where he was able to observe everyone's face except for Tyson.

'Are you enjoying the work?' Shane eyed Nathan and didn't miss the relieved look he shot at Chris, which set up a new range of questions. Why Chris? Ah, yes, Chris had interviewed him and let him get away with his dishonesty.

'Yes, so far it's interesting.'

'How about the team members, any problems with them?'

'Um, no. All three are helpful… explain things well. We get on all right.'

'Is this the sort of work you were doing at…,' Shane opened the file and leafed through until he found one of the company references. He flicked the page in front of Nathan. 'This company.' There was no way Shane could have missed the sudden tightening of jaw muscles, but he doubted anyone else would have noticed, except maybe Tyson, who would be alert and know what to look for.

'Um, no,' came out strangled from Nathan's mouth.

'So, what did you do at this particular company?'

'What's going on?' growled Chris. 'Why the questions? I rang the referee.' He wore an expression Shane couldn't read, but Chris sounded angry.

Shane moved back to his seat and eased into it while eyeing Chris. 'You didn't write in the interview notes what this...' he tugged the paper back and searched for the referee's name, 'Susan Spriggs said.'

'She told me Nathan was a hard worker, knew his stuff and recommended him.' Even though Chris spoke with confidence, his left hand was drumming on his notebook. Shane couldn't be sure if the drumming was a habit, for he'd seen the same action more than once over the past week, or could it be guilt?

'Well, I find that very interesting because there is no Susan Spriggs at this company and this phone number,' he stabbed his finger on said number, 'has no association with the company named on the paper.'

Muffled imprecations came from everyone except Tyson, who sat back in a relaxed pose. 'Same with these other two references and as far as the qualification certificates... no-one by the name of Nathan Boyd has ever been enrolled at this university, especially in the science department.' Shane turned towards Nathan. 'Do you want to explain?' He didn't miss the quick glance Nathan shot towards Chris again. Was there a reason for such a guilty glance? No, it had to be because Chris had been duped by Nathan. Shane folded his arms at the lengthy silence and stared at the reddening face which had gone stony still.

'I needed the job,' Nathan finally stuttered. The others might have believed him, but Shane didn't.

'Well, tough, because you no longer have one. I'll show you out.' Shane stood and waited behind his chair. He could read the surprise on each face and waited for any of the others to say something, but silence reigned, except for the hushed movements Nathan made as he rolled his seat backwards, rose and pushed the chair back in with a defiant *whack*.

'I've got personal stuff upstairs,' Nathan mumbled as he preceded Shane to the door.

'I'll have it boxed up and delivered to the address we have on record. I assume the address, at least, wasn't a lie.'

'No.' Nathan stalled as though he wanted to add something so Shane shoved him in the back with one hand.

'Good, now go before I completely lose my cool because right now I'm beyond angry. And don't think for one second I don't know why you are really here. It's not because you needed a job.' A sucked in breath of shock was barely audible but the man was definitely shocked.

As they reached the reception area, Shane grabbed Nathan by the elbow and tugged him towards Shelley. 'Could you please do the paperwork to finalise this man's employment. Calculate his pay until the end of today and give the details to Steve. Our Mr Boyd here will need a termination certificate. On it I want you to outline the truth: tendering false employment references and qualifications, stealing, breaking and entering. I'm still considering whether to call the police but will discuss it with Tyson first. He has the connections.'

Shane turned to Nathan. 'Now get out and don't ever set foot on these premises again. The two keys you stole will be useless because I've already called a locksmith and the locks were changed today. And as for the papers you stole from my office… well, good luck.' He didn't miss the stiffening of the body nor the spike of fear in the man's eyes as Shane folded his arms and tapped one foot until the stunned looking slime-ball turned and dragged his feet as he tried to walk tall to the front door, but how tall can one look when they carry the weight of guilt on their shoulders?

'Are you okay?' Shelley asked as Shane turned to go back to the meeting. 'I presume he was the fire escape person.'

'Yes, and yes,' Shane muttered in response to both questions. A sigh of relief exploded before he swore profusely then apologised to Shelley yet again for his foul language. 'I'm glad to be rid of him but now I have to figure out who sent him here.'

'What do you mean?'

'He's a spy.'

'I don't believe it… and the things he stole… they are important?'

Shane managed a grin. 'He thinks so.' He blew out his cheeks at the thought of what came next. 'Now I've got to go and face the others. Can you get onto the paperwork ASAP? Thanks.'

As he strode back to Conference Room Three, Shane sucked in long deep breaths to calm his ire. He wasn't sure if the other execs had been talking among themselves while he'd been away but the room held an expectant hush the moment he stepped inside the door. It wasn't until he was seated before anyone said a thing. All three opened their mouths at the same time. There was a pause as they glanced at each other and were about to open their mouths again when they all released an awkward laugh.

'What just went down?' Bill finally said after both the others indicated to him to go first.

'Nathan Boyd lied about his qualifications and work experience, so I sacked him. The last thing we need around here is an employee who can't be trusted, especially after last year's debacle.'

'How did you know?' asked Steve.

'You employed Tyson to check on security. He earned his pay.'

'I'm sorry,' butted in Chris, 'I should have been more thorough.'

Before answering, Shane studied the man, in search of some sign of guilt but Chris looked like the Chris he knew. 'It's not all your fault. You gave me his papers to check. I read them and never had an inkling they were fake. Look at it as a lesson learned. In future it might be a good idea if we actually ring the institutions and companies from listed numbers and not those given by the applicant and ask for the relevant people to verify the paperwork.'

'But why would he do it?' asked Steve.

Stunned, Shane shook his head in amazement. 'You really need to ask? The same reason you guys employed Tyson.'

'Come on,' said Bill, 'you think he's after your research?'

Ensuring he could catch a glimpse of all three, Shane swung his head from one side to the other. 'I don't think, I'm almost certain.'

'How…' cried Bill, who looked genuinely shocked.

'What do you mean?' came from Chris at the same time but in a more measured voice. There was nothing overacted in the look of mystification on his face.

'But nobody knows.' Steve was the third voice coming on top of the others. They looked at each other in silence. To Shane, they all sounded so innocent and equally shocked, but one was an excellent actor for any knowledge about Prancer could only have come from one of these three and now Shane was certain Steve was the culprit for he needed money. All Shane had to do now was prove it. It amused him how Tyson calmly sat back in his seat, taking it all in and not contributing a single phrase. His eyes held no expression, but his lips quirked at the corners as though amused. How Shane wished he could read minds right now.

'You said you had results,' said Steve with a look of anticipation.

Bastard, Shane thought as he sank back into his chair as though he wasn't miffed. 'I never said the results to what. I've given you the results of Tyson's investigation.' He waited for the explosion but all he received were three stunned stares and another lengthy silence.

'Oh, come on, what about your research?' Again, it was the over-eager Steve. And then it hit Shane. Why was Steve so keen to hear about results if he already had the stolen paperwork? Damn, was he wrong? He glanced at Bill who was looking confused then at Chris who seemed relaxed with his fingers no longer drumming. Now Shane wasn't so certain he had this pegged. Maybe it was time to drop another bombshell to get reactions.

'Okay, guys, here's what I can tell you about the research.' It didn't surprise him to see all three lean forwards, looking eager.

'It takes time for Petrie samples to grow. I'm still waiting for results, but I think, and only think, I know what went wrong. I need to adjust the formula and run another series of tests. It's going to take me at least another week, possibly two.' He held up his hands to stop the outbursts as all three opened their mouths to speak. 'I'll let you all know as soon as I can. But there is one important thing I need to know.'

'What?' asked Bill as he relaxed back in his seat.

'I'm getting a bit jacked off at you three for keeping me in the dark about things around here.'

'What the hell do you mean?' asked Chris as he stood and shoved his chair back. The vehemence on his face was not of the pretend variety.

'Why haven't I been told this company is insolvent?'

Bill leapt from his chair at the same time as Chris yelled, 'No way!'

A split second later, Steve swore and paled to a scary white. He staggered upright. 'We're not insolvent, fellas. You've all got the latest quarterly auditor's report. It is accurate.' He stumbled as though drunk while he made his awkward way towards the door. 'Shane, I need to speak with you in private. Your office,' he muttered in Shane's ear as he staggered past.

'I guess the meeting is over,' announced Tyson as he stood, collected his papers and followed Steve, with a certain swagger.

Ignoring Bill and Chris's volley of questions, Shane hightailed it after Tyson, in search of Steve. Time to get some answers.

Chapter Twenty-Two

If dejection could have a range of depths, then Steve was at the lowest as he leant against the wall opposite Shane's office door.

'When did you speak to Grace?' Steve muttered before Shane could unlock the door he now ensured was secure every time he left the room, even if it was a two-minute bathroom break. Since the new lock had been installed, he was the only person to have a key. The master wasn't going on the board until the patent was secure and not even Shelley would have a copy.

'Sit,' Shane said as he relocked the door so they wouldn't be interrupted. To give himself time to calm his agitation he took his time moving around the beige desk and folding into his chair, which he'd filched from the boardroom because it offered more comfort than his previous chair. Hoping to appear nonchalant, he leant back and gripped his fingers behind his head. The man sitting in front of him appeared to be carrying a ten-tonne weight on his shoulders. 'I had a very interesting chat with Grace a couple of hours ago and met your beautiful daughter. Why didn't you tell us about Chloe?'

Steve eyed him in a such way, Shane got the impression the man didn't know what the hell to say or do. He huffed out a long breath. 'Grace didn't want me to.'

'Why? Surely you aren't ashamed of Chloe's condition, she's gorgeous and smart.'

'No!' The defiance was immediate and heartfelt with a stare daring Shane to say any different.

'Then why?'

'It was tough accepting there was a problem at first. Grace blamed herself for Chloe's affliction; thought she must have done something wrong or eaten the wrong foods during pregnancy. She became depressed. After counselling and joining a group who had children the same, she came to grips with things but since Chloe was already one we didn't know how to broach the subject. I know I should have but I'm not and never will be ashamed of Chloe. We both love her to bits.'

'You need to bring Chloe in to meet everyone here. Hell, we do medical research here, among other things. I can't think of anyone in this building who won't understand and accept her for who she is: a beautiful, intelligent little girl.'

'I know and I will – now you know. It's kinda like the ice has been broken, which is such a relief. It's like when you tell a lie and you have to go on creating more and more lies to cover the first one.' The flush rising up Steve's face said much more than the words flowing from his mouth. Shane had a feeling they came unbidden from the subconscious.

'And now we get to the nitty-gritty.'

Steve's eyes flicked towards him but just as quick, flicked away again. 'What do you mean?' he said to the floor.

'Come on, Richo, for some reason you've been lying to your own wife and if I know you as well as I think I do, there must be something serious going on.' The man sitting opposite him was not the Steve who Shane knew. Everything about him screamed defeat: slumped shoulders, sad, hollow eyes and a worry-worn face all said the same thing.

'Do you remember the conference we went to last year?' Even though the words were directed to Shane, Steve's eyes remained fixed to a spot on the floor and if Shane was right it was because they held unshed tears.

What could possibly be so bad to bring Steve to tears? 'Yes, almost a year ago.' It was hard to not get up and give the man a hug, but gut instinct told him to do so would change things and cause Steve to clam up and possibly even flee.

'Not quite eleven months,' murmured Steve, so soft it was barely audible.

Okay, for him to be so specific about the time must mean it was important, thought Shane. He felt his heart begin to race when Steve's shoulders dropped even more at the end of a long drawn out groan.

'I got drunk.'

'Huh, no way!' Shane shot forwards and leant over the desk. 'You barely had any alcohol. Neither of us did.'

'I must have had more than I thought. I woke up in a strange woman's bed,' raced out of Steve's mouth so fast as though he didn't dare pause.

'You what? You cheated on Grace?' Shane flopped back in his seat, shocked to the core.

'I don't remember,' said Steve, his voice raw with pain.

Shane sucked in a long breath to force his body to calm. 'What do you mean by you don't remember?' he said much quieter. 'How can you not remember getting into a woman's bed: one who is not your wife? I would have thought such an incident would leave an indelible memory.'

As Steve folded back in his seat, his eyes were awash with moisture, 'I honestly don't remember a thing.'

'You must remember something because you said you woke up in a woman's bed.'

'I sure as hell remember that bit and everything after but nothing before.'

'Not even being with me?'

'Of course I recall you and the sessions I attended – it's the parts in between.' Steve jerked up out of the chair so sudden, the seat spun around on the swivel with a whirring grind.

'Steve, calm down.'

He whipped around, leant over and thumped the desk with a clenched fist. 'How can I calm down? I'm screwed.'

Now Shane was not only horrified but also mystified. 'What do you mean?'

Instead of answering, Steve removed his phone from his shirt pocket, slid one finger across the screen, tapped, waited and finally turned the phone towards Shane. A photo showed a clear image of a baby sitting propped up on a lounge chair.

'Is this Chloe?' Shane asked.

'Hell, no!'

'Then who?'

'My son,' was rung from Steve's throat on a long husky wail.

It was a struggle to recall the name of Steve and Grace's first born. 'Joshua, he must be about five by now, so why are you showing me his baby photo?' A sudden thought came to him. Maybe something had happened to the youngster. Maybe this was why Grace and Steve had been acting so out of character.

'No, not Josh. This is Adam.'

'Adam? I didn't know you were expecting another child.'

'Nor did I,' Steve muttered on a long groan as he flopped back into the seat.

'Now you've lost me,' said Shane.

Steve swore as a fierce look returned to his eyes. He leant forwards with elbows on his knees and his fingers interlocked so tight, the knuckles turned white. 'Three weeks ago, a woman was waiting in the car park here at work. When I reached my car to go home, she came up to me. I didn't know who she was, didn't recognise her. She was holding a baby – this baby.' He tapped the screen bringing it back to life. 'She said it was mine.'

'Yours? Ah, the woman from the bedroom. But… you slept with her? How could you cheat on Grace?'

'She said I did but honestly, I don't remember. I mean, I wouldn't ever cheat on Grace. I love her too much. She's my life, my everything.' Poor man slumped back in the seat looking devastated and for some reason Shane believed him. But something didn't add up and he couldn't figure out what was wrong.

'Let me look at the photo again.' A niggling sensation chipped away while Steve brought up the photo and spun the phone around so Shane could study it in more detail. He put two fingers on the screen to enlarge the face. 'How old is this child?' he asked as he enlarged it even more to get a closer look.

'Not quite six weeks.'

'Have you seen the birth certificate?' Shane swung his eyes away from the phone to Steve.

'Cathy says she hasn't got it yet. Why?'

'My sisters sent me weekly photos of their kids when they were born, and they still do but not quite so often these days. To me, this child looks to be more than six weeks old, more like three or four months. A six-week-old wouldn't be able to sit so upright, wouldn't have such a full, rounded face.'

'I thought the same, but Cathy said he wasn't full term, born a few of weeks early.'

'Which would make the child even lighter when born. I would have thought a six-week-old premature baby would be scrawnier with weak muscle tone.' He eyed Steve. 'Let's go back to the conference. Which night are we talking about?'

'Sunday.'

Shane's eyes widened. 'And you never said anything to me at work on Monday? Why?'

'Get real, man! I didn't know how or what to say. I was in shock.'

This was something Shane could understand. 'So, tell me what you recall. We finished the afternoon session around five and went to the cocktail party. I think I only had one glass of wine because I was driving home, and I can recall you having only one glass of light beer for the same reason. I left around eight and you were talking to three others when I said goodbye and if I recall, you said you would be leaving soon.'

'Yes, those details I remember. The other three were from the children's hospital research foundation. After that things are hazy. I know I suddenly didn't feel so good, so I went to the men's room and from there my memory deserts me.'

'Nothing else? Not even what you did in the men's room? Did you throw up?'

'I peed.' He looked thoughtful as one hand scrubbed through his hair. 'I washed my hands and splashed water over my face to get rid of the giddiness. The rest is blank.'

'Really? The woman, was she one of the three?'

'No but I had been talking to her not long before and several times during the day. She introduced herself when we were paired up in the problem-solving workshop. We talked about what we did, what we enjoyed… general stuff. After lunch she sought me out and we chatted some more. I couldn't seem to get rid of her.'

'What did you talk about?' It was interesting she sought him out. 'Did you tell her you were married and had kids?'

'Not sure but I don't think so. I like to keep my private life – well – private and why would I? It was more about where we worked, what we did.'

'Where does… um… this woman work?'

'She's not there anymore because of the baby but she was the personal assistant to Kevin Sutherland from…'

'I know who he is. Works at BCI Chemicals,' Shane cut in. 'What's the woman's name?'

'Catherine Ellery - Cathy.'

'Have you had anything to do with her since… well, since you woke up in her bed?'

'No, nothing, I swear!'

'Tell me about the Sunday night. You know, when you woke up. What happened?'

'It was dark when I woke. I felt weird and kind of groggy and needed to pee. I got out of bed, stumbled around, bumped into things because I didn't have a clue where I was and couldn't seem to find my balance. A light came on and I saw – hell, man, I saw this naked woman sitting up in the bed I'd just gotten out of. I was furious… asked her what the hell she was doing there. I was horrified when she told me we had… you know… had sex. Oh, God – I still can't believe it.' Steve rubbed both hands down his face then one slid up and down the nape of his neck as he stared back at the ground.

Shane couldn't believe it either. Steve had never been the kind of man who would be indiscriminate or cheat on his wife. All the years Shane had known him, he'd never two-timed a woman. 'What happened next?'

'I dragged on my trousers and shoes and got the hell out of there. I discovered I was still at the hotel where the conference had been. Even though I still felt weird I drove home.'

'You said trousers and shoes. What about the rest of your clothes?'

Steve rocked back against the chair as another hand tunnelled through his hair. 'I still had them on. Shirt unbuttoned.'

'Including your jocks?'

'Umm, yes, I think so. Yes, because I took them off when I got undressed at home.'

'Doesn't that seem strange? How can you have sex without knowing it and still have your underwear on? And this… er… Cathy rocks up here nine months later to claim you're the father. Steve, did you even think this child might not be yours?'

'She was adamant and since I couldn't remember, I believed her.'

'I take it, from what Grace told me, you have been seeing this woman and giving her money.'

'Grace knows where I've been going? Oh, hell.'

'No, she complained about the extra hours you'd been working and the serious cut in your pay.'

'Oh, Lord. I didn't know what else to tell her. This is such a mess. Cathy had contacted the Child Support Agency the day after Adam was born. She used her address as the mailing address and presented me with the orders when she turned up. I was forced to hand over ten per cent of my pay from the date of birth. I had to tell Grace something and I'm not sleeping with Cathy – I could never. Hell, I don't even like the woman. I only go to see the boy. I didn't know what else to do.' Steve leant forwards. 'Do you really think it might not be mine? Why would she do that to me?'

'Because the real father ditched her is the probable answer and she needed a scapegoat, so why not choose a good-looking guy who owns his own thriving business and is on a better than average income? It makes me wonder how many other men she *interviewed,*' he made air quotation marks with the word, 'over the two days of the conference. She could have spent all Saturday sounding out other guys and not finding anyone to fit the bill, honing onto you. You don't wear a wedding ring and didn't mention a wife and kids so come in sucker - you'll do.'

'Shit, what am I supposed to do now?'

'I have a question. If you were so drunk you have no recollection of what happened, how could you… um… get it up? You know what I mean? And there's no way you were drunk enough to be out to it. You had one low alcohol beer over three hours. Even after half a dozen of those you would still be able to remember things. I've seen you in the past after having drunk six or seven. You might have acted stupid, but you were never in such a state to be unconscious. It sounds more like your drink was spiked.'

'Spiked! You mean someone spiked my beer?'

'Not someone – Cathy. And if you were drugged, there's no way you could have had an erection or had sex.'

Steve flopped back in the chair and swore. He glanced at Shane, around the room then back at Shane. 'What can I do to prove this?'

'You know, for an intelligent man who has a master's degree in commerce, you're not being too smart.' Shane stood, walked to the laboratory, unlocked the door and went inside. Being so organised he knew exactly where to look for what he needed. He slid open a drawer and withdrew two identical sealed plastic bags. Next, he yanked out a pair of latex gloves and dragged them over his hands before returning to Steve. Within seconds he opened one of the sealed bags and withdrew the contents. 'Open your mouth,' he ordered Steve.

'What, why?'

'I'm going to take a swab for a DNA test. Open.' When Steve opened his mouth to argue, Shane grasped his lower jaw and tugged it down with one hand, swirling one swab around the inside of his right cheek. He used the second swab for the other side. Satisfied he had enough saliva and surface cells he popped the swabs into the glass phials and screwed on the lids.

'You know how to do these tests?' Steve asked after a long glare which cursed Shane to hell and back.

'Of course, I do them all the time but usually on rats.'

'Gee, thanks but fat lot of good that will do when we have nothing to compare it with.'

Shane returned to the lab and placed the sealed containers on the stainless-steel bench. 'That's what you are going to do now - tonight.' He returned to Steve and stood in front of him. 'I'm going to call Grace and tell her we're going for a coffee to have a heart-to-heart for a couple of hours to see if we can resolve our company problems. But you, my friend,' he jabbed a finger in Steve's chest, 'are going to visit your so-called son because you are desperate to spend time with him. You tell the mother you want to hold the boy and give him a long cuddle so the two of you can bond. When, and only when, you have the boy in your arms, you mention how you are desperate for a coffee. The minute she leaves the room you open this,' he handed him the other sealed packet, 'but make sure you handle the contents with the child's clothes or blanket because we don't want any of your DNA on it. Hold the wooden end with the fabric, do what I did with you. Rub the white tip against the inside flesh of one cheek. Use the other swab for the other cheek. Pop them into the glass tubes and screw on the caps. Shove them in your pocket.'

'But surely I need Cathy's permission.'

'She claims you are the father, so you have the same parental right as she does. If she catches you in the act, it's what you tell her. But I'd advise you to not get caught. Bring the samples back here and pop them into my message cubby-hole downstairs. I'll begin the test in the morning.'

'You can't do it tonight?'

'No, I have another appointment at 7.30.'

'How soon before we know?'

'A few days but if the DNA is way off and has very few similar markers, I could be relatively sure sooner.'

'If you are right, what do I do?'

'Demand your money back. If she doesn't give it back, you threaten to sue her. We can use the DNA results to notify the Child Support Agency if needed.'

'You don't think its mine, do you?'

'No but the DNA test will confirm my suspicions. Now go. I'll ring Grace.'

'I owe you, Shane, big time.'

'And I know a way you can repay me, but we'll talk about it tomorrow. I've got to go.' He grasped Steve's arm, yanked him from the chair and shoved him out the door.

Chapter Twenty-Three

The cartons of Thai take-away tantalised not only his salivary glands but also his stomach which kept clenching in discomfort, telling Shane he had been an idiot to miss lunch. He was tempted to pull over, stop and dig in but if he did, he would be late for the meeting. Instead, he put up with hunger pangs, planted his foot a tad more and continued driving for a further fifteen minutes, sighing in relief when he spied his driveway. He pressed the garage door remote as he slowed to mount the kerb. By the time he reached the garage, the door was up far enough for him to be able to creep in without stopping.

As the door slid shut behind him, Shane grabbed his laptop in one hand and the food in the other. It was a pain having to unlock the internal door between garage and kitchen but since the first break-in he had been extra cautious in locking every damn door he'd never thought was necessary before.

Once inside, he plonked the food on the kitchen bench, disarmed the alarm and continued to the bedroom where he dropped the laptop on the bed, unbuttoned his shirt and shrugged it off. A shower was tempting but one glance at the bedside clock told him there wasn't time. Instead he pulled a fresh collared T-shirt from the shelf, shoved arms in and tugged the top into place. He took off his shoes and hopped on each foot while yanking off socks and tossed them, along with the shirt into the laundry basket. Hand went to his belt to change from trousers into something more comfortable when he heard the *brnng, brnng* of the front doorbell. Bare feet padded on the polished wood as he strode down the passage and retrieved the now hidden key to unlock both deadlocks. He would be overjoyed when this was all over, he thought as he pulled the door open. He could leave keys in locks and internal doors unlocked.

'Jessica, just in time.' He clicked the latch to unfasten the security screen door and pushed it out. 'Come on in.'

'Umm, can we talk out here?'

It shocked him to think Jessica Simmonds was afraid to come into his house and yet she was afraid: the fear in her eyes was unmistakeable. He recalled how she had kept her distance while sitting on the shopping centre bench, so there must be a reason she didn't trust him or maybe it was men in general she had an issue with.

'We could, but right now I'm starving.' He laughed when Jessica took two steps back. 'Look, I'm one of the good guys, I promise you. Tyson, the man you met who was looking after my house over the weekend, is head of his own security firm. He can vouch for me. I can give you the number of my mum and two sisters if you'd like to ring them. One is married to a lawyer. No, on second thought, you're not speaking to my sisters.'

'Why not?'

'They'd probably give you the third degree. Little brother has a new woman in his life – let's check her out. No, I can't let them loose on you even though you are here only to give me some information.'

Jessica seemed to relax enough to smile at his comments.

'Look, Jessica, I've only just arrived home. I have enough Thai take-away sitting on the kitchen bench, to share. If it makes you feel safer, we can eat out here on the veranda. I suppose I should ask if you've eaten yet.'

'No, I don't eat before my run.'

'Do you like Thai?'

'Yes, as long as it's not too spicy.'

'Let me do this right. Miss Simmonds, would you care to join me for dinner? Six different dishes to choose from and only one has enough spice to make your eyes water. If you're game to join me in the kitchen, I'll leave the front door open so you can escape if you feel unsafe. Or I could set up a picnic table and chairs out here on the veranda. You decide but make it quick. I missed lunch and am hungry.'

The woman in front of him visibly relaxed and joy of joys, a shy grin softened her face.

'Okay, I'll come inside but let me do this right. Mr Douglas, I'd love to join you for dinner as long as I don't have to share the eye-watering dish.'

Delighted with her sassiness, Shane stood as far back as he could and held the door open to let Jessica pass. 'The kitchen is at the end of the passage to the right. You can't miss it.' True to his word, he pulled the screen door closed to keep out annoying night bugs, which would sneak in, stay hidden until he'd dozed off then they would buzz and bite to ensure sleep was short-lived, but he didn't lock it and left the heavy wooden door open. The rain band had moved inland leaving a cloudless sky. The night was cool but not yet cold and a waft of fresh air would do more harm than good. Remembering he was going to give the formal front room he never used, an airing, he flung open the door as he walked past, following his guest down the passage.

The awed look on Jessica's fac as she shot a glance around his kitchen, was unexpected. 'This kitchen is fabulous!' she exclaimed.

'Thank you. One day the rest of the house will get updated to match. Then the garden,' he added as an afterthought, recalling her comment about the jungle outside he hadn't yet tamed. 'Sit at the table, I'll get the plates. We'll eat first and talk later. You said you have something to show me.'

'Yes,' she said as she pulled a phone from a pocket in the front of the purple and black training top she wore over tight-fitting work-out pants. On her feet were white socks and running shoes, which matched the top in colour.

When Shane moved towards her to pull out the seat nearest the passage, he noticed how she flinched and seemed to shrink back. He paused and raised both hands in the air. 'Jessica, I promise I'll keep away. I was going to suggest you sit in this chair,' he pointed towards the seat to which he was referring, 'because it's closest to the passage. As promised, I left the front door open. I'll sit on the other side and at the other end. Is that okay with you?'

As she nodded she mumbled, 'I'm sorry.' She eased into the chair but with her legs skewed towards the passage, ready for flight.

Shane grabbed two dinner plates and cutlery, ensuring he kept away from her as he placed them in the middle of the table. Gut instinct sent him the definite message Miss Jessica M. Simmonds had been hurt, probably in the physical sense, by some unscrupulous animal. 'You have nothing to be sorry about. You don't know me well enough to trust me.' Next, he carried the bag of food to the table and tore open the plastic before prising lids off each container and placing them next to each other within Jessica's reach. The spicy aroma hit. He could make out soy sauce, ginger, coconut and chilli. Before sitting, he scooped small amounts from all but the spicy carton onto a plate and slid it towards Jessica. 'No spice. If there's a dish which doesn't take your fancy leave it and help yourself to more. Not knowing what you preferred, I chose my favourites.' He filled his plate and settled at the far end, diagonally opposite Jessica. They ate in silence for a few minutes before Shane remembered he should offer his guest a drink. They both settled on water.

When his hunger was slaked, Shane cleared the table, being careful to keep his distance. Re-seated, he leant back in his chair and folded his arms. 'Now what can you tell me about those two men?'

'On the weekends I go running early in the morning instead of evenings. Since Monday night, I've altered the course every day, so I don't come along your road so often and aren't seen to have a regular routine. I know it's unlikely the same thing will happen but…'

'They scared you. I understand better now.'

'Yes. Saturday was the first time I came down this road again. Well… I didn't end up coming all the way because I spotted one of the men, the one you spoke to. He was parked up at the next corner.' She pointed to the west. 'He was standing beside his car and was looking through binoculars towards your place.'

Shane's heart did a double take before racing at a frantic pace to catch up with the missed beats. 'Are you sure?'

'Absolutely certain.'

'What time was this?'

'Not long after six. I was too scared to go past him, so I double backed to the next corner. I was going to return home but figured something wasn't right. To ensure I wasn't seen, I went around the block so I would come out down the next street.' This time she pointed east. 'But the other man from that night was next to his car, also watching your place. I didn't know what to do so I made out I was resting and sat behind a thick shrub in someone's garden a couple of houses back, pretending to sip from my water bottle while I watched to see what they were going to do. I was about to call the police when you drove past in your car.'

'Yes, I was going to the south-west to visit my mother and sisters.'

'Well, the man I was watching phoned someone, I presumed the other man but can't be sure. After a short conversation he got into his car and followed you.'

'What?' And then it hit him. This man must have followed all the way to Pinjarra from home. Shane leant forwards and placed his forearms on the table. 'Can you describe this second man?'

A sly smile crept out from the corners of her mouth. 'Even better, I took his photo. After he left, I managed to get a photo of the other man as well and their cars. I've even got their number plates.'

'You did? Brilliant. Clever thinking.'

At the sudden slam of a door, they both jerked around. Jessica froze as she peered down the passage. Shane shot from his seat and raced towards the arched opening, ignoring Jessica's yelp as he tore past her. He came to a grinding halt when he recognised the person marching towards him. Damn, this was going to be awkward.

'You didn't ring me, Shane Douglas.' Carol didn't sound the slightest bit happy.

Planting his hands on his hips, Shane stood tall to prevent her from coming any further. 'I rang but you didn't answer.'

Carol pulled up and glared at him. 'No way. I've had my mobile with me all the time and not once did you ring me.'

'I didn't call on your mobile.'

'What... oh.'

'Yes, oh.'

'Shane, I can explain. Can we talk? I'm sorry.' The sudden change in demeanour was unbelievable. From the fierce look of anger, her face changed in a split second to frantic. This was the old Carol: the one he knew. The one he loved, and his heart hitched at the sight of her, but his head was yelling at him to damn well get her out of here.

'Now you're here you might as well come in.' Damn, why did he ask her to stay?

'Well, don't sound so overjoyed to see me.' Now this was the new Carol: the angry, spiteful woman who had arrived in his life - was it only three nights ago?'

'I have company.' Shane stood aside and held out his arm, inviting Carol to pass. The word *fireworks* came to his mind as Carol stepped past him and froze.

'Well it didn't take you long,' she hissed over her shoulder.

'Long for what? I think you might be jumping to conclusions: unfounded conclusions. This is Jessica Simmonds. She has some information for me. Jessica, this is Carol Maguire.'

Carol stepped into the kitchen and glared at poor Jessica, who wriggled as though she didn't want to be there. 'Information about what?'

Shane sighed. 'Things which don't concern you. Would you like a drink?'

'Thank you yes, White wine if it's chilled, otherwise red. Why the big secret?' Carol pulled out the chair directly opposite Jessica and plonked into it, keeping her eyes planted on Jessica, who looked downright uncomfortable.

Shane laughed at her audacity; he couldn't help it. 'It's no secret but doesn't concern you and who the hell are you complaining about me having secrets when you have spun me nothing but a pack of lies?'

'I think I'd better go.' Jessica stood. Poor woman looked embarrassed.

Shane stepped towards her, but recalling her fear, retreated and moved around the bench to get the wine and glasses. 'No, please stay. It's of vital importance we finish our conversation: more important than you realise. Please join us for a drink. I'll make tea or coffee if you prefer.'

Jessica hesitated but thankfully, eased back into the chair. If she went, he feared Carol wouldn't hold back with her words. It wasn't hard to realise Jessica wasn't feeling comfortable. Well, nor was he. 'Thank you. Now what would you prefer?'

'Wine will be fine. I could show you the pictures and leave.'

'No stay. We have more to discuss.'

'What's going on?' asked Carol as she flicked her questioning glance between Jessica and Shane.

'Carol,' Shane admonished, 'give it a rest. Maybe, you can tell me why you are here.' He unscrewed the metal cap and poured wine into three glasses, swinging his eyes between the two women, wishing he could read minds. He carried the two full glasses to the table and settled them on coasters, in front of each woman. Instead of sitting where he had been before, he carried his own glass to the far end so he could watch both faces.

'I came to find out why you didn't return my call, but now I know.'

It amused Shane to see a blush of guilt rise up Carol's face. 'Now you know, I know about you being dismissed from your job and Friday night, you lied to me about it as well as other things.'

'I can explain,' she muttered as the blush deepened. To hide her guilt, she went to take a sip of her wine but instead gulped more than she intended, causing her to choke. In one sense Shane felt sorry for her as she coughed, bringing water to her eyes. The entire situation was awkward but she'd brought it on herself. She knew he didn't like a relationship based on lies. Right from the time they'd met he'd insisted on honesty after catching her out on a few half-truths: he couldn't help it for it was the way he'd been brought up. And now he wondered about the earlier half-truths.

'And I came to apologise for Friday,' she added after wiping the moisture from her eyes with the back of one hand and catching her breath.

In an instant, sorrow changed to disbelief. 'Yet you were demanding an apology from me over the weekend. What has changed?' Carol's startled glance in his direction said a lot. He bet a week's pay she hadn't realised Tyson had mentioned the way Carol had behaved.

Her eyes slid towards Jessica. 'Can we talk in private?'

'I'll go,' said Jessica.

'No, you stay where you are. I'll see Carol out.' No way was Shane going to allow Carol the upper hand. He stood and moved behind Carol's chair. 'Come on, we can talk out the front. I'll give you five minutes.' He should have dropped dead on the spot from the furious glare Carol speared through him, but she stood, swigged down the rest of her wine and slammed the glass onto the table so hard it was a wonder it didn't shatter. Without acknowledging Jessica, she stormed down the passage.

'I apologise for this,' Shane said to Jessica. 'I'll be back in five. Feel free to look around.'

Once outside, Shane stood with arms folded to one side of the veranda and waited. There was no doubt Carol was furious because he had been rude to virtually dismiss her in front of a stranger. Deep down he didn't care, well, he did care, more than he liked and it was killing him to act so overbearing but she was the one at fault, although it was possible she was too embarrassed to admit she was sacked. It would be a difficult situation for anyone. On the other hand, there had to be a reason a team leader was summarily dismissed with an underling being promoted into the position.

'Shane, can we start again? I know you're mad at me and I deserve it but I'm truly sorry.'

This conciliatory tone was a surprise. 'Do you want to explain why you lied to me?'

'I was embarrassed about losing my job. I didn't know what to say?'

'There had to be a reason why you were dismissed.'

'I was made redundant, not sacked,' she emphasised. He was beginning to feel sorry for her. Maybe he was being too harsh but hell, the entire past two weeks was so out of sync he wondered if he hadn't been transported to some alternate world.

'Why you? Were you the only one?'

'I was the first. You know how the economy is going. There was a downturn in business.'

The way she said it would normally have had him believe her but the person who had taken her place had been an underling from the same team, so her actual position was still viable and there's a huge difference in *being dismissed* and *made redundant.* 'What about this holiday you mentioned?' Even in the half-light streaming from the passage, Shane could make out the guilt washing over her face. The way she masked it with a demure look within seconds made him wonder how much of an act she'd been putting on, not only over the past few days but all during their relationship.

Why hadn't he ever noticed this before? Now, he felt sure tonight was an act to suck him into believing her and now he wondered how much of this entire relationship had been a lie.

'I figured I could go away for a few weeks before looking for another job. I've worked long and hard, not daring to take a long vacation. I've been putting money aside my entire working life and have a healthy nest egg. Surely I deserve a month or two seeing the sights other people enjoy all the time.'

It was funny how the few weeks had turned into a month or two when Shane knew she already had a one-way ticket, which indicated a long term away. 'Of course, you deserve it so where do you intend to go?' This was going to be interesting. If she told the truth, maybe he would believe her about the rest and forgive her. His heart wanted to believe her. Please, please be honest, he thought.

'I thought I'd start in Venice, travel along the Mediterranean coast to the south of France, exploring each town as I went. I'll probably end up in Paris and maybe continue to London.'

A sense of disappointment hit. The continual lies were unbelievable but instead of calling her out on them he wanted to find out more. 'When do you plan on going and why didn't you mention this to me?'

'I was going to tell you, but you've been so busy with your research and I know you wouldn't be able to take time off.'

His ears pricked up. Not once had he mentioned his research to her, especially since making the pact with the other execs. So how did she know or was she guessing because he had worked more hours than normal over the past few months? So maybe she figured it out. It was more than possible for she was an intelligent woman. 'I could have taken time off. I've got several months of accrued leave and you didn't answer my question, when are you going?'

'I haven't decided. I just want things to go back the way we were. We are good together and I know you more than like me.'

'I was stupid enough to allow myself to fall in love with you,' Shane blurted but immediately regretted it. He sucked in a long breath. 'But we're done,' he added.

'Done, why?'

'Because, despite how I feel about you, I can't live with the lies and you are still lying through your teeth. I have no idea why you can't be honest with me but since you can't, I can't trust you and a relationship without trust is doomed, so we're done.' He spun around and yanked the screen door open.

'Shane, no, I'm sorry,' he heard before the slammed wooden door muted further words, which couldn't be heard by the time he'd raced back to the kitchen with everything inside him tugging and wrenching and twisting into a tight tangle like the fine knots of a fishing line.

At the kitchen bench he leant over, arms extended, forcing the turmoil inside to calm.

'Are you all right?' came from directly in front of him.

'Yes, no, I will be.' On a final sucked in breath, Shane glanced up to see Jessica wiping a fork with the tea towel. Over her shoulder he could see clean dishes stacked in neat piles on the bench at the end of the sink. 'I appreciate you doing my dishes, but it was unnecessary. Thank you.'

'You're welcome. I put the leftovers in your fridge.' She laid the fork next to the other cutlery. 'You don't have a dish washer, or at least I couldn't find one.'

'No.' Shane straightened, waiting for the usual snide comment of disbelief.

'Nor do I. Can't see the point when there's only me. It would take me over a week to fill a machine and the thought of all the yucky food residue festering for days makes my skin crawl. Besides it takes all of two minutes to rinse off under hot water.'

Shane laughed. 'My reasoning exactly but you have no idea how much ribbing I get.'

'Me too.' Jessica folded the towel in half lengthways and fed it through the handle of the oven. 'Is Carol your girlfriend? Oops, sorry, it's none of my business.'

'Was, not anymore and since we aired our differences in front of you, I guess you have a right to know.'

'You caught her lying. Are you sure she was?'

'Absolutely and when I gave her the opportunity to come clean, she compounded her lies, which is one thing I can't tolerate in a relationship. If you don't have trust and respect, I can't see how a relationship can work.'

'I agree. Can I show you those photos now? I need to get home to prepare for work.'

'Of course. Let's sit.' Since he was closer to the table, Shane sat first at a centre chair, giving Jessica the opportunity to choose to sit where she felt most comfortable. It was a pleasant surprise when she settled into a chair next to him. It surprised him even more when she pulled up the photos on her mobile phone and leant closer so they could both look at the same time. Somewhere, somehow, he must have done something right to gain her trust, but he would take care to not lose it again.

'I recognise this man,' Shane stuttered in shock when the first image came to life. 'He followed me all the way to Pinjarra. When I stopped suddenly at a crosswalk he almost rammed into me and an hour later I spied him trying to break into my car.' Using one finger, he flicked to the next image, which showed the rear end of the car with a clear number plate. 'Would you mind sending these photos to my email address?' He twisted his head to catch Jessica's eye. 'It's important because I'm almost certain this person was responsible for the beating up of an elderly man I befriended on Saturday morning. The poor guy died from his injuries.'

'Oh!' Jessica jerked back but Shane didn't think it was from fear of him.

'The police will need this information.'

'I understand. Yes, of course. What happened?'

While they finished the forgotten wine, Shane related the weekend's events and handed her a business card, which contained not only his contact numbers but also his email address. By the time he walked Jessica to the door, she no longer kept her distance, which was the most positive thing in his life since she'd first hidden on his veranda.

Chapter Twenty-Four

Even though the rain had moved on, it had left behind enough humidity to create a dense drifting fog which sent long fingers curling through gardens, keeping low to the ground as though it was too afraid to rise more than a metre or two. Driving had been a nightmare with cyclists, pedestrians and the rear of vehicles looming out of nowhere. It defied logic as to why one would cycle in such weather. To Shane, it was a kamikaze exercise after he'd almost cleaned up two of them shooting across an intersection against the lights, causing his heart to beat like an eagle caught in a canary cage for almost the entire thirty minutes it had taken him to reach his building.

Relief surged when he turned into the car park entrance, drifted through the scattering of vehicles and came to a rest in his designated spot. Here, there was no mist, as though a magnetic field was set up around the building to keep such phenomena away.

For once he wasn't early; there was no need now his research was complete. Today he was arriving along with most of the other workers in time to clock on minutes before opening. This morning he'd lingered under the doona for an extra half hour, lapping up the warmth. After a long shower, he'd taken the time to cook a decent breakfast and had even watched the early morning news on the television, something he hadn't done for so long, he couldn't remember the last time. To him it felt slovenly but so damn good.

The way Will Tyson stood in the foyer it appeared he was waiting for someone to arrive. Shane hoped it wasn't him for Tyson seeking him out usually meant bad news and Shane had had more than enough bad news of late. When Tyson stepped in time with him towards the staff cubbyholes, where Shane retrieved his mail and Steve's DNA test, then kept pace to the elevator, Shane sighed, resigned to another bad day.

'If it's good news, talk. If it's not, go away.' Shane said out of the side of his mouth as he punched the elevator button.

Tyson laughed. 'Having a bad day already, are you?'

The door swished open and Shane stepped in, wishing he could shut the door in the dratted man's face, but no such luck. Tyson stepped in after him, along with four others.

'My day so far, apart from the suicidal fog, has been brilliant. I'd like to keep it that way.' They were the only ones to alight on the second floor. Like a shadow, Tyson tagged along as Shane headed for his office. The shadow stilled when Shane paused long enough to unlock the door but it followed him inside where finally he and the shadow parted company. Uninvited, Tyson sat while Shane removed his warm jacket and dropped it over the back of his chair.

'Since you're still here I take it you have good news.'

'My, we are tetchy this morning. What happened?' asked Tyson while Shane labelled the plastic bag to ensure he didn't get the DNA samples mixed up.

On a long sigh, Shane plopped into his chair. 'Carol turned up last night.' He paused, glanced at Tyson and grinned. 'While Jessica Simmonds was there.' The laugh which echoed around the room wasn't funny from Shane's point of view but Tyson obviously thought it was.

'Interesting, I bet she wasn't pleased,' said Tyson after he'd contained his glee.

'Who, Carol or Jessica?'

'Either.'

'It was awkward, so I took Carol out the front and gave her the opportunity to come clean.'

'And?' Tyson asked as he lolled back in his chair looking way too smug.

'She didn't. All I got was another pack of lies. Now, since your payment is coming out of my research grant, I would like you to do something for me. It's unrelated to why you were employed.'

'Sounds intriguing.'

Shane jotted down a phone number and two names and grinned as he slid the yellow paper towards Tyson. 'I'd like you to ring this number, ask for either of these people and tell them Carol Maguire has applied for a position with your company. Ask for a reference. They might give you a hint as to why she was dismissed from her job.

Tyson shot upright. 'Holy Moley! Dismissed? She got the sack?'

'Not sure, but I think so. Carol says she was made redundant which would mean her position was no longer viable. However, her exact same position has been filled by a woman lower on the ladder, one who worked under Carol but on the same team.'

'Sounds like a sacking to me but why don't you ring?'

'Most of the people there know me and would recognise my voice.' Restless and uncomfortable, Shane stood and moved to the small fridge nestled under a bench. He withdrew a bottle of chilled water and held it in the air in question.

'No thanks,' said Tyson as he relaxed back again.

As he filled a glass with water, Shane found himself wondering if he should share details of Jessica's visit.

'What happened with your other visitor?'

Surprised Tyson was echoing his thoughts, Shane spun around, spilling a little water from the glass as he picked it up at the same time. Licking the dribble from his hand, Shane returned to his seat, took a sip and settled the glass on the desk. 'I'd appreciate your advice.' He sat back and related all Jessica had told him. 'Who do I take this to? Pinjarra police or the ones investigating the break-in. I'm certain it's the same culprit. Come to think of it, I'd rather it not be Pinjarra.'

'Why?' asked Tyson as he flicked through the photos again, taking time to study each.

'The sergeant in charge is a pompous jerk. He had me hung, drawn and quartered for Jim Daniel's death.' Shane didn't appreciate Tyson's smirk

'Do you have contact numbers for the guys here? You know, the ones you got to arrest me.'

This time it was Shane who let loose with a laugh. 'Somewhere. I'll dig it out and give them a call,' he said. 'Now there are a couple of things I'd like to know. First, why didn't the alarm for this building go off when young Boyd entered via the fire escape?'

'I wondered the same thing because it would take more than thirty seconds to reach the monitor board to disarm it, which I did when I came in. I checked. The door isn't connected to your security system.'

'Why on earth not?'

'My guess is, whoever designed the system didn't think it would be necessary since it is basically a door which is designed as an exit only in an emergency situation.'

'Not good enough. I'll make sure we have it rectified.'

'My company can connect it.'

'This is the other thing I was going to ask. What does your company do?'

'Security in all forms. I have twenty staff members. Two private investigators, a couple of electronic whizzes who love playing with the latest gadgets, designers for building security systems, two forensic auditors who can trace hidden financial transactions, computer specialists and a few highly skilled personal bodyguards, who are in constant demand for high ranking officials and visitors, mostly of the star variety. We do a lot of government work, both local and federal.'

'What's your specialty?'

'All of the above but I prefer delving into secrets, picking off each layer of the onion until I reach the sweet centre. I'm enjoying this job, which reminds me, you have a couple more staff members hiding a secret life.'

Adrenalin spurted, causing Shane's heartrate to quicken. His thoughts immediately went to Steve and he wondered if it was one of the people Tyson was talking about. He didn't want to ask and just in case it wasn't he wouldn't mention it. Today's task was to search for DNA and prove the two samples were incompatible. Even though he'd lost faith in Steve, this problem wasn't related to Prancer and didn't concern anyone else. Steve didn't deserve what this woman was trying to do to him. 'I thought I mentioned something about only good news.'

'They aren't a threat to the company: more personal secrets so nothing to worry about. But, and here's the not so good news, until about six months ago Nathan Boyd didn't exist. I can't find a single shred of evidence a man with his name, born on the day he had as his birth date, ever lived.'

It was as Shane had suspected so he couldn't figure out why he felt so shocked. 'Will you be able to find out who he is and more important, who he works for?'

The smile spreading across Tyson's face was wicked. 'I won't give up until I have the answers. This is what gives me the biggest high and now I'm eager to continue searching for the truth.' He stood, pushed the chair back against the wall. 'Have a great day.'

To ensure he did, Shane stuck the sign, *Do Not Disturb* on the outside of the laboratory door and locked himself inside. Everyone knew it meant he was undertaking critical tests from which he couldn't be distracted barring a bomb or civil emergency. Fellow executives would think he was working on Prancer which was what he wanted. While preparing the two DNA samples, he ignored the regular ringing of both the landline and his mobile phones until they became annoying. Fed up, he took the landline off the hook and switched off the mobile but not before he noticed the number of times Carol had either rung or messaged. He didn't like the way his heart wrenched at the sight of her number and wasn't sure what to do about it. It was a pity one couldn't switch off their feelings the same way one could do with a telephone. The thought sent a sudden wave of sadness through him. Carol had been an integral part of his life and he was going to miss her, probably more than he wanted.

Determined not to let his heartache get to him, he forced her image to the back of his mind and concentrated on the delicate task of preparing the two samples on separate ends of the long bench to ensure there was no cross-contamination, double checking every single item was labelled with the correct name.

Three hours later he emerged to deal with the small pile of letters he'd dropped on his desk and the dozens of emails people were determined to send each day. Most, he ignored or deleted, only reading the internal ones, answering scientific queries or giving suggestions to fellow employees. It was impossible not to notice the number of times Carol had emailed short messages, begging his forgiveness and apologising, with each becoming more demanding for his response. After a quick scan of each he pressed delete.

He was still pondering what to do about Carol when his office door opened. Miffed by the lack of a knock, he looked up to see the usually immaculate Bill slide into the room. It shocked him to see the creased striped shirt with the top button undone and the dark blue tie loose and askew. Either the man had slept in his clothes or he'd been having a tough day. Shane couldn't recall ever seeing the man looking so bedraggled. The creases on his face mirrored those on the shirt.

'Are you okay?' Shane asked as Bill slumped into the chair opposite without bothering to pull it away from the wall.

'Yes, of course, why do you ask?'

'To be honest, you look like hell.'

The man frowned then huffed out a long breath before looking as though he was searching for the right words. 'I slept here last night. You've been working on Prancer. Any results yet?'

It wasn't what Bill said which sent a shiver down Shane's spine but more the way he said it. Eyes were evasive and Bill shifted in his seat in an awkward, uneasy manner. No way was Shane going to correct Bill on his assumption and besides he hadn't asked what Shane had been working on. 'First, why did you sleep here?'

'None of your business,' he growled in such an aggressive manner Shane held up his hands in submission.

'Okay, sorry I asked but if you want to talk about it, let me know.'

'I don't, not yet. Now, Prancer.'

'I'm sure I mentioned yesterday it would take up to two weeks. You know what the process is. It's not like I can put microscopic samples in a Petrie dish or test-tube, look at it and say yes or no. Petrie samples must grow. Live cells need time to react. Cancer cells grow, reproduce or die. It's not instant. They take time, during which I look, I study, I record before drawing substantiated conclusions based on fact.'

'Surely you must have an idea about what is happening. I mean, you've been working on this for years. You must be able to have an educated guess.'

'I might think I know what's going to happen but educated guesses are not conclusive facts. I *think* I know what went wrong. I *think* I know how to rectify it, but I still must *prove* it. Wrong guesses will ruin not only our reputation but also ten years of research. I'm not prepared to do put everything on the line because of a bad guess and nor should you. After so many years, the only difference another couple of weeks will make is certainty.'

'Where do you keep your research?'

The question was so unexpected Shane was dumbfounded and didn't have a clue how to answer. Why such a blatant question?

'Do you keep it at home?' came before Shane could respond.

'No.'

'In this office?' Bill swept an arm around.

'Not anymore,' Shane said before snapping his mouth shut. He hadn't told anyone about the weekend snooper and he was getting a real weird feeling about this inquisition.

'Why? What do you mean?'

Shane sat back and linked his fingers. 'There was an attempted break-in at my office on Sunday.'

Bill shot from his seat. He swore, spun around with one hand on his hip and the other gripping the nape of his neck. The look on his face was pure agony. If he wasn't worried about the antics, Shane would laugh at the way the genteel man was behaving so out of character.

'Why the hell wasn't I told about this? Who knows? What happened? Who was it? Were the police called?' After the rapid-fire questions Bill dropped like a bomb back into his seat but his face had turned white.

'Tyson checked it out. Isn't that why you employed him?'

'Wasn't my idea. I didn't want him here.'

The shocks kept coming. It took supreme effort for Shane not to show how stunned he was. This was not what he'd been told before.

'What happened?' Bill continued to fidget in such a way, Shane's warning system was clanging with loud bells and flashing red neon lights.

'I sacked the culprit.'

'You what? Oh, Nathan Boyd. Hell, what was he hoping to gain? He didn't steal Prancer, did he? Dear God, no.'

'I don't have my research here. How stupid do you think I am?'

Bill's hands were everywhere like he'd been in receipt of an electric shock. They wrung tight before one swept down his thigh and thumped while the other grubbed through his hair and down his face. The one on his thigh began jabbing like it was a jerking battery-operated toy.

'Bill,' Shane said but didn't seem to penetrate the man's agony. 'Bill!' he shouted loud enough to still the man and get his attention. 'Boyd didn't get any information on Prancer.' The man slumped forward on a long drawn out breath. There was a lengthy pause before he sat upright, looking suddenly alert. 'Where is it if it isn't here or at home?'

This time it was Shane who stood. Everything inside him was shouting – warning! Why did Bill want to know? Had Shane got it wrong? Was Bill the culprit? But if he was, he wouldn't have been so shocked about Boyd. The reaction to the news about Boyd was definitely not feigned.

'Just so you know, my research is in a safe place: a place only I know about.'

'You gave it to someone on the weekend, didn't you? You said you were visiting friends, but can they be trusted? Who did you give it to? I have a right to know.'

Now Shane was more than worried. He moved to the door and yanked it open. 'Bill, I gave it to no-one. I've already told you it's in a safe place and I am the only person who knows where it is and to be blunt, I don't appreciate this aggressive inquisition. This is *my* research, not yours. Now get out.'

'But…'

'OUT!'

Chapter Twenty-Five

With frustration and anger simmering, Shane needed to find some fresh air and a place to think. He snatched his jacket from the back of the chair and strode to the door while shoving arms in sleeves. There he found Steve and Chris coming from the direction of their respective offices.

'What's all the ruckus about?' asked Steve as he approached.

'What's up with Bill? I've never seen him so rattled,' Chris demanded at the same time.

The last thing Shane needed was to stand here and explain things about which he had no idea. 'Beats me. He got aggressive so I told him to go and now I'm going to find something to eat.' He kept walking towards the elevator. 'While I'm away, see if you two,' he punched the button and thankfully the door opened straight away, 'can find out what's eating him.' He stepped into the lift and pressed the down button. 'He looks stressed and the fact he slept here last night might give you a clue. I'll see you later.' Shane shot a glance skywards to acknowledge any or all deities for letting the door hiss shut, blocking the other two from entering.

On his way through the foyer he paused long enough to speak to Shelley. 'If Carol Maguire rings, I'm either not here or can't be disturbed. Also, a police officer is coming at three to discuss my burglary. Can you please bring him to my office when he arrives? I'm going out for lunch.'

'Again?'

'You have a problem with me taking my lunch hour?'

'No, of course not. I'm sorry. I was just surprised because it's so unlike you.' Poor Shelley tried to smile but it looked like her smile was too afraid to emerge. Hell, he must have come over too strong.

'It's me who should be sorry. I apologise for taking my frustration out on you. Forgive me.'

The smile emerged. 'Forgiven. I can never be mad at you.'

Shane turned and headed for the door.

'Unless, of course, you forget your marker,' Shelley called after him.

Shane laughed and detoured. Thank goodness for Shelley and her sense of humour, he thought as he made his way to the café down the road. This time he didn't much care where he ate. All he needed was space away from the office to collect his thoughts, scroll through them and come up with some logical explanations. When he spied Tyson sitting at a table not far inside the door, Shane cursed under his breath and went to walk past so he could find another table and dine alone, but the strength of Tyson's grip on his arm pulled him to a halt.

'Join me. I have news about your lady friend.'

Shane paused before relenting. He could handle this since it had nothing to do with Prancer, or Bill, or Steve, or Boyd. He pulled out the chair opposite Tyson and folded his body into it.

'Have you eaten yet?' he asked Tyson.

'I've ordered. I came to your office earlier but noticed the sign. Thought I would eat first and catch up later.' He waved a hand in the air to attract the attention of a server.

Order given; Shane settled back. 'Spill all.'

'I rang the first of those names you gave me but was immediately put onto speaker with both. They wanted to know what company I was from. Both women laughed at the word, *security*. It seems the lovely Carol stole a hefty sum of money.'

'What? You must be kidding me. No way.' Shane rocked back in disbelief.

'As yet, they can't prove it but Carol oversaw an account for her section. Small sums have vanished from the account over the past eighteen months with some creative accounting covering the transactions until recently when one of the bosses became suspicious and took a closer look. It adds up to close on $125,000.'

'You're kidding! Eighteen months – which is only six months longer than we've known each other. Are they sure it was Carol, because I can't see it?'

'They're still investigating but Carol was the only one responsible for that particular account. They've been able to trace where the money went: to a company called Evici Pty Ltd. The Companies' Registration Board has Graham and Lauren Cross as the registered owners. Here are the details.' Tyson slid three folded sheets of paper across the table.

Shane studied them. 'Let me guess, these two people don't exist.'

'I knew you were a smart man.'

'Have you had any luck tracing Boyd?'

'I haven't had time. I've been looking into this.'

When lunch arrived, Shane concentrated on his open steak-burger with caramelised onions, fried egg, oozing cheese and tossed salad on the side until it was finished. Food gone, he set the plate aside and picked up his hot chocolate. Eating usually gave him time to think but this time things were no clearer in his mind.

'I still can't believe Carol stole money. Why would she? She's thirty and has worked since completing her degree. She says she's saved all her working life and has a tidy sum put away. She owns her unit, so has no payments to make. No, it has to be someone else.'

Tyson set his empty mug next to his own plate. 'They have a court order to trace all her financial transactions since she was employed. They've taken me up on my offer of a forensic auditor. He's already working on this. The tidy sum you mentioned, any idea how much?'

'No, of course not.'

'And she owns her unit. It's in a classy area isn't it?'

'Well, yes, but I own my house and I'm not a lot older.'

'But you must earn a lot more than Carol.'

'I suppose so but I've never asked what she earns. It never mattered and not something I would ever ask a woman I was dating. After all, she was a team leader so must have earned more than her peers.'

'Do your team leaders earn more?'

'Yes, of course, they have the extra responsibility.'

'How much more?'

'About five thousand per annum.'

'I wouldn't think five thousand on top of a normal employees wage would be enough to pay off a high-end apartment and save a tidy amount by age thirty. She wouldn't have been a team leader since the time she was employed. Surely she would have had to climb the ladder to reach such a status.'

'Yes, but we don't know how wealthy her parents were or if she had some type of inheritance when her father died, although I assume he would have left everything to his wife but he still could have left her some form of inheritance.'

'True, but to me it's worth looking into.'

Shane shook his head in disbelief as he leant back. 'How I wish I could wind back and delete the past two weeks. It's been one startling shock after another but I still refuse to believe Carol stole from her employer.'

'Everything will work out. We'll find who is responsible for this.'

Shane sighed. 'I suppose so but it's so damn frustrating. By the way, would you be able to sit in on my interview with Snr Sgt Mitch Jenkins? He's the guy who arrested you. Three o'clock in my office.'

After an *hmpff* of disgust, Tyson glanced at his watch. 'If we leave now, we might make it back in time.'

'What? It can't be so late.' But one glance at his own watch told him the day was a couple of hours older than he thought.

After paying on the way out, they strode side-by-side in what was now calm, clear air which held a hint of iciness. Summer had finally departed and winter was threatening, not that Shane minded. He enjoyed listening to the rain pounding on the iron roof at night, appreciating every drop of water to fill dams and water sources in one of the driest countries on earth. He also didn't mind the cold for it was easy to add another layer to keep warm and curling up in front of a roaring cosy fire with a good book and a glass of red wine was one of his life's pleasures.

They reached the main entrance at the same time as another man who Shane recognised despite the lack of uniform. 'Sergeant, come on in. Are you off duty?'

'On my way to work. Had lunch with my wife where I prefer to be incognito. I'll get changed at the station. You have something for me.'

'Let's go to my office.' Shane stood aside to let Tyson and the sergeant enter the reception area then followed them inside where he paused long enough to move his marker and inform Shelley his guest had arrived.

Once in his office, he moved the desk back to give more room and found another chair to make a circle. So the sergeant would have a clear picture of how things evolved and why Shane suspected the incidents were related, he started at the beginning. Tyson was a great help, only interrupting when he thought Shane had missed a point or glossed over a fact which might be important. The sergeant wrote like crazy to get all the details down, pausing at regular intervals to slot in questions. Jessica's photos were sent to yet another email address after being passed around and examined thoroughly.

Satisfied he'd given all the details, Shane relaxed back but jerked upright when he noticed a green light flash on then blink in rapid succession.

'What's wrong?' Tyson asked as he twisted his head to see what Shane was staring at.

'That's Shelley's panic button. Something is wrong downstairs. I have to go.' He didn't wait for a response but bolted out the door and down the passage. Running footsteps followed. He didn't bother with the elevator – it would take too long but instead raced for the staircase and took the steps two at a time, slowing near the bottom to pause and peer over the balustrade. He couldn't see anything untoward but loud moans, thuds and crashing furniture came from the far end. Tyson and the sergeant caught up with him as Shane called Shelley's name in a harsh whisper. Her head bopped up from where she had been hiding under her desk.

'What's going on?' he asked as he reached her.

'Two men with Bill. They're in Conference Room One.' Tyson shot past them with the sergeant on his heels.

'Do you recognise them?'

'No, I've called the police.'

'How about locking the front doors then scoot out the back and lock it from the outside? Go around the front and wait for the police.'

Shelley hesitated.

'Go, I'll wait here until you're safe.' Shelley grabbed a bunch of keys, raced to the front door, jammed the top bolt up and the bottom one down. She spun around and high-tailed it to the back, kicking off her high heels as she went.

Shane waited only until he was sure Shelley would be safe before he twisted around and raced towards the continuing hubbub. He rounded the corner.

Whummp! Something hard wrapped around his throat and yanked hard. His legs crumpled but being jammed against what felt like a brick wall, kept him upright. Scrabbling for balance, he bucked and twisted to reel away, managing to free one arm, which he tensed as he curled it back and let fly with a clenched fist. Knuckles connected with hard bone and juddering pain rebounded up his arm before the wave of pain registered. Still caught in a headlock with vice-like fingers squeezing his throat tight, he was punched between his forehead and nose, which hurt like hell. A second punch landed in the same place before he'd had time to react. When the blood spurted at the agony he was sure his nose was broken. The pain increased when his body landed on the hard, cold tiles and a booted foot stomped into the small of his back, followed by one to the head. Agony descended with the weight of an entire body slamming into him and pinning him to the floor. Acute pain burrowed inside as a volley of punches pounded into his flesh as though he was a gym punching bag. He felt like he was drowning, with every ounce of breath forced from his lungs by the crushing weight.

Lying there, he wanted to get up but his limbs felt heavy, his chest encased in lead. He felt his brain becoming sluggish from lack of oxygen. He fought to remain conscious but was losing the battle until, all of a sudden, the weight lifted and a thought shot through his mind – was this what it felt like to die?

'Shane, Shane, are you okay?' he thought he heard through the fog.

'Shane!' The voice was clearer, louder. He tried to sit up, scrabbling around on limbs which had forgotten how to work, but it wasn't going to happen so he flopped back down, gulped in some air to get lungs working again. Blurred vision began clearing but he thought he was hallucinating when all he could see was red. He managed to lift his head and realised the red was blood – his blood.

'Shane!' It was a voice he recognised.

'Tyson,' he croaked. With a supreme effort he managed to push himself over and looked up. Tyson was squatted beside him with Chris standing behind. Both were peering down at him, worried frowns marring their features.

'What the hell happened?' Shane gasped through a throat which felt so thick it struggled to swallow.

'Sorry,' said Tyson. 'I got caught up helping Hazelby. An ambulance is on its way.'

At the thought of being carted away, Shane pulled himself into a sitting position, gasping at the pain. 'I don't need an ambulance.'

'You haven't seen yourself in a mirror,' Chris quipped. 'How do you feel?'

'You know those huge roller machines they use to compact gravel on a new road? Well one of them has run me over and reversed back again.'

Chris dared to let a grin sneak out. Why the hell did he think this was funny?

'The ambulance is for Bill,' said Tyson. 'He's in a bad way.'

'What happened?' Shane managed to get up on all fours. It was a struggle to fight his way to a standing position. He stepped tentatively. Feet felt fine but each footfall felt as though the tiles beneath had turned to jelly. Tyson grabbed him around the waist to support him to the nearest door and guided him to a chair. Sitting never felt so good even though all those supposedly solid things around him, like walls and chairs, were wavering the same as a heat haze.

'On second thoughts, you need an ambulance as well.'

'Like hell, just tell me what happened,' Shane demanded.

Before Tyson could open his mouth, loud voices interrupted them. Four uniformed police officers filed past the door followed by two paramedics wheeling a trolley between them. Shane shook Tyson away and tagged onto the end of the parade, following on unsteady feet into the conference room. It was a weird sensation, walking on legs which felt as though they didn't belong to him.

He stood in the doorway and was too stunned to say anything. Chairs were upturned, the table shoved to one side and a man Shane didn't recognise was sitting slumped against the far wall, wrists handcuffed together in front of him. He appeared to be unconscious with a red and blue swelling over his left temple.

Shane swung his eyes to the comatose man lying outstretched on the floor. Both paramedics were working frantically on the mangled bloodied remains of Bill. One was staunching flowing blood from open gashes while the other was inserting a catheter to feed him fluids. Shane doubted they would have enough fluid to make up for the amount of blood already lost. But if they were working on Bill, he must still be alive.

'You recognise this man?' Shane heard Tyson ask from behind.

It took an effort to stay upright as Shane turned around to see Sgt Jenkins drag in another man. This had to be the low life who jumped Shane. Tyson yanked the man's head up and Shane recognised him in an instant. 'That's the man from Pinjarra, the one who was staking out my house and the one who probably murdered Jim Daniels.' He turned to Tyson. 'I need some answers… now.'

'All in good time. Do you recognise him?' Tyson pointed to the man against the wall.

'No, I've never seen him before.' His eyes tracked back to Bill, who was being lifted with utmost care onto the trolley, by two officers and the paramedics. A trail of blood followed. There was only so much blood a person could lose before the body shut down and it looked like Bill had lost enough for three men. Gut instinct told him Bill was in a bad way. It would be touch and go unless they could replace the lost blood quick smart.

Everyone shuffled backwards to let the grim parade through. Once gone, the officers regrouped, one each side of the two perpetrators of this bloodbath. They hauled the still semi-conscious men out and along the passage. Shane followed, grateful for the supporting arm of Tyson as he trod warily along the passage, wincing at the puddle of his own blood which had already darkened.

They were met in the reception area by what looked to be every member of their staff. All wore grim expressions of disbelief. When Shane stopped, Tyson tugged him forwards.

'I'm taking you to the E.R. to be checked over,' he said.

Shane baulked. 'I'm okay.'

'You took several blows to the head. I'm not afraid to toss you over my shoulder and will if I must. While the doctor is giving you the once over, I'll detail everything I know, which is going to add to your list of startling shocks for the week.'

ent horizontal text.

Chapter Twenty-Six

At last, he could get horizontal and cushion his thundering head in a pillow. He had kept his eyes shut for most of the journey as Tyson carved a way through the afternoon peak hour traffic with horn blaring. Shane had faith in the man's driving skills but the flickering of vehicles, buildings and people as they passed at speed, had increased the pounding in his head as well as the level of nausea. It had been a darn sight more comfortable to keep his eyes shut.

All the while, Shane had held a wadded handkerchief to his nose for every time he thought it had stopped dripping blood and he'd taken the handkerchief away, the blood decided it wanted to ooze even more. When he'd dared a peek, it was to see the road sign with a big arrow telling them they'd reached the hospital.

Alighting from the car had been agony with certain areas in his lower back protesting strongly at his daring to move. Now the adrenalin from the attack had subsided, the aches and jabbing pain had taken its place with a vengeance.

'Tell me one thing,' Shane said without opening his eyes, 'where did that cretin come from?'

There was a shuffle of feet and a screech of a chair being dragged across the linoleum causing Shane to wince. 'At a guess I'd say he was the lookout. He must have been inside the first room. Neither the sergeant nor I saw him when we raced past. While we paused outside the conference room door long enough to assess how many people were inside and where they were, we heard demands for money.'

'Money?' Shane interrupted as his eyes whipped open, instantly regretting the action when bright overhead lights arrowed into his eyes and speared through his brain. 'Who was demanding the money, Bill?'

'No, the other man was demanding money from Bill, who had taken a hell of a beating. While I did my best to staunch the flow of blood, Bill managed to gasp out a few words before he passed out – enough for me to conclude his wife, Lisa, has amassed huge credit card debts, which Bill didn't know about. The pair of them got caught up in a gambling syndicate to pay off the cards. As with all gambling, they lost. Now they owe to the syndicate, which I assume is an illegal outfit. Stupid fools. Hazelby should have known better.'

A deep groan rumbled upwards from deep inside Shane's chest. He didn't have to be told any more. He was an intelligent man, smart enough to figure out the rest. 'Bill promised a payout when I announced my research findings but when there was a delay, they, whoever they are, decided to steal the research instead which would give them a far bigger payout but they couldn't find it, so retribution has been meted out. Oh, God!' He tented the fingers of both hands around the outside of his face in anguish and to prevent his thundering head from splitting apart. 'The man who attacked me must be made of steel. It was like hitting a solid block of concrete. How did you know to come back?'

'You don't remember? You yelled my name.'

The swishing back of curtains interrupted them. The next, what felt like hours, were a mixture of torment and relief as Shane was prodded, examined and x-rayed. They even insisted on examining his urine for signs of blood which would indicate damaged kidneys. Apart from a mass of agonising bruises, a nose which felt like it was twice its normal size and had been mashed into a million pieces, a mild concussion and a thumping headache, he was finally given permission to leave. He wasn't sure if he was peeved at Tyson's continual hovering or thankful but when he attempted to stand so they could leave, he was grateful for the man's steady arm, which kept him upright as they made their way to the ICU where they were told they would find Bill.

They knocked on the door and stepped inside the private room. Three faces turned to stare at them. Two kept attending to the patient who hadn't been long out of surgery. The other had streaks of moisture down her distraught face which contrasted with the impeccable hair and clothes. The mass of gold jewellery looked so out of place it gave Shane another wave of nausea. He recalled Lisa being fond of the latest fashions but she looked ridiculous, especially in the critical care unit.

Bill's dark hair had been shaved away revealing two ragged lines of sutures. His hospital gown was open at the chest to accommodate several white adhesive patches attached to his chest, each with a cable leading to a monitor, on which a beeping heartbeat showed. The blood-pressure reading was alarmingly low. Most of Bill's face was covered with an oxygen mask but what they could see of the flesh was ashen gray. Among the stickers were newly sewn together wounds which looked more like stab wounds than surgeon's precise cuts. Other tubes snaked from catheters to drips and machines. There seemed to be more machinery than man.

Nobody spoke. The two nurses continued reading monitors, adjusting drip flows and taking down notes. After sending Shane a vicious glare, Lisa turned back to her husband and simply stroked his hand. It was all she could do.

'How is he?' asked Tyson.

A blue-garbed nurse paused in her writing, looked up and shook her head. 'It's not so good. He had a cardiac arrest on the table. We managed to resuscitate him but he's lost a great deal of blood. As fast as we could put it in, he bled it out until the wounds were closed. We don't know how much internal damage has been done.'

A loud sob split the air and Lisa collapsed forwards onto the side of the bed. Suddenly she jerked her head sideways. 'It's all your fault,' she spat.

Shane rocked back and almost stumbled but Tyson tightened his grip to steady him. Shane opened his mouth to say something but words eluded him. It was the second time the same accusation had been hurled at him but by two different women, both wives of his peers.

'There's no need for such an insult,' Tyson said. 'Shane almost lost his life today while trying to save your husband. If you want to lay blame, take a good look in a mirror.' He immediately used pressure with his arm to turn Shane around. 'I think it will be best if we leave.'

Again, words defied him as Shane tried to keep up with Tyson's angry stride. What the man said was probably true but it was a low blow to a woman in shock. 'Don't you think you were being a bit harsh and how about slowing down?'

'Sorry but her comment made me see red,' Tyson muttered as he shortened his stride. 'It was her accusation which was harsh and uncalled for.'

'Maybe she's unaware of what we now know.' They reached an open elevator and stepped in with three others.

'She's not unaware any longer. Do you have any objection to me going through Bill's office tonight? See what I can find before the police decide they may need to investigate.'

The lift door opened and everyone filed out into the vast echoing reception area. When Tyson suggested Shane wait at the entrance while Tyson retrieved his car, Shane paused for several seconds but since the painkillers he'd been given had decided to finally kick in, he kept pace with Tyson as they traversed the well-lit car park. While he'd been inside, day had turned into night and he didn't have a clue how long the sun had been gone. Didn't much care either.

'What are you looking for?'

'Evidence to back up what Bill told me so I can get a clearer picture.'

'Go for it.'

Now the strong sedatives were dulling the pain, the drive home was less traumatic, but it was silent with both lost in thought. The silence was a relief, so Shane let his eyes slide shut, hoping for sleep but an over-active mind plastered images of the day into his brain in bright technicolour. He couldn't recall ever having spent a more dramatic day. He snorted to himself, make it a dramatic week. Pictures of the two thugs came to the forefront. Only one he recognised, which meant the two men from the first night of this continuing ordeal, had something to do with Bill but they were on the scene before the Tuesday meeting when Tyson turned up and before Shane decided something wasn't all hunky-dory which caused him to delay his announcement. Therefore, his earlier estimation about how things evolved must be wrong. But, and of this he was certain, Bill was instrumental in the burglary and the incidents in Pinjarra. Which left at least one other man on the loose and Nathan Boyd: how did he fit in? And the dopey duo, as Tyson had dubbed them. Where did they fit in?

'Something doesn't add up,' he muttered as they turned into his street.

'We are on the same wave-length – Boyd. I know you weren't asleep,' said Tyson on a laugh. He pulled into Shane's driveway, his headlights shining on the house. 'I'm only staying until your nurse arrives.'

'Excuse me?' Shane straightened, twisting his head to stare at the man but immediately regretted it when every nerve ending from the waist up, protested. Far slower, he sank back into the seat. 'I don't need a nurse.'

'I was there when the doctor mentioned something about hourly observations and heard you promise they would be done so he would release you into my care.' Tyson brought the car to a standstill, laughing way too loud at Shane's curse. 'Ah, here she comes now,' Tyson added as he glanced into the rear-vision mirror.

Shane swore again when he recognised the car which pulled up alongside. 'You called my mother? And I was beginning to like you but not anymore.' He turned to the grinning man. 'How did you get her number?'

'It was easy and you know how much I enjoy snooping. There aren't many Douglas's listed in the south west directory who live in Australind. It took two minutes on the internet. I think she was in the car before I'd finished telling her you were in the E.R.'

'Shane Benjamin Douglas,' he heard through the closed window before his door opened. 'Oh, my God!' followed when he turned his face.

'Mum, I'm okay.'

'Mrs Douglas, he has mild concussion, whopping bruises on his back, neck and skull and you are to take him back to hospital at any sign of – well, being a trained nurse, you know the signs.'

'You're a dead man, Tyson,' Shane muttered as he eased his body from the passenger seat. 'My car is still at the office,' he added as an afterthought. Lord, why is he even thinking about his damn car?

'I'll check your car. Go to bed, oh, and here is your prescription.'

Before Shane could move, his mother reached in, grabbed the box, glanced at the label and frowned. 'What time did he have the first two?' she asked.

'Mum, don't fret,' said Shane then suffered her fierce look of determination as Tyson gave the time.

'I'm your mother, I'll fret if I want to. It's what mothers do when their child is beaten to a pulp. Now get inside and into the shower and see if you can't do something about removing the layer of dried blood.'

'I'm going.' Shane turned and took cautious steps towards the house, flicking one finger at Tyson's laughter. His mother was by his side by the time he began searching his trousers pocket for keys, Tyson remaining until the door was open and Shane flicked on the hall light. When she took his elbow to guide him down the passage, he wanted to protest but figured it would be a useless exercise. Mama Bear could be ferocious when one of her cubs or grand cubs was hurt. It was easier to keep his mouth shut and accept her ministrations with grace. When he turned right for the kitchen she tugged left.

'Shower,' she said.

'Fine,' he answered with a grin she couldn't see, 'but you'll have to deal with the police when the alarm goes off because it hasn't been disarmed.' He grinned again at her whispered, 'smarty pants,' but she allowed him to turn into the kitchen but only long enough for him to press in the code. Before he had a chance to say or do anything she tugged him around and refused to leave his side until they reached the en-suite of his bedroom.

He caught sight of himself in the mirror and let loose with a four-letter word at the vision staring back at him.

Caked blackened blood filled all the creases on his face and around each bristle of his day-old beard. Both eyes wore dark panda-like bruises with a red and blue emu-sized egg at the top of his nose. Red zebra stripes adorned his neck, where the life had almost been squeezed out of him.

'While you are in the shower, use the soap to wash out your mouth,' his mother said as she left the room and pulled the door shut after her.

'I love you too, Mum,' he called.

'Ten minutes and I'm coming in,' she yelled back from the other side of the wood.

Shane opened the door and stuck his head out. 'The way I feel, it's going to take ten minutes to get undressed.'

'Thought you said you were okay,' she quipped with one eyebrow raised.

'I'm going to kill Tyson for daring to ring you,' he said as he retreated, 'and don't you dare come in.'

'Nothing I haven't seen before,' she yelled back.

'Not since I was three.'

'You're the spitting image of your father. I was married to him for fifteen years and still remember what he looked like.'

Embarrassment didn't begin to describe how he felt. Shane opened his mouth to respond but thought better of it, instead stripping off his blood-soaked shirt and dropping it into the shower stall. Maybe the blood would wash out. If not, it would be binned. As he stepped into the shower, he twisted his head to see the reflection of his back in the mirror. Good grief, no wonder he felt like he'd been torn in two. Tyson wasn't kidding when he said there were whopping bruises. There wasn't much of his lower back shining its normal pink. No way was he going to let Mum see this.

The warm water felt brilliant, so Shane lingered while dabbing gently at his face until the flannel came away clean. He shampooed his hair, soaped his body and rinsed off before taking time to towel himself dry. When he realised he had no clean clothes with him, he bet dear Mama Bear was waiting behind the door. Resigned to his fate, he wrapped the towel around his hips and twisted the ends together into a tight knot. It was a surprise to find the bedroom empty but since he didn't possess anything resembling pyjamas, he had to make do with struggling to don a well-worn T-shirt and loose track pants.

He was about to track down his mother when there was a knock at the door seconds before it opened.

'Bed,' she ordered with one finger pointing towards his bed. In her other hand she held a tray on which stood a bowl of soup, a spoon and a small plate of buttered toast triangles, bringing back fond memories of his childhood. He'd always insisted on triangles while his sisters preferred their toast to be cut into squares. After the tray was settled on his bedside table, he swung one arm around his mother's shoulders and gave her a hug. 'I appreciate you being here, Mum, it feels good but Tyson is going to pay for ringing you and causing you to worry.'

'He did the right thing and I wouldn't want to be anywhere else right now. You need to rest so get this into you. I'll check on you every now and again…' she held up her arm to stop him from arguing. 'I know the concussion is mild. When he rang the second time, Will told me everything the doctor said. Your skull isn't fractured but you were kicked and punched. There's still a slim chance of a brain bleed. It's much easier and safer to deal with it the moment it happens rather than waiting until it does major damage. I won't let it happen. You're my son – allow me to take care of you for the next twenty-four hours so I don't have to worry myself sick.'

Shane eased his body onto the side of the bed, ate every spoonful of the soup and every crumb of toast. The plates were whipped from his lap the very second he set the spoon aside. A pointed finger appeared before his eyes, so he lay down and allowed Mama Bear to tuck him in, kiss his cheek and turn off the light. He wasn't about to argue with being given a huge dose of T.L.C. but he wouldn't stay longer than the night. He had too many questions to be answered.

Chapter Twenty-Seven

'Ah, you're awake. How do you feel?' The door opened further to admit his mother who trod quietly across the room wearing socks on her feet, carrying a glass filled with water and what he assumed were pills clenched in her other hand.

'The drummer in my head has ceased pounding on his big bass drum. Now it's more like the wire snare scraping across the vellum.'

'And the rest of your body?' She dropped a single pill into his hand.

'I'm not game to tell you,' he said before popping the pill onto his tongue and washing it down with a sip of cool water. Shane wasn't one for taking medication unless it was vital. Today it was vital. It felt as though every damaged sinew had contracted into a tight spasm after tying themselves into knots so tight, they were impossible to undo.

'Why not?' A cool smooth hand settled on his brow to check the temperature. After so many years of nursing it was probably an instinctive habit but it gave him a sense of being treasured.

'Because you would make me wash my mouth out again.'

'That bad, huh?'

'Just stiff and sore, which will ease once I get up, warm the sore parts under a hot shower and start moving.'

His mother settled on the side of the bed. 'You need to stay in bed.'

'Mum, I can't. I have no choice but to go into work for a couple of hours. There are two DNA tests I can't neglect, which are vitally important. I also need to check up on Bill and talk to Tyson. Three hours at the most then maybe I can take you somewhere quiet for lunch.'

There was a long sigh from his mother followed by a searching look. 'Okay, but I'm coming with you and we're still on hourly obs. By the way, Will Tyson asked for you to ring him the moment you awaken.' She gently pressed one thumb against the top and bottom lid of his right eye, forcing them apart and studied the pupil. The other eye followed. 'Looks good, normal reaction. I'm happy. Here.' She handed him his mobile phone which she withdrew from the pocket of her fleece jacket.

Shocked, Shane glanced at his bedside table where he'd dropped the phone after sneaking a call to the hospital during the night.

'Don't think I didn't hear you. I slept in the room next door and heard every moan and groan as well as your two calls. Now ring Will.'

'Tyson is going to pay,' Shane grumbled. 'Give me twenty minutes and I'll be ready for work.' After his mother left, Shane wasted no time in dialling Tyson's number, hoping to waken him from a deep sleep, but he answered on the first ring. Payback would have to wait.

'Morning Shane, how's the body?'

'Better than yesterday. You wanted something?'

'So, you still feel like crap. I wanted to tell you about the man outside your front door. He's one of my men: your personal bodyguard.'

'What the hell? I don't need a bodyguard.' Shane tried to scramble out of bed, but a sharp jab of agony forced him to slow and move with a great deal more caution.

'If I didn't think it was necessary, he wouldn't be there and before you get all uppity, I spoke with the higher echelon in police headquarters. They know the two men arrested yesterday. Both are heavies for the worst crime gang boss in the state. Hazelby couldn't have picked anyone worse to get involved with. The police have a guard on Bill's room.'

'So, he's still alive.'

'Barely. He had another heart attack during the night. It doesn't look good. He lost too much blood, his brain was without oxygen for a dangerous length of time and he is now in a coma, on life support. I spent a couple of hours in his office last night; found what I was looking for. I gave some info to the police so they could act ASAP. His wife is a piece of work. Racked up huge debts on the finer things of life; all unnecessary.'

'Like what?'

'Twice a week massages, hair appointments, beauty treatments. Plastic surgery, Botox, clothes, clothes and more clothes – all top end and very expensive. Jewellery worth tens of thousands. Poor guy didn't have a clue. She used one credit card to pay off another with several maxed-out credit cards all in her name only, which she'd probably kept from Bill. From what I can gather, Bill used up everything he had to pay them off but it wasn't enough so they tried the gambling gambit to make up the shortfall. I can see signs of desperation in his paperwork. The trouble is, the more he paid off the more she spent. I suspect she has an addiction they couldn't control. From what I can make out, she's been spending up big since their marriage, but he only found out about six months ago.'

'What has this got to do with me needing a bodyguard?'

'This particular arse-hole will still want his money, plus interest, at an exorbitant rate. It is more than obvious they know your research is worth a lot. They won't care how they get paid. They've already committed murder and serious bodily harm. They won't baulk at kidnap and torture to get what they want.'

Stunned, Shane fell back onto the bed. 'And you dared to put my mother in danger.'

'Hence the reason for a bodyguard. I wouldn't have rung your mother if I had known who we were dealing with. There's been a man watching your house all night. They are good, the best, black ops trained. I suggest you stay home for at least another twenty-four hours.'

'I can't. I have vital DNA tests on the go. I must check them. The dragon lady has given her approval but insists on coming with me.'

'I heard you, Shane Douglas,' came a voice from the passageway and Tyson must have heard her for his laughter was wicked.

'Jeeze, you two, give a man a break,' Shane said loud enough for them both to hear.

'Take Phil with you. He'll protect you both if you stay together. I'll see you in the office.' There was a click and the line went dead.

Exactly twenty excruciating minutes later, Shane presented himself to the kitchen, where he found a cooked breakfast being placed on the table. Even though the thought of food turned his stomach, he sat and ate most, even the over-sweet tea. He normally never took sugar but presumed it had been added to give energy or overcome yesterday's shock. It didn't matter the reason; he knew better than to complain. Plates and cutlery were swept away the very second he slid them to one side and were washed before he could protest.

'We'll have to use your car,' Shane said as his mother wiped her hands dry. 'Mine is still at work.'

'Perfect,' she picked up her handbag and keys, 'because I wasn't going to let you drive in any case.'

It took a monumental effort to stand and walk to the security panel as normal as possible without showing how much it hurt. If he showed the slightest limp, wince or sign of weakness, he had no doubt Mama Bear would tie him to the bed. 'I presume you know about…' he wavered his hand in the direction of the front door.

'The security man, yes, and after what Will Tyson told me this morning I'm more than grateful. Here I was, thankful my son had taken up a nice safe career and look what happens. I never would have imagined how researching in a laboratory could result in such chaos and danger.'

Much to his disgust, Shane was relegated to the backseat for the journey to work while Phil rode in the front. He was fortunate his mother had an SUV, which was big enough to cart grandchildren to various sporting activities with all the required paraphernalia, for he would have struggled to get into a smaller sedan. As it was, bending and folding tortured flesh into the back seat with a jovial smile, was testing. After his shower he had used a mirror to study the black boot print on his lower back. It was at its worst and he was damn lucky the skin hadn't broken, nor more damage had been done to the kidneys. Tomorrow, the miracle of the body's healing powers would mean he would feel a tad better and maybe he could do without the painkillers, but not today.

The scene in the reception area of the normally quiet building he worked in, was a shock. Navy and white police tape blocked off the passageway leading to the crime scene, which was going to be inconvenient for it was the only access to the storeroom. He baulked at the sight of the dark patch of his own dried blood. Surely it could have been cleaned up by now. Nobody needed to match it to any suspect, but police investigators had their methods and arguing was going to achieve nothing but angst and him losing.

The normally ebullient Shelley was sitting at her desk looking pale and drawn as though she hadn't slept. Shane shuffled across to her. 'You should have taken the day off. We would all understand. Sonia could have stood in for you.'

'So should have you but I need to keep busy, so my mind ceases this constant loop of replay. Seeing you beaten… and poor Bill,' a shiver wove itself across her shoulders. She sucked in a breath and pointed to her private little office where a man seated on what was normally her chair and her chair alone, lifted his hand in greeting. 'I brought my bodyguard. He insisted.'

'Hi, Pete,' Shane waved back to Shelley's husband. 'Sorry your wife was caught up in this.'

The man stood to join his wife before shaking hands with Shane. 'At least she wasn't in the line of fire. I can see she wasn't glamorising the facts.' He indicated towards Shane's face. 'You don't look so good. I hope you don't mind my being here but Shelley insisted on coming in, even though she had a sleepless night and has been jumping at the slightest sound or movement. I took the day off work.'

'Feel free.' Shane turned and indicated his two companions. 'I have my own security detail.' After a round of introductions he left Phil guarding the door with instructions to only let in those Shelley indicated were okay. There would be few visitors for they were not the type of business where customers came and went all day. Shane ushered his mother upstairs to his office where he settled her at his desk with a book while he moved to the laboratory.

The serenity of working at mundane tasks at the bench had a deep calming effect. Carrying out processes with practised ease seemed to numb the brain from mental torment; or maybe it was the strong painkillers he was dosed up on. He'd read the contents listed on the packet and understood why his mother had halved the dosage to only one. He would have done the same. The medication was highly addictive so tomorrow he would cease taking them or maybe, if the pain became too much, he would switch to an over-the-counter brand with no codeine.

The only interruption over the two hours of peace had been Mama Bear checking his vital signs. They both knew he was medically fine but if it gave her satisfaction, he was happy to oblige. Deep down he enjoyed the mothering, something he would never verbally admit to.

Shane turned at the knock on the glass panelled door. At the sight of the posse, his heart clawed its way up his throat and jammed itself in a really uncomfortable spot so he couldn't breathe. Steve, Chris and Tyson stood as one on the other side. Grim faces told the story. Damn, damn, damn. No matter what Bill had done, he didn't deserve to die. They could have worked things out.

The door opened to a heavy silence. Three sets of staring eyes caught his. All glistened with suppressed moisture. A long huff of breath forced itself out of Shane's clogged throat, letting his heart drop and rebound, feeling like a lump of lead-shot dropping from the very top of a tall shot-tower. His mother stood, came to him and put her arm around his shoulders.

'I'm so sorry,' she whispered.

'So am I,' said Shane as he stripped off his lab clothes and dropped them in a hamper.

Chapter Twenty-Eight

It amazed Shane how Bill's passing affected him. All afternoon and evening it had felt as though he was fighting through a dense dark fog, unable to focus or find a way out. The vacuum hadn't eased when he'd awoken after a restless night spent chasing away vivid pictures of bloodied bodies.

The somewhere quiet for lunch he had promised his mother yesterday, had ended up being delivered pizzas shared with Chris, Steve, Shelley and her husband. The silence in the small room had been wretched and nerve-racking with everyone seeming to be in their own world of stunned disbelief. Often a mouth would open to say something only to close again, having uttered nothing but a long huff. There was little discussion and what little there was, was only about essential work matters.

After passing on the news to the staff, they had sent home those who weren't working on vital components of their projects. Sometimes you couldn't up and leave when watching for reactions or results, so a skeleton staff had remained to oversee the necessary. It had surprised Shane when Chris had offered to stay and man the phones for the afternoon, giving the others the option to go home. Shane had no idea what the others had done but he chose to return home, tailing his mother's car, with Tyson's security guy seated next to him, ready to pounce should anything untoward happen.

Having spent many years dealing with grieving loved ones after a patient's death, his mother had used her skills, coaxing Shane to talk about Bill. She began by asking about how he met the man, followed by their experiences at university, drawing out stories of their less than decorous antics, and there had been more than he was game to admit. Some things you never tell your mother. At times it had felt wrong to be relating happy or humorous events when the poor man had died only hours previous after such an horrendous assault but over the two hours they talked, his agonising grief eased to an accepting deep sadness. He would be forever grateful for the friendship and forever sorry for the way it ended. It depressed him to know Bill was driven to betray, not only Shane but the entire company. To a certain extent he could understand the reasoning, but the treachery cut deep.

There was only one positive outcome: he now knew who was behind all the unfortunate mishaps. He snorted as he negotiated a way through heavy traffic: not mishaps but disasters, including three vicious beatings and two murders.

Thank goodness the two culprits had been caught and were now in jail but one they knew of remained on the loose. Were there more? Were the twins a part of this? They were unknown quantities and more than a little scary.

Turning into the office car park, Shane forced his mind back to the sunny but frigid new day, hoping it would be far more peaceful. His hope was dashed the moment he spied the distinctive navy and white markings on two police vehicles parked in the *Visitors Only* bays. Damn, there would be more questions, most to which, he now knew the answers.

It still hurt to alight from the car, especially since he had forgone any painkillers this morning, but walking was easier if his stride was kept short and unhurried. He entered the rear door to a buzz of excitement. A police photographer was snapping shots at Shane's dried blood dotted with triangular markers, while another stood by jotting down notes. It made sense that now this was a murder investigation, the police would be thorough but heck, it was his blood, he was alive and the perpetrator behind bars.

The crime-scene tape had gone, but mumblings emanating from the conference room indicated similar action was happening inside. Shelley wasn't at her desk but a single glance into her office gave the answer to her whereabouts. She was being interviewed by another officer.

There goes his quiet day but maybe there was still a chance he could get relative peace while he studied the results to Steve's DNA tests. If he failed to move his marker on the board to indicate his presence, few would know he was here. Instead of being obvious by crossing the foyer to the elevator, he turned and took the stairs one at a time, wincing each time he lifted his left foot. Taking the stairs hadn't been his most brilliant choice, he thought as he paused on the halfway landing long enough to suck in his breath for courage to complete the upward journey. A long sigh escaped when he reached his office where he slowly sank into the comfort of the office chair. To allow time to ease the aches, he turned on the computer to deal with emails even though he felt desperate to analyse the DNA results. Steve would have to wait a little longer while Shane's battered body ceased reminding him he was a fool to have taken the stairs.

The first thing he did was to log on the electronic version of the daily paper to search the death notices. It saddened him when there were only two notices for Jim Daniels, confirming his suspicions the general community didn't give a damn about their so-called local hero. It was a blot on society when so many aged citizens are brushed aside. Well, he was going to make darn sure he was standing by the graveside of the man who touched his heart in such a short time.

Shane was about to send the final reply to the important messages when the internal phone chirped its distinctive tone. Reaching across the desk, he lifted the receiver and frowned at Shelley's message. Steve met him at the door, looking as mystified as Shane felt.

'Why would Lisa be here, today of all days?' asked Steve as they stepped together towards the elevator where they were met by Chris. It appeared Lisa wanted to speak to all three of them and not only Shane.

'Maybe she has details of funeral arrangements,' Shane suggested as they stood waiting for the elevator. It was the only logical thing he could think of. A shiver wound its way down his body at the thought. It barely gave a person time to get over the shock of someone passing away when they had to go through the trauma of making funeral arrangements. Next week was going to be as traumatic as these last few with two unnecessary funerals to attend.

The only sound as they rode down one floor was the soft whirring of the elevator machinery. Normally it wasn't noticed but today, for some reason it made its presence felt and the ride seemed to take forever. The walk along the passage to the small conference room felt as though Shane was going to the guillotine with the tension rebounding off the walls. He had no idea how the other two were feeling but for some perverse reason he thought the guillotine would be a far better option than what was waiting for them when they reached the door three metres away.

Two metres.

One metre.

Steve stepped inside first, followed by Chris while Shane hesitated long enough to suck in a long breath to give him the courage to take the final step. When he saw Lisa sitting in the far end chair he choked on the held breath. She looked anything but a grieving widow. Her blonde hair was immaculate as though she had come straight from the hairdresser. Maybe she had if what Tyson had said was true. The make-up was over the top, caked on thick but it could be hiding the ravages of devastation; he hoped it was so. The one thing belying his thought was the slight smirk around her mouth. What really threw him off kilter was the brightness of the slinky multi-coloured dress, which clung to every curve and hollow, highlighting her figure: not in an elegant classy way but more of a sleazy sexual manner. At least three gold chains hung around her neck, each a different length. The longest held a jewel-studded pendant. Dear heaven, he hoped she was dressed to counteract her distress but it wasn't the impression he was getting. This over-the-top pussy cat was lapping at the richest and most expensive cream. A wave of nausea overwhelmed him as he dragged out the chair nearest the door. Unable to take his eyes from the woman, he took his time to ease his aches and pains downwards.

'We're very sorry for your loss,' said Chris.

Lisa sat forward. 'Thank you. I'll let you know about the funeral in a few days.'

Shane straightened. If she wasn't here about the funeral, why did she want this meeting?

'I need Bill's share of the company,' she blurted without any preamble.

'Excuse me?' Chris exploded as he shot from his seat.

'What did you say?' asked Steve at the same time while Shane's mouth gaped in stunned surprise.

Silence followed while all three men glanced at each other before turning their eyes back on Lisa. Chris slid back into his seat with his mouth agape.

'I need it today.' Lisa hunched forwards, perching on the end of her seat with her arms on the table and her hands held together in a loose clasp. There was at least one bejewelled gold ring on each finger with two on her ring finger. None of them looked like cheap costume jewellery. She eyed each one of them, giving Shane enough time to come to his senses.

'Why?' he asked as he took out his mobile phone and messaged Tyson to come immediately with Bill's paperwork.

'I need the money.' Lisa sat back, appearing relaxed. Shane wondered how much of an act she was putting on for she certainly wasn't behaving like a woman who had lost her husband to a vicious attack less than a day ago.

'Why?' he asked again, this time incurring a fierce glare from Lisa.

'It's none of your business,' she snapped.

Shane leant forwards. 'That's where you are wrong. It is our business,' he stressed the word as he indicated each man, 'as in our company, which you want to disrupt at the click of a finger.'

'It was Bill's company too.' The beginning of anger flared in her eyes and only then did Shane realise how stiff her facial features were. The skin was so rigid it was impossible for her to form a frown line or even smile creases, which explained the half-smile she'd given. She'd either had a serious face-lift or injected copious amounts of Botox. He suspected both if Tyson's words were to be believed.

'Yes, it was,' said Steve, 'but I don't think you understand the structure of the company.'

Shane held up a hand to prevent Steve from saying more. 'Why do you need the money?'

'I have bills to pay.' Her eyes dropped and her arms folded in an obvious defensive pose.

'Bill receives a good wage every fortnight, more than enough to cover any household bills.' Shane shook his head at Steve and Chris when it looked like they were going to interrupt. He figured Tyson hadn't divulged to them what he'd found in Bill's paperwork. 'Steve can transfer into the normal account; the amount Bill is owed for this pay period. He can do it today.'

'That's not enough, it won't even pay the deposit for the funeral.'

'Surely he has savings,' said Chris. 'On what he earned a year he must have put money away.'

A tinge of colour heightened Lisa's neck and cheeks. 'If he did, it was well hidden.'

'Why would he hide it from you? You're his wife,' said Steve.

'Because Bill Hazelby had the misfortune to marry a gold-digger with a penchant for spending way beyond his means,' came from the doorway.

Lisa's head jerked up. 'Who the hell are you?'

'Will Tyson.' The man introduced himself as he settled in a seat opposite Lisa who looked both terrified and angry.

She glanced around at the other three. 'What's he got to do with this?'

'We…' began Steve but Tyson interrupted him.

'I'm a licensed private investigator, employed by this company to investigate why Shane's house was broken into and ransacked, why his house was being watched, why he was followed during the weekend and why a frail man in his nineties, with whom Shane had a brief conversation, was tortured to death before his house was also ransacked. I can now add two more items to the list: why Shane was almost killed in this very building and why your husband was beaten and stabbed viciously enough to cause his death.' He turned to Chris. 'Would you mind asking one of those police officers out there to come and join us?'

An obscenity came from Steve while Lisa plonked back into her seat, but she didn't sit easy, instead fidgeting as though the seat was made from the sharpest of needles. Shane eased back into the padded leather backrest, wondering what Chris and Steve were thinking for much of what they'd heard in the past few minutes, he hadn't divulged to either.

'This hasn't got anything to do with why I am here,' Lisa said but it came out more of a mumble.

Tyson didn't respond but waited until Chris returned. While both men sat, Tyson asked the officer to be a witness and take notes. The tension increased when he took his time to place the file on the table and carefully align it as though highlighting its importance before opening out the top cover. Tension increased even further as he ran a hand over the cover as though to smooth it. He sat back and eyed Lisa long enough, she began to fidget under the scrutiny. Shane noticed how everyone else was staring at the file.

'To answer your last statement, Mrs Hazelby, this has everything to do with you and why you are here. You and you alone, are responsible for the murder of two men, one being your husband.'

'No, you don't know anything. I didn't kill anyone.' She stood. 'I don't have to sit here and listen to this garbage.' She grabbed a large garish bag from the floor and hoisted the handle over one shoulder.

'Sit down!' Tyson bellowed.

Shane wasn't the only one who jumped at the roar. At the resultant stabbing across his back he swore under his breath as he took his time to ease against the backrest.

Lisa didn't sit but stood stock still with eyes wide and mouth agape.

'You will listen, Mrs Hazelby. I have already spoken with the police and given them copies of these papers.' He jabbed one finger on the pile. 'Please sit because this officer will arrest you if you attempt to leave this room.'

Lisa flicked nervous eyes towards the officer before sinking ever so slowly onto the very edge of the chair. Shane didn't think she was humbled, more like petrified, for which he was pleased.

'Thank you.' Tyson sat back with his forearms on the arm rests, his fingers splayed together. 'Before your husband passed out from blood loss yesterday, he spoke with me. Among some of his garbled words, he indicated there was paperwork in his office; these papers.' Tyson tapped the open file. 'Last night I spent several hours going through them and have been here since five this morning. Among them is a detailed diary he kept for the past six months or so.'

Lisa gasped and turned pale. There was a definite shake to the hand she placed on the edge of the table.

'It outlines your deception and has minute details of your addiction to spending money, including exactly how much debt you have created. When I first read the bank statements with details of your credit card spending, I thought Bill had been the one to begin gambling to find more money to pay off those debts. But when I discovered the hidden diary, I realised getting involved with an illegal betting syndicate was all your doing, which only compounded your losses. Now you not only owe several banks large sums of money, but you couldn't pay this notorious crime gang.'

Tyson leant forwards. 'It was you, who informed this crime boss about the value of Shane's research although I believe you got the amount wrong. One million you told them, which was probably a guess on your part for your quote is far short of the true value.'

Chris stood on a curse while Steve mumbled something equally uncouth.

'It was you who suggested they could have all the money if they stole Shane's work and it was you who gave them details of his home.'

'You don't know what you are talking about.' Her voice quivered as though afraid but the hand was shaking even more.

'Yes, I do know. Bill wrote down every word of your phone conversations which he overheard. He also followed you and jotted down the times and places of your gambling trysts.'

An agonised trembling groan rumbled from Lisa's throat as she slumped forwards and dropped her head on the table.

'You owe seven different banks roughly half a million dollars in total and the crime syndicate another $250,000. All of it in your name only.'

A round of gasps was accompanied by shocked retorts. Stunned, Shane could only stare at the woman who, when she lifted her head, had turned a pasty shade of gray.

'Which is why I need Bill's share of the company,' she finally blurted with bravado. The woman wasn't giving up. 'He loaned the company money when you set it up. He gets a quarter share of Shane's research and this company must be worth… what… several million?'

The laugh which gurgled out of Shane's mouth was one of disbelief. Just as stunned, both Steve and Chris stood and began spouting different arguments, creating bedlam. Tyson sat back, allowing them all to vent their opinions. Lisa had nowhere to go and nothing to say that wasn't going to dig her hole in the manure pit any deeper. Shane couldn't get over the nerve of the bitch. Did she honestly think she could get away with this?

When things quietened, Shane held up his hand to indicate he wanted a word. 'Lisa, first, all four of us borrowed money to get this company up and running. We have all been paid back with interest so not one of us is owed a single cent for the initial loan. The money was repaid years ago, before you came on the scene. We all borrowed money again to purchase this building. Again, we have all been paid back and again, before your time. As for my research – it is *my* research, not Bill's, not Chris's, not Steve's and certainly not yours. Any profit I make from my research goes where I dictate and not necessarily to the company or to you or any other individual.' Once again he held up his hand to prevent Steve or Chris from saying anything different for they understood the terms, but no way was he letting this evil woman get a cent.

'It has been over a week since I figured out someone was trying to steal my work, so I locked it away in a very safe place. Your friends' attempts to steal it were never going to succeed for there was nothing to steal in my home nor this building. All my computers have had any research notes deleted. As for Bill's share of the company, you need to study the original documents outlining what happens if one of us were to have an untimely death. It is all there in black and white, legally signed, sealed and registered. First, any remaining partners have the opportunity to purchase the deceased's share if they so wish, either individually or as a group. The money is to go where the deceased person's will, dictates. I don't know how your husband's will is worded but regardless, it must go through probate first, which usually takes at least twelve months. You, as a spouse, get nothing from this company. Nor would Steve's wife unless it is stated in his will. We remaining partners also have the option of bringing in another partner who would purchase Bill's shares in the company, which would also take many months. There are a few more minor, but equally important details.'

'You bastard!' Lisa hissed as she stood with a jerk. There was tense silence before she screwed her eyes in thought. 'What about his superannuation? That's mine.'

'Maybe,' said Steve. There was a supercilious smile on his face. Now he had recovered from the shocks of the revelations, he seemed to have a handle on things. He winked at Shane. 'It depends on who he has named as his beneficiary and since the fund was set up ten years ago, maybe you aren't listed. You may be if he altered the paperwork when you married. I don't know.'

'You must know,' Lisa squealed. 'You are the treasurer.'

'Accountant,' he corrected. 'I pay the money into his super fund each quarter. I don't deal with his private paperwork.'

Shane grinned to himself for Steve knew every detail of all their superannuation.

'You can't do this to me!' Lisa screamed.

'These guys aren't doing anything to you.' Tyson flicked through the papers in front of him. 'Everything that has happened is a result of your actions and Bill has made sure you suffer the consequences.'

Lisa spun around, alert but her hands were shaking. 'What do you mean?' she asked as she faced him again.

'As I said, Bill kept a detailed diary. It outlines the arguments you and he had, how you were given a chance by not spending any more money and liquidating some of your assets such as selling your jewellery, but you blew your chance by spending the same amount Bill paid off with his savings. It outlines how the marriage ended four months ago, something Bill registered with the Family Court so he could apply for a divorce as soon as possible. It also outlines how Bill went to his lawyer and…' Tyson paused to flick through the papers and withdrew a few stapled together, 'changed his will.'

Shane was certain the pause Tyson made, was for effect.

'Bill suspected your criminal friends would come after either you or both of you and predicted it was possible things could get nasty if they did. He even referred to possible physical attack. He'd had several threatening emails outlining what would happen to both him and you if all money owed wasn't paid within a certain time. Copies of those emails are here. The new will is very specific. The house and furniture are to be sold with the proceeds paying out his housing loan. Any money left over goes into a trust fund for his nieces and nephews and can't be accessed until the youngest is twenty-five. His shares in this business are to be split evenly between the remaining three partners. You get what you took from the house when he threw you out:

your car, jewellery, clothes and personal belongings, which Bill suggested you could sell to pay off some of your debt. Since you have already ruined your husband financially, you get nothing.'

'I'm his wife!' Lisa yelled with a stamp of one foot, reminding Shane of a recalcitrant child not getting their own way. She half stood before thinking better of it. As she sat back, a stiff smile began. 'I'll contest the will.'

'Go for it but there is a lengthy section where it specifies his request for any contest be denied and the reasons why. The will is ironclad: Bill made sure it would be by using a top lawyer to write it up.'

Lisa surged forwards; the smile replaced with a sneer. 'We'll see.' She stormed to the door. 'Watch your backs you bastards! I'm going to make sure you all get what you deserve.'

The police officer barred her exit by slinging an arm around her shoulders and drawing her against his body in a hold so tight, she had no way of escaping, although she twisted and wriggled in a useless attempt to get out the door.

Tyson twisted his head. 'You think your criminal cohorts are going to help you?'

Lisa stalled and shot Tyson a look, which Shane could only describe as hopeful.

'Bill had access to your internet account because you failed to alter your password. He printed off every single detail on times and places, so the police raided the gambling party in the early hours this morning, arresting the lot of them. The police might thank you for them being able to nab the most notorious crime boss this state has seen. But I doubt it. The superintendent I spoke to this morning even hinted at ways to have you arrested, after all you instigated, aided and abetted two murders, one of them being your own husband, which will probably get you a life sentence. Being a party to a crime gang won't get you any time off. Oh, and by the way, don't even think of trying to get into the marital home. You know, the one you were barred from entering four months ago with a restraining order and is now under police guard. And as for leaving the country, your passport has been revoked. Have a great day.'

Lisa screamed filthy epithets, damning them all to hell as she ploughed through the policeman and ran full pelt, loud sobs following in her wake.

Chapter Twenty-Nine

'Well, that was interesting,' said Steve, lolling back in his seat, looking bemused.

'What's even more interesting,' said Chris, 'is why Shane has been keeping things from us. What's this about your house being watched and you being followed and another murder? And where in hell's name is your research?'

Ever so slowly, Shane slid his eyes shut while one hand tunnelled through his hair before settling on the nape of his neck which he gripped to prevent his fist from flying free with a punch. He so didn't want to discuss this but both men needed some sort of explanation. His sucked in breath to gain control was long and audible. 'All of what Tyson said is true. It has been a hellish week.'

'But why not tell us?' Steve asked, appearing to be genuine in his concern. His entire demeanour yelled hurt and mystification.

'I didn't know who I could trust.' At the gasps of protest, Shane eyed both men who looked put out, especially Steve. 'Look guys, what would you have done in the same situation? Only the four of us knew about Prancer and the only reason someone was after my research was because one of us didn't keep their sworn promise and blabbed. It certainly wasn't me, leaving three suspects. You guys employed Tyson without my knowledge, which put the wind up me. I even suspected he had been employed to gain access to my work, so I downloaded every single file onto thumb drives and hid them. I erased the files from all my computers. I've been working with Tyson ever since, to do exactly what you employed him to do; keep Prancer safe.

'Now we all know I had a reason to be wary and we know who the culprit is so if you aren't happy with the way I handled things, then tough.' Shane stood quicker than was wise, wincing at the resultant stab of pain. It was ridiculous the way he felt like an old arthritic man. 'Now if you will excuse me, I have tests waiting to be analysed.'

Taking more care in the way he moved, he reached the door when a thought came to him. He turned. 'I have a suggestion. I feel it would be the right thing to do if either we three, or the company, paid for Bill's funeral. It's clear the poor man wanted nothing to do with his wife. I wish Bill had come to us. Together we could have come up with a solution. He didn't deserve this ghastly outcome.'

'I agree,' said Chris.

'I'll look into it,' Steve added as Shane left, eager to get away. The last half hour had been intense and damned eye-opening. He still wasn't sure how he felt about Bill: better than he had before, now he knew a few more revealing facts but still Lisa had got details of Prancer from somewhere. As he stepped into the elevator, he heard running footsteps. He rushed inside to escape but when the door didn't close, he turned to see Tyson holding it open.

'Can we talk?' Tyson didn't wait for an answer but sidled beside Shane.

'Do I have any choice?' As Shane glanced up at the taller man, he couldn't help but grin. 'You lied to them.'

'About what?'

'What you said to Lisa about why you were employed.'

'Yes, well, she set the goalposts. I just moved the boundary a little to fit her game, but we still have a problem.'

With his eyes shut, Shane groaned. 'You have to be kidding. What else could possibly be wrong?'

'One name - Nathan Boyd.'

'Why is he still a problem? I figured he was a stooge sent by this infamous gang.'

'Maybe, it's possible but names were named in Hazelby's diary: all except Boyd. There is no mention of the man, not even a hint. If he was a plant, Bill would have known. Everything else is detailed. Even after he'd tossed his wife out, he accessed her computer, printed off all her messages to and from the syndicate. She didn't think to alter her password. I'm sure he was collecting evidence to take to the authorities and probably you three. There's mention of the two tailing you, the details she gave to them about you and everything I revealed today. Even the dopey duo cracked a mention. They were employed by the gang but nowhere is there even a hint of Boyd.'

A long groan rumbled from deep down in Shane's gut as the elevator door whooshed open. The familiar chemical smell, peculiar to laboratories, hit. He didn't mind the aroma, it felt comforting, especially after the last few days of horror. 'I really don't want to know this.' He headed for his office eager to find privacy and solace.

'I'm sorry but I wanted to warn you to be careful. By the way, Bill has given details on what he wants for a funeral. I mentioned it to Steve who said he would sort it. We might need some legal intervention to have the body released to the company and not his wife. He specifically decreed she is not involved. The way he wrote about her indicated he was more than furious with her and no longer cared a damn what happened to her.'

Shane paused at his office door. 'That's a small mercy. I now understand why you called her a piece of work but you were giving her credit she doesn't deserve.'

'Prancer, eh?'

'It doesn't matter any longer. Now I've got work to do and I'd appreciate a few hours of un-interrupted peace.'

'The police will want your statement.'

'Ah, hell. Ask them to leave me until last. I really have important test results to analyse and a report to write.'

'I'll see what I can do.'

It was a relief when Tyson strode away and Shane was able to lock himself in the lab with the *Do Not Disturb* sign stuck outside. The only way he was going to give his mind any peace was to immerse himself in work.

Two hours later he finished typing up a report for the Child Support Agency and emailed it off. Before hunting down the man concerned, he printed a copy for Steve and one for the mother of his purported son. A tap on Steve's door was greeted with a mumbled word Shane took for a *yes,* so he entered. Too bad if it was a *no.*

'I thought you might like this.' Shane slid an envelope over the desk. It spun around and landed right side up against the pen Steve had been using. Steve stared at the large manila envelope, glanced up at Shane and swung his eyes back at the envelope. His hand shook as he reached out and scooped up the envelope. After opening it and withdrawing the contents, he took his time to read the report. The papers dropped and Steve looked up.

'It's not mine. Are you sure?'

Shane dragged a chair away from the wall and eased his aching back into it. 'Testing for paternity of a male child is relatively easy and provides very conclusive results. Males have a single Y chromosome which is passed on from father to son. That Y chromosome is shared by all male members of a common male predecessor. You inherited your particular Y chromosome from your father and him from his father. Any male child you have will have the same as you. I extracted the DNA from both samples and compared the polymorphic sites. If Adam was your child those indicators must match at each locus. If you compare the two graphs you won't find any matching indicators, so it is impossible for the boy to be yours.'

'I don't know what to say.' His shocked surprise turned to a grin. 'Thank you. This is such a relief but…' He sat back. 'What do I do now?'

'First, you pay no more money. Second, I've already emailed my official report to the agency with the suggestion they recoup all the money they have already collected. Third, if it was me, I'd sue the woman but to do so would involve being honest with Grace. I presume you haven't said anything.'

'Hell no! How could I? I adore Grace and never want to hurt her. This would destroy her. If it had been mine, I would have had to find a way to tell her.' Steve leant forwards. 'Do I confront this woman?'

Shane thought. 'No, I wouldn't. The less you have to do with her the better. Why don't you go home tonight and tell Grace everything has been sorted at work and is back to normal? Maybe associate the problems with Bill's wife creating havoc. You have to explain Bill's death so shove all the blame onto his wife, after all, Lisa deserves it.'

Steve smiled. 'Brilliant idea but what if this woman comes here looking for me?'

'Give me her address. I'll confront her with the evidence. I could threaten her with legal action if she attempts to contact you and if she doesn't return every cent to the agency. It makes sense to handle this via a third party so there's no need for her to contact you. Does she have your phone number?'

'Not my personal ones but she could look up the company number.'

'I'll threaten her. If threats don't work, we could put Tyson to use. He's big enough to scare the pants off anyone.'

'He certainly scared Bill's wife.'

'Nothing less than she deserved.'

'I can't thank you enough for this,' said Steve.

'There's something you can do for me in return.'

'What? Anything.'

'You can swear on your life you had nothing to do with stealing my research.'

'You think I would steal from this company?' he yelled as he stood. 'How could you?'

'Calm down, Steve.'

'Calm down? You know I would never betray you or the company. This is my life and it provides me with a far better living than I ever expected. Why on earth would I risk losing it?' Steve paced, across the room, around in a circle and back again. Fury marred his features: a fury which couldn't be faked.

'Steve, please, I had to be sure. Please sit.'

He plonked, sending up an embarrassing puff of air as buttocks hit leather. 'If I was involved, do you think I would hire Tyson? Really?'

Shane shook his head and sighed, now certain Steve wasn't involved, which delighted him. 'How did you get Tyson here? The last time I spoke to Bill he denied wanting Tyson.'

A sheepish grin spread from Steve's mouth. 'I guess now is the time to be honest. I tricked the other two. This thing with Adam had me running scared. Losing ten per cent of my pay was impossible to explain to Grace. I figured I could cover it up as soon as Prancer became viable, so I panicked. I was terrified the same would happen with this discovery as what happened last year.

'Seems you were right to be scared.'

'Yes, well, hindsight is pretty bloody amazing. I'd heard of Will Tyson and his outfit from a friend. I knew he was the best so I went to Chris and told him all of us agreed to hire Tyson's company. Chris was dead against it but I told him we had a majority, so he had no choice but to agree. After getting Chris to agree I went to Bill with the same story. Bill wasn't quite so stroppy about it but once I explained the reasons to him, he was more willing. Now I think he was hoping Tyson would find the truth.'

'Could be, but you didn't come to me.'

'I didn't have time with you being closeted away so I hired Tyson. With it a *fait accompli* I figured you would go with the flow.'

'I was pissed.'

Steve grinned, eyes flashing with mischief. 'I know but maybe, now you know I was right, you might forgive me. I'm sorry but I was plain terrified at the time.'

Shane stood. 'We still have a problem.'

'What do you mean? How?'

'Nathan Boyd was also after my research and he has nothing to do with Lisa.'

Chapter Thirty

With its deep but narrow porch and neat front garden, the unit was modest but modern. As he unlatched the gate and stepped onto the leaf strewn concrete path, Shane wondered how much of Steve's money was used to rent this upmarket place: or maybe Catherine Ellery owned it for she wasn't a young teenager but had to be close to thirty, so has worked for a number of years.

When he pressed the button, the resultant chimes played a sickly cute tune, which went on way too long and would drive Shane nuts within a week. He now regretted offering to do this. It really wasn't his business and he had more than enough on his plate but to save Steve and Grace's marriage, it was worth the effort. He wondered if he would do the same if Steve had been the culprit. Probably not.

This could be a way of assuaging his guilt for blaming Steve of being the traitor.

The click-clack of footsteps neared, followed by the porch light being switched on and the turning of a key. The wood panelled door opened about thirty centimetres.

'Yes?' Even on a single word, there was a strong English accent which tickled his memory into awareness. Her accent was so noticeable he recalled hearing this woman talking at the conference but he couldn't bring her picture to mind.

'Miss Ellery?'

'Yes, how can I help you?' The door opened wider to reveal a smallish woman with dark hair doing its best to escape two short pigtails. She was pretty, with a smattering of freckles across the pert nose separating dark eyes. Still, he didn't recognise her.

To appear friendly, Shane smiled and took two steps back so she wouldn't feel threatened. His manoeuvre worked: the woman stepped out, which is what he hoped would happen.

'Hi, I'm Dr Shane Douglas.'

'Doctor? You must have the wrong place. I didn't phone for a doctor.'

'You are Catherine Ellery?'

'Yes.'

'I have the right place.' He held out the buff coloured envelope, which Catherine took and read her name before glancing up with a frown wrinkling the band of freckles.

'What's this?'

'The results of the DNA test I undertook on behalf of Mr Steven Richards, comparing his DNA with your son's DNA.'

Fear replaced the frown. Brown eyes widened and flicked from side-to-side while her mouth gaped. 'You have no right. This is an invasion of privacy.' As she waved the envelope in the air her hand shook, giving the impression he'd hit a nerve.

'Since you claimed Mr Richards is the biological father of your child, he has every right to proof of such an allegation. And since there is no chance your child is his, he is demanding all the money you have received from him under false pretences, to be returned to the Child Support Agency within seven days. Failure to do so will result in him having you charged with obtaining credit by fraud. He is also considering laying charges with the police about the way you set him up by using an illicit substance to render him unconscious.'

There was a gasp, followed by silence but Shane didn't miss her trying to sneak back inside by creeping backwards with one hand searching around for the door. Shane grabbed the door handle and held it rigid with enough of a gap so the door wouldn't shut. He would hate her being locked out so she couldn't tend the boy.

'I haven't finished,' he said in a tone stern enough to make her still and pay attention. She shrunk against the door as though willing her body to pass through the solid wood. 'Any attempt to contact Mr Richards, or any member of his family will result in him taking you to court. I have already emailed a copy of these results to the Child Support Agency and in case you think there were no witnesses to what you did to him, I was with him at the same conference and I can assure you he drank very little alcohol that night – certainly not enough for him to be classed as drunk or to fall into an alcoholic stupor. I also know what a philanderer your old boss, Kevin Sutherland, is. I presume he is the real father.'

The way she paled on a hiss gave him his answer. 'Go to him. I'll even do the DNA test for you since I already have your son's on record. I really don't know how you could even think you would get away with your scam. It defies logic.' He released the handle. 'Have a great evening.' Shane turned away and retreated to his car, grinning at the slamming of the door. For once he enjoyed being the bearer of bad news.

The visit had taken him on a lengthy detour, so it was another hour before he drove into his garage and pressed the remote for the door to close behind him. A fabulous aroma of roasting meat stirred gastric juices into action the very moment he stepped into the kitchen. Yum.

'Something in here smells wonderful.' He stopped in his tracks. Mum wasn't alone. 'Jessica?' His surprise turned to a grin as he placed his laptop on the bench and stepped closer to the two women seated on opposite sides of the table. He bent and gave his mother a peck on her cheek while eyeing Jessica. 'So, you're not scared witless by Mum but give me a wide berth - interesting.' He enjoyed the blush which pinkened Jessica's cheeks.

'You're afraid of Shane? Why? What did he do to you?' Shane received a glare from his mother before he settled by her side.

Poor Jessica looked mortified. 'Nothing, he's been very considerate.'

'Just as well. So why are you afraid of him?' asked his mother.

Seeing the way Jessica fought to find words, Shane figured she needed saving. 'I think it's not me as a person she's afraid of but more of men in general. If my guess is correct, I get the feeling some idiotic moron did a number on her. Am I right?'

A shy nod was his only answer.

'I'm sorry you were treated with enough disrespect to make you afraid of all men. Mum, here, would tan my hide if I treated anyone, man or woman, with disrespect. Let me assure you, I have never used my strength to harm a woman.' He grinned. 'Actually, that's not quite true.'

'Shane!' His mother looked both shocked and fierce.

'One time I punched my sister in the stomach. I was ten and have regretted it ever since.'

A warm hand gripped his arm. 'At the time you were angry with the world.' His mother turned to Jessica. 'The father Shane adored, had passed away from cancer. It was a tough time.'

'Oh, I'm sorry,' said Jessica.

'Thank you,' both Shane and his mother said at the same time.

'Are you joining us for dinner?' Shane asked. 'I'm starving and if I'm not mistaken, Mum has baked us her famous lamb roast.'

Appearing to be shy, Jessica glanced down at her hands. 'I wasn't intending to. I came to ask a favour from you.' Despite her head hanging low, she couldn't hide the deepening blush rising up her neck.

'Which is? Shane asked, delighted with her coyness. This must be something serious, the way she was reacting.

'I teach at a high school. The seniors have their annual ball coming up next Friday. I umm... have to attend but I... err... need a partner, otherwise I will have to dance with all the hormone driven seventeen-year-old boys,' raced out of her mouth so fast, Shane couldn't help but laugh. He dared to reach out and cup her chin to draw her face up so they could see eye-to-eye.

'It would be my pleasure.'

'It would? Are you sure?' She jerked back, releasing his hold. He didn't think it was from fear but more from shock at his ready acceptance.

'Absolutely. How formal is it? Lounge suit, tux?'

'Oh, God, thank you, lounge suit is fine, I'm sorry...' She sucked in a long breath before a grin escaped. 'I'm gabbing but I was so nervous. I've never asked a guy out before.' She indicated with one hand towards his face. 'Your mother told me you were attacked. It looks painful. Are you okay?'

'I'm getting there. Hopefully the bruising is gone by next Friday otherwise you might want to change your mind. By the way, this,' he tapped a finger against the dark blue smudges under each of his eyes, 'is courtesy of the man who followed me.'

'Really? I'm sorry.'

'You have nothing to be sorry about. In fact, the police are appreciative of your information for it has given them some clear evidence of intent. I'm pleased to inform you this hood is now in jail along with his cohorts, including the other man you photographed. So now we should be safe.'

A plate laden with juicy slices of roast lamb surrounded by baked root vegetables and a variety of greens was placed in front of Jessica. A second plate was placed in front of Shane. He glanced up as guilt swamped him. He hadn't even noticed his mother leaving the table or heard her plating up the meal.

'Thank you.' He glanced at Jessica. 'Looks like you're staying for dinner. I can guarantee it will be superb.'

It was one of the most pleasant experiences of the past two weeks to be eating one of his favourite meals with his beloved Mum and a woman he still wasn't too sure about. Did he like Jessica? So far, yes. It was difficult coming to grips with how easily he'd agreed to her request but what harm could it do? A high school ball wasn't on his list of places to take a woman on a first date, but it could be fun. It could also be as boring as watching paint dry, but what the heck. He was no longer committed to one woman, wasn't betraying anyone and was a single man, free to date whomever he pleased.

Shane was about to pop the last morsel of gravy covered meat into his mouth when a knock on the front door interrupted him. He eyed the crispy end knob of lamb – his favourite bit, which he'd saved till last, slid it into his mouth before settling the cutlery in neat alignment on the plate and pushing his seat out. He excused himself and strode down the passage, annoyed at the interruption. It seemed fate or karma or whatever it was, wasn't going to allow him more than thirty minutes of joy.

Another more insistent knock echoed down the passage. 'Coming,' he called as he unlocked the door and immediately regretted doing so. Damn, he must have done something bad to be on the receiving end of this. Carol stood to one side of the doorway.

'Hi, Shane, can we talk?'

Undecided what to do, he switched on the porch light, glanced down the passage and back at Carol who had either been out somewhere or had dressed for the occasion in smart evening slacks with an emerald green camisole under a sparkly three-quarter sleeved jacket. If it was a social call, she was going all out to impress him which sent the hairs of the nape of his neck to full alert. Why?

'I have dinner guests?'

'Oh, a woman?'

Now why should it concern her what gender guest he had? Surely his refusal to respond to any of her numerous messages after he'd told her they were over, would have indicated he was no longer interested in her. His heart tumble-turned, reminding him he still had strong feelings for Carol, something he couldn't just switch off, but her perfidy was something he couldn't live with.

'Two women, not that it's any of your business.' It took a second for his words to compute.

Carol winced as she took a step back. Her eyes lifted and screwed while peering at his face. 'What happened?' She swept one hand around indicating the injuries to his face, which now resembled a raccoon, accompanying the black tiger stripes adorning his neck.

None of your damn business, he thought. 'It met with a solid object.'

'Ooh, nasty.'

'What is it you wanted to talk about?"

'I… I… I'm sorry, really sorry.' She searched his eyes. 'I didn't realise I would miss you so much. I want to explain everything, to be honest. Isn't that what you wanted?'

One hand ran through his hair in frustration. He didn't like the way those words came out as though she was merely pandering to him to get what she wanted. It was something she had never done before, at least not that he was aware of, so to act like this now gave him a clear message she was up to something. What to do? Did he give her the opportunity or not? How he wished Tyson had come back to him with answers about the search of her bank accounts. He eyed her while he thought. Let's see how honest she was going to be.

'Okay, but we'll talk out here.' He stepped outside, crossed the veranda and went down the steps. 'Sit.' He indicated the top step.

Carol swept her eyes up and down the bare wooden planks. The glare she sent him wasn't of the friendly kind, as if to chastise him for daring her to sit on dusty wood. 'No thanks. I'll stand.' The heels of her stilettos wavered on each step as she descended and came to a standstill about a metre along the path. The shoes appeared to be new, as did the outfit for he couldn't recall ever seeing them before and after twelve months of dating, he'd seen most of her wardrobe.

'Fine, I'll sit,' and he dropped to the top step, regretting the action when his bruised back protested. Taking up as much room as he could so she wouldn't sit next to him, he rested elbows on knees, clasping his hands under his chin, watching her, waiting.

In the heavy silence Carol took a fidgety step back, delighting him to see she was feeling uncomfortable.

'Can we start over? I miss you.'

Shane skewed his head to one side, staring at her and wondering how much truth was in her words. Why now? Why was she so eager to resume their relationship? 'I've missed you as well but I wasn't the one who couldn't be honest and you have always known honesty is important to me. Why did you leave your job?'

Her lips formed a straight line and somehow he knew she was blushing even though he couldn't see so well in the dimness. 'I've already told you I was made redundant. There was a downturn in work coming in. Someone had to go and it was me.'

Still she lied but he was determined to go further to see how far she would go. 'What about the rest of your team? Were they made redundant?'

'I was told they would all be going. There wasn't enough work to keep us on.'

Shane's insides began to simmer in rage but he fought to keep the anger under control, while in his mind he counted back the days from the previous Sunday. Tyson had said Carol was leaving in ten days. Today was Thursday so there were six more days. So why was Carol so eager to resume their relationship if she was leaving on Tuesday? 'Tell me more about this holiday you are planning.'

A startled expression with widening eyes lit up her face. 'What do you want to know?'

Shane was certain her voice quivered. Let's see how nervous she can get, he thought. 'How long will you be away?'

'Umm… about three months.'

Now it's three months when before it was a few weeks. He wondered if she remembered what she'd said before but if she had definite plans she would know exactly, to the day, how long she would be away. 'When are you leaving?'

'Soo… um… I haven't finalised the details yet but am getting there. I'm leaving in about four weeks.'

She almost said soon, which confirmed what he already knew. 'Are you still going to Europe?'

'Yes, definitely. I've got a tentative booking to fly to Athens.'

Now it was Athens and not Venice. Did she even remember what she's said before? Shane leant back, balancing on straight arms. 'A tentative booking means you must have a date.'

There was a long pause. 'Only a tentative one.'

It amused Shane how Carol had crossed her arms and was looking down at one foot, which was making little semicircles in front of the other. He could tell she was disconcerted by the barrage of questions. 'Are you going alone?'

The foot stopped mid-swing. There was a pause before she shuffled from foot-to-foot as she looked around everywhere but at him.

'Yes.'

'Hmm, there's one thing puzzling me.'

Finally, her eyes connected with his. 'What?' she asked as she straightened.

'Why would you want to resume a relationship when you are planning on spending at least three months overseas – alone?' He emphasised the last word because for some reason he had an inkling it wasn't true. Was it a female she was going with or had she been two-timing him? The thought hurt but with the lies she continued to spout with such ease he figured it was now a strong possibility she could be hiding even more and had probably been lying for months.

There was a quick sucking in of her breath. 'I miss you.'

'We've been apart for less than a week and you swear you miss me yet you're planning on being away for three months. If you missed me so much, why aren't you inviting me to join you? I've already told you I have accrued leave owing.' But with Chris's annual leave already booked and coming up, Shane wouldn't be able to take time off yet. It was something she didn't need to know for these details were irrelevant. Although, come to think of it, with Bill gone, Chris might have to delay his leave for a few months while they sort things out with the company.

The play of emotions crossing her features was amazing. There was shock at his suggestion, followed by a tightening of muscles around her mouth while her body went rigid. It was obvious she hadn't been expecting him to turn things around and it was obvious she was searching for some logical answer: one he would believe, well he had news for her and it wasn't of the good variety.

'There's no need to answer because I wouldn't come with you in any case. I need time to give you an answer.' Like hell he did. A perverse idea came. 'I'll let you know on Tuesday.'

Her head snapped up. 'Oh… I was hoping we could spend the weekend together. I could come over.'

Now he was downright mystified. Why was she so keen?

'The weekend? You've always been unavailable for weekends.' And now he wondered why. 'Always spend it with your mother, you said.' And now, some perverse voice told him it wasn't her mother she spent the weekends with. 'Besides, I have guests to entertain.' He eased his body upright. 'I'll ring you Tuesday evening. I have to get back to my visitors.' He climbed the steps. 'Goodnight,' he said over his shoulder, 'Enjoy your weekend.'

'What about tomorrow night?' she called after him in a voice hinting at desperation. 'We could go out for dinner like we always do.'

Now certain something weird was going on, Shane turned with one hand on the door handle. 'I said I have guests. We have plans I can't change. What do you really want, Carol?'

'Isn't it obvious? I want to spend time with you.' The lady was way too desperate.

'Carol, I know you were sacked. I know your place was taken by Sarah James, a junior on your team who has now been promoted. Therefore your position is still there so it's impossible you were made redundant. I also know the rest of your team are still employed and I know *why* you were fired. Without honesty there is no trust. Without trust there can be no relationship and I certainly can't trust you any longer because of your blatant dishonesty. Goodnight.'

'What...?'

It wasn't normal practice for Shane to slam doors but he did this time out of sheer frustration, mixed with a large dose of anger along with a heaped ladle of mystification and there was no way to describe the hurt burrowing into his heart. There had to be a reason for her persistence. Why was she so keen to get back with him? To gain equilibrium, he leant against the door and sucked in a few long breaths before striding along the passage, determined to enjoy the rest of the meal with two far more pleasant women.

The rhubarb and apple tart he'd spied cooling on the bench, had his name written on it and with a bit of luck Mum had made her special creamy custard to go with it. His problems could be put aside until tomorrow when he would set Tyson the task of peeling off the layers of one Carol Maguire to find the core, which he was now convinced was rotten, mouldy and festering.

Chapter Thirty-One

The chinks of glass touching metal, the murmurs of voices discussing minor details and social events along with the occasional hushed chortle of laughter felt so comforting, so normal. A tap turned on with a rush of water to rinse either hands or an instrument. The whirring of exhaust fans sucking away the worst of chemical fumes created a rhythmic syncopation while Shane moved from project to project, watching, discussing, solving minor problems. For the past three hours he had relished in the normality of life in a laboratory. Despite the humdrum sounds, it was more subdued than normal as though everyone was showing respect for the one person no longer with them. Most had quietly commented on Bill's passing, showing their shock, their horror but mostly their sadness for the man they admired. There had been a collective request for all to attend his funeral en-masse.

It was a sombre visit to the upper floor labs yet at the same time there was a beginning to the healing process, especially for Shane.

As the first shift began leaving for lunch, Shane joined them to retrieve the lunch he was looking forward to, from the refrigerator. A plastic container held leftover roast while a second, larger dish was filled with custard-drenched rhubarb tart. To ensure he could enjoy the meal without interruption, he rode the elevator to the ground floor, exited the front door, turned right and strode to the intersection. Movement was easier with the sharp stabs now more of the duller tug variety. When the little green man flicked on, Shane crossed the road and kept walking two blocks until he reached a park where he settled on a bench under the shade of several massive eucalypts. Ten metres in front of him sat a dark pond bedecked with a variety of waterfowl doing what they always did: gliding, racing, slowing before dunking under the water in search of yummy delicacies. The park appeared to be a popular lunch-time haunt with business attired men and women sitting on the many benches or on the expansive lawns, many seeking warmth in the sun for the day still held a chill crispness despite the cloudless sky. Most were eating, others relaxing, many with eyes closed.

Shane lifted the lid on the roast and hoed in, not caring it was cold. It still tasted delicious and there was enough left residing in his fridge at home for the evening meal. It had been a wrench seeing his mother depart soon after breakfast. Despite the reason for her being there, he had wallowed in her company. It might not be macho for a grown man to admit enjoying being mothered but Shane didn't care. The pleasure had been all his and Mamma Bear was now happy her cub was out of danger.

When he peeled off the cling wrap from the other dish, a sigh of pure pleasure escaped. He lifted the bowl, sniffed with a smile and fished out the plastic spoon, licking off the layer of fluffy yellow custard. Social graces could go to hell. He licked, he scooped, he slurped and enjoyed, even to the extent of licking the bowl clean, not caring two hoots if anyone was watching. Replete with his mother's home cooking, Shane dashed across the road to purchase a small bottle of water, which he sipped as he meandered a different route back to work.

All signs of police activity had gone. The reception area was its normal quiet self and the cleaning staff had been permitted to scrub away the blackened remains of his blood, thank goodness. Seeing the area back the way it was, made it difficult to believe less than two days ago it had been the scene of a bloodbath. A shiver of unease at the memory wove its way down his spine as he slid his marker next to his name to indicate he was present. Sonia Wosniak, the assistant receptionist who was filling in for Shelley while she was at lunch, nodded as Shane passed. With a bit of luck, he could reach his office and lose himself in work for the rest of the afternoon. It felt weird to be having such a normal, pleasant and relaxing day after the turmoil of the past week and a half, but it was such a darn good feeling.

Reading and answering emails were such a waste of time when he could be studying samples through the microscope, he thought as he ploughed through the thirty-seven new emails. The sudden knock at the door was a relief until he glanced up to see Tyson entering.

'Please let this be good news,' he said as he pressed *send* and closed the emails.

Tyson grinned while he dragged the visitor's chair closer to the desk. 'Yes and no.'

'Give me the yes, I don't really want the no.'

'Can't have one without the other. Write down this name.'

Shane picked up a pen and poised it over the pile of scrap paper he kept on hand for jotting down notes.

'Nathan Boyd.'

Shane's head jerked up to stare at Tyson. He wrote on a growl.

'Now put the letters 'JO' in front of his first name.'

Shane wrote, read and frowned. 'Jonathan Boyd. It still doesn't ring a bell but it's a smart way of creating an alias.'

'Even smarter when you consider Boyd is his middle name.'

'And you know the surname, don't you?'

'Yes and this is where the bad news comes in.'

'Do I want to know?'

'Definitely not.'

As Shane slid his eyes shut on a groan and sank back in his chair, a whole host of surnames flew through his mind. Evans, Hazelby, Simmonds began the list before thinking of the other workers before swinging back to Bill's wife. He couldn't recall her maiden name but it had to be the one. It was the only one which made any sense. His eyes opened to see the grim mouth of Tyson. Ah, hell, he wasn't going to like this.

'Okay, sock it to me.'

'Maguire.'

The pen dropped as Shane jerked forwards. 'Excuse me?'

'Jonathan Boyd Maguire, first cousin to one Carol Janine Maguire. I'm now certain your relationship with Carol was a set up from the beginning, with only one aim in mind and it wasn't to find an everlasting partner but to find your research especially when you consider her mother lives in Queensland… with her father.'

A ten-tonne block of concrete slammed into Shane's chest at the same time as his blood thundered through his veins. His mouth opened in denial, but no sound could get through the blockage in his throat. He stood and spun around as awareness slammed into his brain. He sat again and before spinning around in the seat.

'You have to be kidding me!'

'Sorry, no. I've checked and re-checked to be certain.'

'Queensland… her father's alive? So what…?' He didn't want to know but now understood why Carol was so determined to get back together – purely to gain access to the research they'd failed to find so far. They must have discovered the papers Boyd stole were fake. But there was a positive. 'They weren't able to get what they were after,' he mumbled to himself.

'What makes you say that?'

'Sorry, I didn't realise I was talking aloud. Last night. Carol came around, begging for us to get together again.' He flopped back in the seat and rubbed both hands down his face as shocked brain cells re-aligned and began computing again. 'Hell, but it all makes sense now.' He leant forward.

'I gave her a chance to come clean but she continued to lie about everything: her dismissal, her holiday plans and everything else. I tried to figure out why she would want to re-ignite our relationship when she was leaving this coming Tuesday. God, I've been a fool. She wanted to spend the weekend together.' He thumped a fist on the desk. 'At my place.' A long groan rumbled out. 'No doubt hoping to find my research.' He slumped back again, 'Dear heaven, I don't believe this.' A grin slipped across his face. 'Wouldn't have done her any good if she did find it.'

'Why not?'

'Because I've already taken out the worldwide patent. I set it in motion during my weekend south. I received an email this morning confirming the patent, in my name only, is pending.'

Tyson looked stunned then he laughed and laughed some more as though it was the greatest joke ever heard but to Shane something still didn't make sense. Frustrated, he stood and paced, thinking. He spun around and stabbed a finger in the air towards Tyson. 'Something doesn't add up.'

Tyson leant back, elbows on the chair rests with fingers together in a steeple but with a smug look. 'Several things don't make sense. First, how did the pair of them know? Did you let it slip?'

'No.' Shane spun around as a tiny memory jabbed away, desperate to be released. He paused, thought and turned to Tyson. 'Monday night, Carol came around. She said... what were her words? Let me think.' He stilled and wracked his brain, recalling the conversation until it came to him. "You've been so busy with your research..." The chair received a pounding as Shane thumped the back and sent it spinning on the swivel. 'Somehow, she knew I was working on my research, but how?'

'Could Bill have roped her in?' asked Tyson but there was a twitch around his mouth.

'You know, don't you?'

'Yes. I figured it out around two this morning but only after I followed her last night.'

'You followed her to my place?'

'Yes, but after your place she went to someone else's place and spent the night. Probably the same place she's spent every weekend since it certainly wasn't with her mother. She's been two-timing you for… I'd say since you met. After seeing her with her boyfriend and working out her accounts, it all made sense.'

Feeling sick to the stomach for being such a sucker, Shane eased back into his abused chair and leant forward.

'What did you find? Tell me.'

'There is nothing untoward in any of the accounts in her name only. Her pay has gone in, costs of living have been taken out. There are no unexplained deposits or debits and guess what? There are no tidy sums put away in any savings account as she intimated to you, but…' Tyson shuffled through a file of papers. 'These are the statements for the Evici Company I mentioned. This is where the money stolen from Carol's business account was deposited and I figured this was the tidy sum to which she was referring.'

Tyson swung the statement around so Shane could scan the numbers. 'Hooley, Dooley, there's over three million in here.' He glanced at Tyson. 'She wouldn't have even earned three million in ten years. To do so she would have to earn three hundred thousand a year. Where did all this money come from?'

'Look at the dates.'

Shane looked and studied the details carefully. The account was opened about a year ago with the first deposit of half a million dollars. Regular $250,000 deposits went in each month for the following six months and totalled… Oh hell!

He knew.

He swore.

He glanced at Tyson who was sitting back with one eyebrow raised.

'She stole and sold our project last year,' came out as a husky growl of disbelief. 'But how? She must have had inside help. It wasn't her cousin for he didn't work here at the time but it could have been anyone because the entire staff knew about it.'

'It probably wasn't Carol who actually stole the project details, but she is involved by being in cahoots with the perpetrator. How did you meet Carol?'

'At a work social function we had in a hotel. She introduced herself to Chris and me while we were standing at the bar.'

'Have you ever thought it could have been a deliberately set up meeting?'

'Oh, God, please no?'

'Why do you think she has a one-way ticket to Brazil?'

'Uh, I don't know, a starting point for a world tour?'

'Australia doesn't have an extradition treaty with Brazil. If she goes there, she can't be extradited back to Australia to face criminal charges. This is why she's so eager to leave this coming Tuesday. It was the first flight she could get, via New Zealand. After realising you figured something was up and after I came on the scene she's running scared. The flight was only booked the day Holly saw the ticket. She thought they had the formula in the stolen papers from your office but when she realised they didn't, she's tried to get back into your good books. And I know who her cohort is.'

Shane could do nothing but stare at Tyson while a fully laden road train slammed into him and ran him over again and again. The pain of treachery was overwhelming.

'Before I tell you the name let me say I wasn't here all morning because I spent it with my friends in police headquarters. I've passed on this information to the fraud squad. They have already sent a team to arrest Carol and there's a team waiting outside for my nod to arrest the other person involved.

'Oh, God!' Shane groaned. 'Who is it?'

'I'll let you discover the same way I did. Write down all the letters in the name of this company and its directors.' He stabbed at the relevant names on top of the Evici documents.

Shane wrote: E V I C I G R A H A M L A U R E N C R O S S

'Now cross out the letters spelling Carol's name.

Shane put a line through each of the letters spelling Carol Maguire.

'Now re-arrange the remaining letters to a name you know well.'

There weren't many letters left and an inkling made it easy, so it didn't take long until his heart stuttered to a standstill before racing to make up for the missed beats. Everything fell into place like a line of dominoes falling onto each other.

'Bloody hell! She's been having an affair with Chris all this time.' Shane stood, turned and raced for the door.

'The bastards set me up.'

He beat Tyson to Chris's door and barged in. 'You bastard. Why?'

Chris turned from his filing cabinet: one Shane realised was being emptied with piles of files on the desk. 'What the hell do you think you are doing?'

Then he spied the edge of an open cardboard carton poking from behind the desk. 'All those files belong to the company,' he added. 'What are you doing?'

'Going on leave.'

'Not until the end of next week.'

'I'm leaving a week earlier.'

'Why?' Bewildered, Shane swept one hand down his face but he knew. Chris was on the same flight as Carol and wasn't coming back, hence the boxes.

'Because I'm sick of you and this place. You are such a sanctimonious prat.'

Shane reeled back at the venom. 'So, you thought you could steal my research, like you did last year, sell it and live off the proceeds.' He stepped closer, so angry he could feel his body vibrate.

'Shit, how did you…' Chris rocked backwards.

Anger took a hold of Shane's sanity. He curled up his fist and let fly, recoiling at the jarring pain when his fist met with the hard bone of Chris's cheek. It felt so damn good when Chris hit the cabinet with a tinny thud. There was a stunned look on his face as he rebounded before sliding down the cold metal. It felt even better when Shane spied the blood gushing from the other man's nose. The look of utter shock on Chris's face gave the same sense of delight Shane had, had as a kid when he had been allowed to lick the icing from the bowl.

When arms yanked him back, Shane fought to free himself so he could have another go, but Tyson tightened his hold.

'Let it go, Shane. He's going to jail.'

Three other men crowded in, hoisted Chris upright and handcuffed him before reading him his rights. The surprise on Chris's face sent the definite message he had expected to get away with his treachery.

Shane was determined to get in the last word. 'Thank, God, I'm a sanctimonious prat. At least I can sleep at night knowing I'm honest and loyal to my friends and family; knowing I have integrity and respect. Far better than being a disloyal, cheating traitor and thief. Far better than letting my girlfriend sleep with another man just to get information.'

'Sleep with you? No way, she wouldn't.'

Shane could do nothing but laugh. 'So glad you are on the receiving end of treachery. Enjoy your holiday in Brazil.'

Oh, how he loved the wince of surprise on the bastard's face as Chris fought to free himself but lost the battle with three officers crowding him against the wall.

'Don't think I don't know about you and your equally double-crossing partner in crime. You both deserve each other.'

He moved closer and shirt-fronted Chris who struggled to get away but was held still by two officers. 'But guess what, you slimy bastard, I win the stakes in double-crossing because I've already patented my research in my name only.'

The look of shock delighted Shane. He turned to the men who were obviously plain clothes members of the police force. 'Take him away. It will give me the greatest pleasure to testify at his trial. I'm so pleased white-collar crime gets far more serious jail time than plain murder.'

Shane stalked out shaking his hand before flexing it several times to ease the ache. It was worth the physical pain to gain the small amount of emotional pleasure to see the double-crossing bastard get what he deserved.

<h1 style="text-align:center;font-style:italic">About the Author</h1>

Even though she always loved creative writing, Tania Park only started writing seriously when she took early retirement from the workforce after a career as a teacher, an underground service locator and company director. Keen to better her skills, she joined a local writer's group and attended as many workshops as she could find, and still does.

The first workshop resulted an a short story, which won third place in a national competition. This gave her the impetus to keep going, especially when the next story came first.

Seven short stories have won places in competitions and been published in various publications, along with four poems and another poem has been etched on the new Busselton jetty in Western Australia.

Recently, a short story, Who Knows, has been accepted in a world-wide hard cover publication by Exisle Publishing in their Timeless Wonder series.

In 2011, she self-published a non-fiction work, The Only Way I Know, which details her husband's traumatic upbringing as the son of one of the last genuine drovers of the de Grey stock route in WA. This book was widely accepted in Canada and the USA during a four-month tour.

She has written several novel length fiction manuscripts, six of which have been self-published in print and e-book form. The third, Blind Justice, was commended in the 2016 FAW Christina Stead national fiction literary awards. The gain national recognition is a triumph.

This seventh book, Double Cross, is pure white collar crime and a little different from the others.